Sleigh Belles

Also by Beth Albright

THE SASSY BELLES
WEDDING BELLES

BETH ALBRIGHT

Sleigh Belles

HARLEQUIN® MIRA®

Recycling programs
for this product may
not exist in your area.

ISBN-13: 978-0-7783-1530-8

SLEIGH BELLES

First printing: October 2013
10 9 8 7 6 5 4 3 2 1

For my Brooks, my son, my precious friend,
the center of my universe. I loved you from the moment I thought
of you and it has grown into the most wonderful priceless love
I have ever known. You are a special soul, and I am the luckiest
mother on earth to have you for my child. This book is all about
family, and you are the very definition of the word. I am so proud
of the man you have become, brilliant and sensitive, thoughtful
and loving. As in everything I do, this is all for you.
I love you more than any words could ever express.

For my Ted, and my precious mother, Betty—
our little family is absolutely everything to me.

Dallas couldn't believe she was having another flare-up. Not now, not tonight, when she had this huge story to report. For Dallas Dubois, trying to get over Cal Hollingsworth was like trying to get over a chronic allergy. You could pretty much count on flare-ups for the rest of your life. Like if you're allergic to bee stings. One little prick and you'll find yourself in the emergency room.

Ironically, that's exactly where she was when she began having the latest of these chronic flare-ups: in the waiting room of the hospital E.R.

Not that anything was wrong with her. She was there to cover a story: Lewis Heart, the Alabama Crimson Tide star football announcer, was rushing to the hospital to see his brand-new baby girl make her way into the world. He had just finished announcing the big win over rival Auburn in the Iron Bowl Classic, and he was sliding into the E.R. just under the wire. Dallas was right there on the scene to cover the birth of the new baby, which was big news in the college town of Tuscaloosa. Lewis was considered Tuscaloosa royalty since he was the "Voice" of the Crimson Tide, the national champion football team, and that was reason enough to cover this big arrival.

"The biggest rivalry in all of college football is going down today, and this is the day that redheaded Vivi chooses to have her baby," Dallas muttered as she ran into the emergency room just barely ahead of Lewis.

"Well, I think this is par for her. Remember, they got married on the day of the season kickoff," Daniel, her cameraman, said as he raced in after her, nearly tripping over the camera cords.

"I know it! Who the hell gets married during football season?"

Lewis dashed into the emergency room, huffing and puffing right past Dallas. His best friend, Cal, was running in right after him, just like the days when they both played for the college football team themselves. In they ran, Cal swooshing right by Dallas without even noticing her. That's when she felt the acute symptoms of this chronic condition coming on again.

Great, she thought. *How can I do my job with* him *here?*

This report had to be good, but Cal always had a way of making Dallas lose her train of thought. Already her heart was racing and her mouth was dry.

How does he do this to me? This is ridiculous. She smoothed her hair and slid her lipstick over her lips one last time, trying to get ready for her live shot.

Dallas had fought this *allergy* ever since high school when she'd first developed an infatuation with Cal, the super-smart quarterback of the Tuscaloosa High School Warriors. Dallas had such a crush on him back then, and that old crush was the source of all these symptoms now because, the truth was, her feelings never really went away.

Dallas forced herself to focus. She smiled into the camera as Daniel counted her down to showtime.

"Good evening, Tuscaloosa! I'm Dallas Dubois, reporting live from Druid City Hospital for WTAL News where we're all eagerly awaiting the birth of the newest addition to our football lovin' town! Our very own Voice of the Crimson Tide and his lovely wife, Vivi, are expecting their first child at any moment, and we'll be right here to bring the news to you firsthand…" Dallas continued her speech into the camera, but she was having trouble concentrating. She stared at the handsome Cal, the "symptoms" taking over her completely.

Thankfully, it was only minutes before Lewis rushed out to the eager crowd that had gathered in the waiting room. "It's a girl! Baby Tallulah is finally here! Oh, my God, she is gorgeous!" Lewis was totally over-the-top excited. "I barely made it," he admitted. "Now I got me two little redheads!"

Everyone clapped and hugged each other, celebrating and high-fiving while Daniel captured the whole event on camera. Before Dallas even knew what happened, she found herself pushed into Cal's arms.

"Hey, Cal." She swallowed hard and forced a smile.

"Hey, Dallas…"

They were face-to-face, inches apart.

He looked at her awkwardly. She pulled away with an uncomfortable grin. Seeing Cal was dangerous. It threatened the thick emotional walls she'd built up over the years to protect her most intimate secrets.

The worst part was, in her opinion, Cal could be such a jerk. He'd never really liked her, always telling his friends she was self-absorbed, the Original Ice Queen.

How could he make her heart always feel as if it was fixin'

to jump right outta her chest if they really didn't even like each other? That little question had always bothered her. But she figured it was pointless trying to make sense of how these things worked. The heart wants what the heart wants and all that. What she did know is that they were never going to be together.

Whatever this was, this chronic allergy she had to Cal, she also knew she could *never* find herself in *this* position again—within inches of Cal's gorgeous face. Being anywhere within five hundred yards of him and she could feel that emotional firewall grow weak and start to crumble. That wall had taken her years to build.

Dallas was a model-like beauty, tall, with long legs and long, bouncy, blond hair. She loved her makeup, too, like any good pageant girl from the Deep South. The saying in the pageant world was *More is better,* and Dallas followed that to perfection. She justified it because she was on TV. But she would have worn that much makeup if she had been an employee at Taco Casa, her very favorite place to feed her biggest habit, sweet iced tea.

Whenever Dallas was around, you knew it. She was just as generous with her perfume as she was with her makeup. *Flowerbomb* was her trademark scent, and, since she always wanted to leave her mark, a heavy cloud of it followed her wherever she went.

Dallas glanced around the waiting room. It was literally bursting at the seams, not even room for a sneeze. Her archrival in all things from beauty pageants to men, Blake O'Hara Heart, was there, of course. She was Vivi's best friend and the two were almost always together. Blake's mother and grandmother were also there, along with Lewis's older brother, newly elected Alabama Senator Harry Heart, who Blake was now divorcing. He was talking to everyone in the waiting room as if he was still on the campaign stump.

And Cal, unfortunately, was part of that little clique, making Dallas even more uncomfortable. She spotted him chatting with Blake and Sonny Bartholomew, the chief homicide investigator and Blake's lover. Cal and Sonny had just solved a huge murder investigation together a few months ago, and they had become fast friends.

Dallas caught herself staring at Cal, and she noticed immediately that he still wasn't wearing a wedding ring. He was tall—about six foot three—which had really helped him as a quarterback. He had dark golden sandy-brown hair that he wore a little long, swept over his forehead. His eyes were a light grayish green, and that body was still in perfect quarterback shape. People had always told him he was heartthrob handsome. He ran the computer sciences department out at the university now, which gave him a sexy-academic quality that made Dallas weak in the knees.

Dallas stiffened herself and put the microphone to her mouth as the camera began to roll again.

Just then, a child from another family in the waiting room zipped by her, slamming into her thigh and splashing her winter-white skirt with red punch.

"Oh, my Lord," Dallas screeched. "Can't y'all keep these kids under control? Look at me!"

Dallas was comin' unglued, but she refused to ruin her broadcast. Her job was everything to her.

"And you're on in five, four, three..." Daniel gave the countdown, and then she was on the air, red stain and all.

He pushed in tight, trying not to show the giant red blemish on her skirt. The kids were going wild, running around and around her in the excitement of getting on camera, their mother chasing them down on live TV.

Dallas kept it together. She was a pro.

She was always perfect when it came to her reporting, since there was nothing in the world she valued more than her flourishing career. She was used to shoving down her emotions and just doing her job. She had been doing that for years, working so hard to become the star reporter she was. Now she was pushing for that coveted anchor chair that would soon be vacant, so there was no room to be anything less than stunning.

"Baby Tallulah Heart has finally arrived," she began, her smile gleaming for the camera, "topping off this incredible night for our Voice of the Crimson Tide. Alabama slammed Auburn in this year's Iron Bowl earlier today, and our own Lewis Heart adds another redhead to his family, so we can count that as two victories this evening. I'm Dallas Dubois, for WTAL News. Good night and Roll, Tide!"

Daniel gave the signal the mic was off. "Okay, we're clear."

"Oh, my God, I cannot stand kids!" Dallas blurted out as soon as she was off the hook. Then she caught a glimpse of herself in the monitor, and the producer began shouting frantically in her ear, "We're live! We're still live!"

Dallas froze. Her career and that anchor chair were hanging in the balance.

"I just cannot, uh, stand kids, uh…to be alone during the holidays," she said trying to save herself.

Daniel had the camera on a tripod and began writing notes on his hand at lightning speed for Dallas to read. She squinted as she spoke.

"So don't forget to join us in a few short weeks for the Tuscaloosa production of…uhm…*Sleigh Bells,* to benefit the… uhm…Children's Home. I'm Dallas Dubois, WTAL News."

"And now we're clear." Daniel knew he was in a heap of trouble.

Dallas was fuming.

"Next time, you idiot, make sure I'm actually clear when you tell me *clear*. My God, you're gonna cost me my job."

She was perched somewhere between infuriated and mortified. With Cal causing a flare-up, kids ruining her skirt, not to mention telling all of Tuscaloosa County that she hated children, Dallas decided it was best to ignore her racing heart and her raging temper, and get the heck outta there as fast as possible.

She ran straight out into the cold November night as fast as her five-inch stilettos would carry her, jumped in the TV truck and switched on the heater. Daniel followed close behind, slamming the double doors in the back and jumping into the satellite truck. They sped away from the happy hospital waiting room, now in full party mode. Dallas had never really been part of that group anyway, although her father had been married to Blake's mother for about ten years at one time, back when the girls were teenagers. Blake could technically have been considered her stepsister. Instead, they'd remained archrivals throughout their lives.

With Vivi and Blake best friends, and Lewis and Cal best friends, the circle was pretty tight, and they purposely left no room for Dallas. Not that she would have wanted to be part of that group in the first place. They all considered her a snob, and Dallas told herself she was just fine with all that. And she thought she was, till she had that flare-up tonight.

"See Cal's back in town," Daniel said, breaking the silence.

"Yeah, I saw. He's been back since the spring, I think," Dallas answered, making small talk.

"Didn't y'all have a fling or somethin'?" Daniel asked her.

"I most certainly did not have a *fling* with him. I absolutely can't stand that man," she shot back. "And if you don't hush your mouth, I swear I'm fixin' to beat your ass," she said with only a hint of sarcasm.

"I know what I saw. You looked a little nervous when he hugged you there."

"No, I was just surprised. You know, caught in the moment, all the excitement." Dallas fidgeted in her seat. "I'm cold, can you please just let it go and turn up the heat?"

Daniel had been Dallas's cameraman the whole time she had worked at WTAL: six years and counting now. He was a smallish man with a dark receding hairline, though he was only about thirty. He had a warm smile and inviting, sweet brown eyes. He wasn't married, and the girlfriends were here and there—no one at the moment. Dallas had never been interested in him romantically. She towered over him for one thing, and she wouldn't be caught dead wearing flats to accommodate a man. She hardly was ever really nice to him, though she claimed it was because he was out to push her buttons, which he was doing right this second.

But then, she was hardly nice to anyone.

"From what I saw, you were already hot back there in Cal's arms," Daniel teased her. He grinned and reached for the heater controls as Dallas yanked her coat up around her neck. Unfortunately, Cal's cologne was lingering on her jacket, making the flare-up continue, even though they had left the hospital.

Something about Cal made Dallas want to hit him. He was so cocky, for one thing, but mostly it was because he ignored her when what she really wanted was to fall into his arms. That wasn't going to happen, so she clung to the idea of hitting him. That way she was safe from her own feelings. Add another layer to that emotional firewall.

Whatever emotions and secrets brewed behind her crystal-blue eyes, she was determined no one would find out. With long legs up to here and her busty cleavage usually visible down to there, Dallas looked like a centerfold. It was part of her armor, and she had absolutely no intention of letting those barriers crumble. Ever. And especially not now with her dream job at stake.

With her future on the line, she certainly could not afford to lose *any* control. And Cal made her lose control. As they arrived back at the TV station, she promised herself she'd stay away from him at all costs. No matter what. She'd managed it since they'd finished college, and she could manage it now.

But with Cal back in town, that might just be a bit harder than she hoped.

Two weeks later

"Absolutely not! There is no earthly way I can take over directing that play. I have no time for that. I'm a professional reporter! I have a busy career! And anyway, the rehearsals conflict with my pedicure appointments." Dallas fumed as she sat at her desk in the WTAL newsroom sipping her sweet tea she'd picked up from Taco Casa. In Alabama, sweet iced tea was a way of life, year-round. Known commonly as the house wine of the Deep South, it was the drink of choice for any time of the day. And after the news Dallas had just received, it was gonna be either sweet tea or vodka.

It was a little over two weeks before Christmas and the director of the children's Christmas play *Sleigh Bells* had come down with the flu. Since Dallas had been at a few of the rehearsals because she was the celebrity emcee, the board of the theater had decided she was the best candidate and had asked her to step in and direct. This was the cause for her latest in a recent string of hissy fits.

"Dallas, I'm sorry, but it's station policy for staff to volunteer for charity during Christmas," Mike Maddox, the news director, told her. "You know the way it works, and this is the perfect opportunity."

"I certainly do, and that's exactly what I was doing by going to the occasional rehearsal—my required community appearances. *Appearances!* I just cannot direct the whole play, Mike. C'mon."

"The president of the board called me and asked if we would support this, and I told him absolutely. It's our duty to the city of Tuscaloosa during Christmas. Imagine the press we'll get over this. Imagine the press *you'll* get over this. I know how bad you want that anchor chair, Dallas, and this ingrains you into the city of Tuscaloosa a little deeper. It's a win-win, you know?"

While the responsibility of directing a play didn't appeal to her at all—and the thought of working with kids appealed to her even less—she couldn't deny that any publicity right now would be good publicity. Dallas rolled her eyes. "Ugh! Fine! I'll just reschedule my standing mani-pedis. I should tell you, though—I'm not an actress, and I don't know the first thing about theater and, oh, by the way, I'm not so great with children either. But, sure, if this is what they want…great."

"Good, I knew you'd see it my way," Mike said as he headed off toward the studio—either oblivious to the sarcasm in Dallas's voice or else just ignoring it.

She looked at her Gucci watch. It was early afternoon in mid-December in Tuscaloosa. The crisp fall air had given way to winter, and Christmastime was twinkling from every corner of this college town. She thought about the Christmas parade next week and her spot atop the WTAL-TV News float right behind the mayor's float. She loved the idea that the entire town would be watching and cheering as she rode on by, but now that she had the Christmas play to direct, her schedule was growing tighter by the minute.

Though she already had another story to cover today, the next rehearsal was in just a couple of hours, Mike had told her, and Dallas knew she had to introduce herself to the kids and try to make this transition as easy as possible. *Just get through it,* she told herself, as if going to rehearsal was like scheduling surgery.

She grabbed her coat as she ran out the door to visit Miss Peaches Shelby who'd had part of her holiday manger scene stolen from her yard. Peaches was so upset 'cause it was the second year in a row that her plastic Baby Jesus was snatched right outta her plastic stable. "They always leave the shepherds, but they take that Baby Jesus every single time," she'd complained on the phone to Dallas. It wasn't exactly big news, but Dallas would never turn down the possibility of camera time.

Climbing into the van where Daniel was already waiting, she buckled in with a loud huff. "Hey, Daniel, let's get this over with as quick as possible, okay? I have a thing at the Bama Theatre this afternoon," Dallas barked as they drove out of the parking lot heading to Miss Peaches's house. "Lucky me, I get all these *lead* stories. This one should *surely* get me that anchor chair," she muttered sarcastically.

"I remember we interviewed her last year about this very same thing," he said.

"I know, and now she says pictures are being sent to her from everywhere on campus showing her Baby Jesus statue first one place and then another."

"Kinda like those little gnomes people take on vacation for pictures everywhere, huh?"

They pulled into the driveway of Peaches Shelby's home,

her little plastic manger scene filled to capacity, except for Baby Jesus. Peaches met them outside, and Daniel began setting up the shot with his camera. Dallas trotted across the cold ground in her usual five-inch heels to greet Miss Peaches.

"Hey, Ms. Dubois," she said, smiling as Dallas showed her where to stand. "I'm so happy to see you again, but of course not under these circumstances." She quickly switched to a sulky frown, visibly upset as she related the story of the stolen plastic statue to Dallas and the cameraman.

"And the very next morning, he was pure ole dee gone, I tell ya. Just like into thin air. And that ain't no miracle! I do believe it's those same boys from that frat house that did this last year."

"Have you called the police?" Dallas asked with her microphone now under Ms. Peaches's nose.

"Yes, I most certainly did. They said they'd be lookin' all over campus."

"Where have these pictures been taken, can you tell?" Dallas asked her.

"Well, there was one with Baby Jesus at Denny Chimes sittin' on Joe Namath's handprints. Then they sent one from the steps of the library. They's crazy, whoever took it. That's just pure awful, don't y'all think?"

"Yes, Miss Peaches. We will do what we can to get the word out." Dallas thanked her and repositioned herself near the empty manger to do her stand-up.

"As you can see, Miss Peaches's stable is empty. There have been sightings of the statue all over the University of Alabama's campus. If anyone knows the whereabouts of Baby Jesus, please call the Tuscaloosa Police department or WTAL TV. I'm Dallas Dubois, WTAL. Okay, Daniel that's a wrap."

She told Miss Peaches goodbye and turned toward the van to wait for Daniel with the heater on high. It was nearly four o'clock, and the kids were going to be waiting at the theater. She was dreading this. It was true that she was not really a fan of kids—anyone's kids—but mostly Dallas just didn't want to be bothered by other people. Call it selfish or self-preservation, she did whatever she had to do to take care of herself, of her career, and that didn't leave much room in her life for anyone else. Especially not for little children in a Christmas play.

"Come on, Daniel! Let's get me to the Bama Theatre. I've gotta pretend I care about this Christmas play," she said as Daniel put the camera equipment in the van and backed out.

When they reached the theater, he pulled up out front to let Dallas out. The Bama Theatre was grand, built in 1937, and was now on the National Register of Historic Places. It was a magnificent old place, one of the last old movie palaces in the Deep South. Dallas and her archrival ex-stepsister, Blake, had been in many a beauty pageant there over the years. But today the beautiful old place would be home to the Christmas play *Sleigh Bells*. The holiday play was a town tradition. Local theater kids would make up the cast, as well as children from the Tuscaloosa Children's Home, a group home for children who, for various reasons, couldn't live at home with their families. Dallas certainly felt sympathy for those kids, but she definitely didn't consider herself qualified to take care of them. She was not looking forward to what she had to do.

She entered the auditorium and stopped in her tracks. The ghosts of Christmas past were all around, hovering over her, haunting her. She stood motionless, looking up at the tiny, lighted stars that filled the painted night sky on the ceiling.

She hadn't seen the stage since they had decorated it and added the sets.

She swallowed hard at the memories that invaded her. The playhouse was covered in Christmas lights, the entire room looking like a winter-white forest, dressed up in its Victorian finest for the holidays. On the stage, a set made to look like a Christmas village sat to the right, with a Christmas wreath hanging on a pretend toy-store door lit by the cutest old-fashioned streetlight.

Dallas was reminded of her first play at this theater, back when she was only eight years old. Her mother almost hadn't made it to the show because of a freak snowstorm—it never snowed in Alabama. Well, almost never.

She took the whole scene in, remembering all the times she'd walked that stage throughout her life. The countless beauty pageants she'd been in, though she'd never really placed better than runner-up. She had stood by while Blake captured most of the titles, while Blake's mother, Kitty, had cheered loudly from the audience. She tried to envision her own mother clapping and calling her name, but since she'd hardly ever shown up to Dallas's events, the memory didn't exist. She began to feel a break in the firewall, so she quickly plugged the dike.

The kids were there already, of course, running around the stage, the choir director trying anxiously, but to no avail, to calm them down. Dallas puffed her chest out, lifted her chin and headed down the aisle toward the stage to say hello and get the worst part over with.

"Children, may I have your attention?" the chubby little lady called out. Ms. Betty Ann had been the choir director at the Bama Theatre since Dallas had been a child in the Christmas plays herself. "Children, have a seat and let Miss Dallas talk to y'all just a minute," Betty Ann said. The children, distracted for a moment by their visitor, obediently sat down on the stage in the middle of the little pretend village. Dallas approached them, coming up from the side stairs. Betty Ann leaned over and whispered to Dallas, "Good luck. They're wound up tighter'n Dick's hatband today. I'm worn slap out already."

"Hey, kids," she started, her heart beating out of her chest. She didn't like to do things she didn't want to do, and she knew she *really* didn't wanna do this. "I'm Miss Dubois and I'm gonna be your new director."

Some of the kids started talking. One little girl even started crying.

"Why? What happened to Miss Fairbanks?" asked one little boy. They were all mumbling now, most of them between the ages of six and ten years old.

"Well, Miss Fairbanks wasn't feeling too well, and she wants to make sure we keep practicing," Betty Ann broke in.

"Exactly, and now I will be the director." Dallas smiled at them, hoping to look enthusiastic.

The kids all looked sad, some more started to cry, and one boy actually folded his arms and went to the corner of the stage, stomping his feet.

Offended, she tried to reason with them. "Look, it's hard for me, too, but here we are now, and Christmas is just around the corner, so let's make the best of this, okay?" Dallas tried to warm them up, but she wasn't very good at it. She was starting to lose her cool façade.

"I don't want you, I want Miss Fairbanks back," announced Sara Grace Griffin, who was nine years old.

"Well, look, I'm not so sure I'll like doing this either, but this is the way it is." Dallas turned and began to walk away, hearing the sound of crying children get louder with each step. She stormed off into the stage wings, arms folded, head down, when she slammed right into—

Cal.

Cal jumped back, obviously surprised to see Dallas right there in front of him in the theater wings.

"Cal! Sorry, what are you doing here?" Dallas asked, shocked at bumping into him here.

"I'm running the sound system for the Christmas play. What are you doing here?"

"Well...guess who's the new director?" She smiled awkwardly, feeling completely out of her element.

"What happened to Ms. Fairbanks?"

"Flu."

"So...you? You're the director?"

"Yep. It's my lucky day."

"Yeah. Well, good luck, I guess. See ya."

Cal walked away, and Dallas turned to watch him leave. It was obvious that he was unfazed by seeing her. She, however, was having another flare-up.

Dallas stepped over to the staircase in the wings and sat

down in the dim amber glow of the footlights. *Unbelievable,* she thought. How was it possible that not only was she stuck directing this ridiculous play, but now she'd also have to do it alongside the one man who never failed at making her lose her cool?

She inhaled a deep breath, trying to get a grip on everything that was happening, but it didn't ease the tension that was beginning to consume her. She felt the pressure building, but for the first time in a long time, she wasn't sure how to take control of the situation. She felt trapped. There was nothing she wanted more than that anchor spot. The announcement, they'd been told, would come just after Christmas. Great timing, she thought, for the person who got the job. They'd be able to start the New Year with an exciting new job. If she didn't get it, she could be one of the two reporters to lose her job to station cutbacks. For now, she knew she just had to stay focused. Worrying about the worst-case scenario wasn't going to make her performance any better. The only thing she could do was to keep her eye on the prize. She had to direct this play and somehow find a way to work with Cal.

Dallas pulled her purse closer, as if it were her only friend in this place. She wore a long winter-white Calvin Klein cashmere coat that she'd bought in Atlanta at a secondhand shop. She drove the three hours over there to shop all the time. She didn't come from much, but she had done quite a job of making it look as though she did. Her dad, businessman Sweeney Sugarman, had divorced Kitty, his second wife and Blake's mother, about ten years ago. Financially, he'd done little more than help pay Dallas's way through college at the University of Alabama. He'd died several years ago and had never even seen her first report for WTAL.

Dallas's mother, on the other hand, had sent her to live with her father when Dallas had only been fourteen years old. The day she'd left was the last time she had seen her mother. They had become estranged ever since. No one in town even saw LouAnn Watkins Sugarman anymore. Last anyone heard, she had tried to become a singing star out in Hollywood, and when that didn't pan out, she'd come back home to some small town in Alabama but had never tried to get in touch. It had been twenty years since Dallas had spoken to her. None of Dallas's family had even come to her college graduation. She was used to being alone. And in control.

With Cal working the sound for the play, Dallas would be running into him almost daily over the next couple of weeks. She huffed out a breath and shook her head. *Okay,* she admitted to herself, *he's still hot. Fine. But I am not going to throw myself at a man who clearly shows no interest in me. I can't let his gorgeous good looks get the best of me at a time like this. Besides, he has nothing I need right now. All I need is to get this play over with, secure my promotion and get on with my life.*

This was typical Dallas. Always thinking of the goal. Always forgetting to actually live along the way. All that armor, the tough-woman mask she donned each day with carefully applied makeup and hairspray, helped shield the real Dallas from everyone. Especially from herself.

"Okay, Ms. Dubois, we've got the children settled down, and they're waitin' for you," Betty Ann said, approaching Dallas in the stairway.

"Fine, please tell that production assistant person I need some Diet Dr. Pepper. I'm already exhausted after that scene out there. I mean, really, what is with all that attitude?"

"Certainly, Ms. Dubois, but you understand they're just nervous. They're only children, for heaven's sake."

"Yeah, well, they aren't the only nervous ones, I'll tell you. Do I look like a theater director to you? I belong on TV, with a camera in front of me, not behind the curtain trying to get a bunch of wild animals to stand in their spots and remember their lines. Let's just be honest—I don't wanna be here any more than they want me here."

"Oh, please don't feel that way. It will all work out just fine," Betty Ann said, though Dallas could see the doubt written all over her face. "Now, I'll get Corey to get your drink and we should get started."

"Great. Thanks." Dallas smiled weakly and exhaled a deep breath. Her stomach was in knots, but she was careful not to let anyone see that. She was totally on edge with her job on the line and that made it tough for her to be sweet to *anyone*.

Cal sat up in the sound booth, adjusting the speaker levels and fiddling with live mic feeds, and trying to figure out how'd he'd managed to find himself working side by side with none other than Dallas Dubois.

He'd always found Dallas attractive—how could you not? With that gorgeous hair, bright blue eyes and curves that should be illegal in most states, Dallas was basically a fantasy on legs.

Not that he was all that that bad himself. He'd been told he was gorgeous by plenty of people all his life, but it never really seemed to sink in. He wasn't a loud braggart like a lot of athletes he'd known in college. He was more reserved. And he was often single.

What no one knew, except maybe Lewis, who had been Cal's best friend in both high school and college, was that he was an over-the-top perfectionist. It wasn't that he was judgmental about the people he dated—it was more that he was tough on himself. He had always been afraid of failing at a relationship, so he'd never got too serious with any one girlfriend.

His grades, however, had been spectacular. He'd pushed himself so hard that it had cut down on his participation in the wild social life that his other friends had enjoyed. Cal was an academic. He took everything super seriously and had gotten his doctorate in computer science by the time he was twenty-six. He had been the star quarterback for the Crimson Tide, leading them to a National Championship in his senior year. He was tough on himself.

That's why he had never married. Not that all the gorgeous beauty queens and coeds couldn't measure up. No. Cal was terrified of failing. His two older brothers had great marriages. His parents had been married for well over forty years. He looked at their success, and he realized he wasn't sure he could ever be that great at it. He'd never met anyone who'd made him feel the things his brothers claimed to feel about their own wives. And he'd always been so focused on school and sports that he couldn't even imagine having enough time left over to properly devote to another person. The last thing he wanted was to let anyone see that he wasn't good enough. For Cal, failure at anything was not an option. Growing up, the minute he thought a relationship might not work forever, he ran. Now, at thirty-four, he still found himself more invested in work than in women.

From his spot in the sound booth, he could oversee some of the action on the stage below. And thanks to live mics, he could hear everything being said. Just now, he could hear Corey, the young production assistant, bringing Dallas her drink.

"Here you go, Ms. Dubois," he said cheerfully.

Cal watched Dallas take the drink from him with a slight nod of her head. "Thanks, and make sure you stay close with that clipboard of yours. I can't possibly write and talk at the same time."

"I'll do my best," Corey said, though his mood had clearly been taken down a notch.

It made Cal sick to hear her unfriendly treatment of everyone. Her bossy behavior, flinging orders around as if she was
throwing rice at a wedding, like this was just business as usual
for her. As far as Cal knew, it was. This was the Dallas he'd
always known. Cold, selfish and self-absorbed. It had been the
reason why, despite how attracted he was to her, he'd never
made an attempt to pursue her.

When rehearsal was over, and he was packing up the equipment for the day, he heard Dallas backstage as she gathered
her things. Corey had run up the side stairs to say good-night.
He knew he should turn off the mic, that he really shouldn't
listen in, but curiosity got the better of him.

"Okay, Ms. Dubois," he heard Corey say. "That's it for tonight. Need anything 'fore I leave?"

"No, that's fine. Can I see your notes from today?"

"Oh, um, well…I didn't really take notes. Nothing really
changed, so I didn't really have any…"

"God, are you an idiot, too? Why do I always work with
idiots? I asked you to take notes of everything we did today."

"Oh, I'm, uh…sorry, Ms. Dubois, but we didn't really do
anything but run over what we were already doing in the
show. But, um…if you want, I can type up something and
email it to you."

"Just forget it. I'll make up the notes myself. Next time just
follow my directions."

"Sorry, ma'am."

Corey was a theater student at Alabama, and his professor
was the flu-ridden Ms. Fairbanks, and Cal could bet he was really going to miss her not being at the Bama Theatre every day.

He'd heard about all he could take. He left the sound booth
and headed down to the stage, running into Dallas as she
headed back up the aisle to meet her ride outside.

"You are really something else. I can't believe you," he said, stopping right in front of her, his hands folded in front of him.

"Excuse me? I don't know what you're talking about, but I have to be back at the station for the newscast so I'm in a hurry."

"Oh, I'm sure you are. But you need to hear a few things before you speed off to your high falutin' TV job."

At well over six feet tall, Cal towered over Dallas—despite the impossibly high heels she was wearing. He used his size to his advantage now, looking down at Dallas with disapproval.

"You haven't changed a bit since high school. Some of us actually grew up but not you. You're still just as full of yourself as you always were."

"What the hell do you mean?" Dallas fought back. "You have no idea the stress I'm under. I don't need this crap. You don't know anything about me, Cal. You never did."

"Well, there's certainly no excuse to talk to everybody like they need to serve you. That's disgusting."

"Cal, I'm late. If you don't like what you heard, then quit eavesdropping and turn the mics off when the conversation doesn't concern you. Now, if you'll kindly move out of my way, I have a newscast to get to." Her face was red with anger and, Cal hoped, a little embarrassment at being called out.

He stepped aside, and she walked past him, her winter-white coat brushing against his pants, her nose in the air as if to let him know she didn't care one bit.

Typical, Cal thought, and he stormed off in the opposite direction.

Dallas was fuming as she made her way up the theater aisle. She held her head up as though she didn't care, but of course she did. She could feel her face growing hot as she made her way outside to Daniel and the van.

How could her entire world be falling off its axis in just one day? She rode in silence back to the station with Daniel, her eyes stinging, but she wasn't fixin' to let even one tear fall. Not until she was in private.

One more thing and her tough façade might become so damaged that the usual quick fix of puffing out her chest with a deep breath and lifting her nose in the air just wouldn't work. Just one more thing and it would be too much for one day. But she had no time to think about falling apart. She had a story to introduce on set.

Dallas arrived back in the newsroom, the Christmas decorations twinkling on the station tree that stood in the corner. A frantic chatter filled the newsroom. It was typical for the time of day, reporters running around and edit bays full as late stories were still being filed. Dallas hurried in at a clip, her heels not slowing her down one bit. Daniel had already edited her story about Miss Peaches. She ran into an empty bay to voice it before it was time to sit on set next to the soon-to-be retiring female anchor and introduce the missing Baby Jesus statue story to the viewers.

Just as she was wrapping it up and preparing to walk into the live studio, the news assistant delivered a piece of paper with a message to her.

Please call me. I need to see you.—Mom

Dallas felt as if she had been pushed off a building. She hadn't spoken to her mother in twenty years, and now, today of all days, she'd decided to call. *Now.* This was the "one more thing" that just might break her. How could she go on the air live in two minutes, right after unexpectedly hearing from the mother who had abandoned her so long ago? She shoved the note into her jacket pocket and marched into the studio smiling. *Take control,* she reminded herself. She knew how to shove down these emotions, and she'd just have to do it again.

Her mother. Wow. All she knew was that she had no time for her mother now. The same way LouAnn hadn't had time for Dallas for the past twenty years. LouAnn had never even attempted to make contact with her. She had purely abandoned her. Dallas had no intention of seeing her now, not ever again.

Still, she was thrown for a loop, her stomach tightening with a painful grip, the years of hurt bubbling up. This was far worse than the confrontation with Cal back at the theater, and she couldn't believe her bad luck.

She barely got through the story on TV, a strained smile pulled across her pretty face. When she returned to her seat in the newsroom, her phone on her desk was ringing. She picked it up without even thinking.

"Dallas Dubois," she said into the receiver.

"Dallas, it's your mother. Please don't hang up." LouAnn sounded nervous.

"Mother. Hi…" she began, then quickly decided there was no need for politeness. "What do you want? I'm really busy."

"I need to see you."

"I'm sorry. Your timing is really bad. Maybe another time." Dallas kept her voice cold, showing no emotion.

This conversation had been years in rehearsal. Dallas had spent a long time imagining that her mother would call her, say she was sorry, maybe cry and beg forgiveness. As she grew older, the pretend conversation took on a different tone, as Dallas grew bitter and developed the hard exterior she'd soon be known for. Now that the moment was finally happening, somehow it wasn't playing out just as she'd practiced.

"Please. It's important," LouAnn begged.

"I'm really sorry. But I've got important things going on, too. So, call me another time, okay? But not anytime soon." And with that, Dallas hung up on her.

A lump swelled in her throat, and she made a beeline to

the ladies' room, locking herself in a stall. Finally alone for a moment, she allowed herself to cry silently into her hands, flushing the toilet over and over to cover the sounds of her anguish in case anyone walking by could hear her. All those years of not hearing her own mother's voice, of wishing that she'd just come home and tell Dallas she hadn't forgotten about her, suddenly made her feel as though she were that young, naïve girl once again. With everything she'd faced today, plus her own guilt of hanging up on a call that had been twenty years in the making, it all became too much. Even for Dallas.

The firewall was down, and Dallas was desperate to put it back together as fast as she could.

That evening, Dallas went home to her empty house. It was a little place near the university that she was renting. If she got that anchor seat, maybe she could afford to buy herself a real place of her own. Maybe she could finally afford to stop running to Atlanta to hide the fact that she shopped at consignment stores. Everyone in town just assumed she had lots of money. She worked hard to make it look that way. But the truth was that reporters didn't make that much. She had bills to pay and, unlike Blake and Vivi, she didn't come from family money. But that wouldn't hold her back. She'd just have to keep climbing her way to the top. Anchors made much more, a lot more. That's what she had her eye on.

She made her way to the shower, petting her big white cat, Wilhelmina. Wilhelmina was her only companion since she had broken up with Dan Donohugh, Harry Heart's campaign manager, right after the election. Both of them had really been using each other, hoping to benefit from Harry's run for the senate, so the brief fling had ended soon after.

Here in her home, Dallas was finally in her safe haven. Just she and Wilhelmina.

Dallas stood under the hot water of her shower thinking of her mother, but trying not to. Why would she be calling after all these years? Dallas had tried to make contact with her when she was still just a teenager. She'd hated living with her father, and she'd really hated living with Blake when her dad had married Blake's mother, Kitty. Blake had let her know immediately it was *her* house, so Dallas hadn't wasted a minute of her time trying to be *sisters* with her.

Instead, she'd spent her time trying to prove herself worthy of her mother's love. She'd become a high school cheerleader just as her mother had been when she was young. She'd worked hard to become the most popular—and that had sometimes been nasty work. You didn't always become popular by being nice, so she'd had to crush a few hearts along the way. Eventually, she had been named the salutatorian of her class. Cal was the valedictorian and had gotten a football scholarship. But Dallas, after receiving a small scholarship of just a thousand dollars, had still been asked to give one of the speeches. She'd pulled together all her courage to call her mother when she found out, but no one had answered the phone. She'd left a message, asking her mother to please come and hear her speak, that it would mean a lot to Dallas to show her what she'd accomplished. She'd never heard back from her mother. *Maybe she didn't get my messages,* she always thought to herself. But she knew it wasn't true.

Eventually, Dallas quit trying to make contact.

As she stood in the shower, the memories of what happened all those years ago haunted her warm oasis.

When Dallas had been only three and her brother, Houston,

had been eleven, their father had walked out on their family. He'd left them to marry his secretary, the woman he'd been with just before he'd married Blake's mother, Kitty. As they'd grown up, Houston had stepped up to become the man of the house and their mother, LouAnn, had leaned on him in that role. The three of them had been an incredibly close, tight-knit family—and, yes, her mother had a thing for Texas and had named her children after her two favorite cities there.

As they grew up, Dallas had loved her brother like no one else in her life. He had been her hero. They had always had an incredibly close relationship. Houston always told her that whoever married her would be the luckiest young man in history, since he would get to have Dallas forever. To say she put him on a pedestal was a major understatement. She used to tell him he was her favorite person in the world. And he'd let her know she was the most special person in his life, too. Even when he'd moved out to campus, they'd still talked all the time and he'd taken her to the movies and out for ice cream once a month. She'd loved him more than anyone. He had been her security.

When Dallas was in the ninth grade, she was basically living life like most teenaged girls her age. Makeup, boys, fashion and cheerleading practice filled her days. Houston, meanwhile, was twenty-two, gorgeous and fixin' to graduate from Alabama.

One day he'd brought a woman, Eleanor Walsh, home with him to meet his family. As smart and charming as Houston was, they weren't at all surprised that he'd found someone special. But when Eleanor walked in the door, she was definitely a surprise, all right. She was about thirty years old, though Houston was just barely twenty-two. He was defensive right away, explaining to LouAnn and Dallas that they were in love and that it was serious. He told them he was planning on marrying her. Dallas, being so young, was actually really excited and wanted to get to know her new "older sister" right away. She trusted her brother's instincts on everything, so if he said this woman was the right one, Dallas was happy to accept it.

As they continued dating, Houston made sure that she and Eleanor became close. They'd take shopping trips together, go to movies and the couple made a real effort to spend time at the house with Dallas and her mother. So one day, Dallas and Eleanor went to Eleanor's house to get ready to go out to a movie together with Houston. It was the first time she'd been invited to Eleanor's place, so she was both nervous and excited. When Dallas entered the house, she immediately was shocked at the mess. The home was filthy—dirty pots and pans on the stove, so much old grease on the floor she couldn't even see the color of the tile. As she moved through the house, following closely behind Eleanor, she heard noises coming from the laundry room. As they passed by, heading up the hall to Eleanor's bedroom, Dallas caught a figure out of the corner of her eye.

A man was sitting on the floor, surrounded by parts from the washing machine, along with screwdrivers and other tools spread out around him. The man glanced up as Dallas walked by. He locked eyes with young Dallas, and instantly she felt a pang in her stomach: that uh-oh feeling you got when things weren't quite right. She had a feeling that Houston might not know this woman as well as he thought.

"Who's that?" she asked Eleanor.

"No one. Just the repairman," she answered casually.

Dallas still felt that feeling. From another bedroom up the hall, Dallas could hear the sounds of children. One was crying. One was arguing with an older woman. As they walked toward the open door, she could see that the older woman was sitting in a small chair designed for a child. She was smoking a cigarette and staring out the window as she "babysat" the kids. As they walked past the door, the older of the two little boys ran out of the room and latched himself on to Eleanor's leg, wrapping himself around her, "Mommy! Hi! Will you stay home tonight?"

Dallas was stunned. The child was about four years old and the other looked to be only two. They were Eleanor's kids. Eleanor had kids! In all the time she'd known her, there had never, not once, been mention of her sons.

"Momma, can't you do something with them?" Eleanor said to the older woman.

"Y'all get off of your momma now," the woman said, ashing her cigarette on the windowsill. "She's goin' out. Go in there and see what yer daddy's doin'."

Dallas couldn't believe what she was hearing. Was the man with the washing machine the father? She froze in place, trying to take this news in for a second. Several seconds.

Dallas got an instant stomachache. She was afraid she had stumbled onto a secret. Surely her beloved brother had no idea he was dating a married woman, with children. Not *dating,* but fixin' to marry!

Dallas didn't want to go to the movies anymore. She wanted to rush home to save her brother from this horrible woman. She wanted to protect him now. She absolutely knew her brother would never be involved with her if he knew the truth. But as she stood there trying to imagine how she'd break the news, Eleanor shuffled her off to her bedroom and began chatting away as she got ready, as though none of this were out of the ordinary. In shock, Dallas wasn't able to do much but follow along and wait for the right opportunity to speak up.

Houston, Eleanor and Dallas made it to the movies anyway, but late that night, after they'd dropped Eleanor off, Dallas decided she had to tell Houston what she'd found out. When they pulled into the driveway of her mother's house, she just blurted it all out in one breath, thinking it might be better to rip it off like a Band-Aid.

"Yeah, I know," he answered, once Dallas had finished.

"What? You *know* she's married and has kids? How could you still want to marry her?"

"I just do, Dallas. You have no idea what the situation really is. Her husband doesn't love her, and they are getting a divorce."

"When? I mean he was there fixing the washing machine and her kids were screaming and crying for her to stay home."

But rather than listen to her concern, rather than talking things out with her as he always did, Houston seemed to have grown cold. "You need to stay out of this. It's none of your business. She thought no one would be home when she took you there today. I'm sorry you had to see all that."

"Does Mom know?" she asked.

"Yeah, and she understands," he said pointedly. "She knows Eleanor loves me and I love her."

"But what about her kids? They were dirty, and her mother was smoking while she was taking care of them. I mean—" she paused and swallowed hard "—is this the kind of woman you really want to marry? Someone who cares so little about her family? Think about how Dad—"

He cut her off midsentence by hitting his fist on the wheel. Houston had had about all he could take from what he suddenly saw as a meddling little sister.

"Don't imply she's not good enough, Dallas. You have no idea what you're talking about. Now just get out, okay?"

She was brokenhearted as she slowly climbed out of his car and went into the house. Her hero had fallen off his pedestal.

The next morning, she asked her mom all about it, and LouAnn confirmed her worst fears. It was all true. But Dallas wasn't going to give up that easily. She'd always thought her mom was far too easy with Houston, trying to make up for the fact that she had depended on him to take their father's place for so much of his life.

"He's happy and that's all that matters," LouAnn said.

"But he won't be for long. He just likes the attention right now. She's older. That's all it is," Dallas reasoned. "You have to know that. Even *I* know that."

"That's enough," LouAnn snapped, stopping the conversation cold. She'd walked out of the room, leaving Dallas alone with her worry.

Over the next few weeks, Dallas continued to try in vain to save her precious brother. Her tears and pleas fell on blind eyes and deaf ears. Until one day it reached the boiling point.

"Dallas, you have to stop this," LouAnn shouted.

"Please, don't let him ruin his life like this," she begged through tears. It was just after Houston had graduated from Alabama. He was standing in the hallway, LouAnn in the kitchen with Dallas.

"I've had enough of this. I can't be around her anymore. She's messing up my life. She's calling Eleanor at home and asking her to leave me alone," Houston shouted. He walked into the kitchen and faced his mother. "Get her away from me or you won't see me anymore."

One threat to LouAnn and that's all it took. She'd already lost one man in her life, and she was not going to let that happen twice.

"That's it, Dallas," her mother said, turning to look at her. "You've been nothing but selfish. Look around! Because of you, my family is falling apart all over again. I will not let you drive my son out of my life. You're going to live with your father. Pack your things right now."

"What? No, Mom, please," Dallas begged. "Please, don't send me away. Look, I'm sorry. I just love Houston and I don't want anything bad to happen to him. But…just give me another chance. I promise I won't say anything else." Dallas was overwhelmed, hysterical that her mother could really do something like this, that she would lose her home and her mother along with her brother.

"No, I'm sorry, that's it," LouAnn said, sitting down in a chair at the kitchen table. She looked older, suddenly. Worn out. Exhausted. And done with Dallas. "I can't take this anymore. I just can't…I'm callin' your daddy. I'm sorry," LouAnn said, head in her hands.

Houston went storming out the front door and jumped in his car. Dallas cried as she packed, as she heard her mother on the phone with her father. On the drive over, her mother looked like a different person. Like the shell of the mother she'd grown up knowing.

At her father's that night, she cried herself to sleep and skipped school the next day. Her eyes nearly swollen shut from tears, she began writing what would be the first of many letters to her brother over the next year. She wouldn't be able to go back to school for several days. Her world had collapsed, snatched away from her by the very people she'd trusted the most, and she couldn't do a thing about it. She thought of running away, but in the end, she developed a coping mechanism. If the people she loved could be so cold and cruel, then so could she. And the armor and the firewalls began to take shape.

She never even knew what became of her brother after all that. She thought he might still be in Alabama somewhere, but she hadn't seen him or looked for him. And he had never tried to contact her.

She took in a deep breath and turned off the water, exhausted from reliving the memories she'd buried so deep and tried to forget. Wilhelmina was sitting at her water dish in the bathroom.

"I do love you, little girl," she said as she reached down to pet her. After drying off, she and Wilhelmina crawled into bed.

Dallas tossed and thrashed all night. Every time she closed her eyes, she remembered one by one the things she'd faced today: the realization that, with Christmas only two and a half weeks away, they'd be announcing the anchor job and, with it, the fate of her career. That she'd been ordered to direct a children's play when she knew nothing about directing or children. That she'd be stuck working closely with Cal until the play was over—a man who she managed to both despise and be drawn to at the same time. And then, worst of all, the mother who had abandoned her so long ago, who had chosen one of her children over the other, had decided she wanted to be in touch. It was all too much for one day, for one person, and Dallas couldn't bring herself to face it.

The best thing she could do was to shove it all down as she had been doing for years. She would have to hold herself together just a little longer to get through Christmas. She exhaled and closed her eyes.

Wilhelmina curled up next to her, purring as she snuggled. Dallas tried to rest and fall sleep, but it was almost impossible to turn her mind off.

How much longer could this coping mechanism work?

5

Dallas woke up early the next morning. Between thoughts of her mother and the house across the street decorated for Christmas with more lights than Times Square, she'd barely gotten any rest at all. She wondered if they were trying to get her to notice them and put them on TV, and she said as much to Daniel as they left to cover their first story of the day.

"They've put up so many lights, I swear, I wake up believing I'm in New York City," Dallas told him as they pulled out of the station lot.

"Why don't you complain?" he asked.

"I think that would just egg them on," she said. Surprisingly, she felt pretty good this morning in spite of all that was going on. It was a new day and that meant she was a day closer to that anchor seat...she hoped.

"I can't believe we're going to cover the Christmas promotion at Lewis's new radio station. That just sounds crazy," she said.

"I know. But he's hired these two new girls from Tennessee and they're doing wonders over there. They're twins but don't look a thing alike."

"I thought we were covering their Twelve Days of Christmas thing?" she asked.

"Oh, we are, but those new girls are so cute…I hoped we could spend some time getting to know them, too. One of them is the promotions director and that's who you're interviewing, Abigail Harper."

"Okay, great. I'll talk to her while you gawk." Dallas smirked at him.

She was happy to be busy with this story today. She'd gotten a message earlier from her news director, Mike Maddox, saying he wanted to meet with her later on. Just thinking of that meeting made her heart jump. She hoped it wasn't about her less-than-stellar performance at yesterday's play practice. She also had another rehearsal tonight, which she was not at all looking forward to.

They arrived at the newly restored Brooks Mansion, a historic building in the center of town that housed the brandnew WRCT—Lewis Heart's new Crimson Tide radio station. This was Lewis's dream come true. He'd fought to save the building when it had faced being torn down, and he'd risked a lot to turn it into the place it had become.

Dallas knew Lewis and his family very well. They all had gone to both high school and college together. Dallas suddenly recalled yesterday's nasty confrontation with Cal after rehearsal. Cal was Lewis's best friend, so he would definitely tell Cal all about her being there to cover the Twelve Days of Christmas promotion at the new radio station. What would Cal tell Lewis about her?

Dallas decided to try her best to get off the naughty list and be nice. She needed a good public image if she wanted to move up in the ranks. She was quite familiar with that whole *more flies with honey* thing, and it was time to use that to her advantage.

"Hey, Lewis, I hear you have a promotion going on around here," she said as she came through the front door. Lewis was just stepping out of his office to head to the studio when she and Daniel arrived.

"Hey, there, Dallas, good to see y'all. Lemme get Abigail. She can tell y'all all about it." He headed to the front office where Caroline Mayfield was tending the phones. She was a local beauty pageant winner with long golden-brown hair and green eyes, and she always kept that gorgeous summer tan—even in the dead of winter.

"Hey, Ms. Dubois, Abigail is expecting y'all," Caroline said, flashing her perfect pageant teeth.

She picked up the phone and announced their arrival. While they waited, Dallas and Daniel wandered around the beautiful lobby, noticing all the exquisite details. Lewis had restored the place even beyond its former glory. The lobby was in a parlor to the left of the front door; a gorgeous wide curving staircase led up to the second floor from the center hall. Just to the back of the stairs on the right was the massive double doorway leading to Lewis's office. Tapestry carpets and sconce lighting created an amber glow throughout the first floor.

Just to the back of the lobby, behind the staircase, a huge studio surrounded with glass windows held all the very latest microphones and technical equipment. Windows from the outside made the studio visible from the sidewalk, so fans could stand on the street and watch the recording of the shows, usually starring Alabama football players and other athletic stars from the campus.

Alabama was the national champion in four different sports some years, but with the reign of the famous football coach,

Paul "Bear" Bryant, having lasted over twenty years, the university was mostly famous for their Crimson Tide football team. Though the Bear had died thirty years ago, the winning dynasty continued under coach Nick Saban. Dallas certainly knew her football well. She'd cheered for the Crimson Tide while Cal was their quarterback.

"Ms. Harper will be right down," Caroline said.

Dallas relaxed a bit in the gorgeous surroundings. The regal Brooks Mansion was all decked out for Christmas. A twelve-foot tree stood in the front hall, greeting guests and tourists with warm, glistening lights. A huge wreath covered in Crimson Tide decorations and crimson-and-white ribbon hung on the beveled glass front doors of the large porch. Christmas carols were even playing over the speakers hooked up throughout the building.

"I'll Be Home for Christmas" began next, and it shot a little pang through Dallas as she waited for Abigail. Home for Christmas likely meant another lonely Christmas alone with Wilhelmina.

Abigail appeared at the top of the stairs. A big smile on her face, she was a Princess Kate look-alike. She wore a dark-colored suit with a Ralph Lauren ruffled blouse and high-heeled black patent leather pumps.

"Hey, Ms. Dubois. Thanks so much for coming out," she said, her hand outstretched to Dallas.

Dallas smiled, but remained guarded. This woman was Lewis's family now. Abigail was Vivi's cousin, a sort of cousin-in-law for Lewis. She knew she needed to at least act as if she was interested. But really, was this the type of story that would get her recognized? Get her that anchor seat? She didn't think so at all. Maybe she needed to mention this to her news director. It was starting to feel as though they were sending her out on less important stories on purpose. Maybe someone had it in for her.

"Hey, Ms. Harper, so nice to meet you. Where would you like to do the interview?" Dallas asked her. "And, please, call me Dallas."

"Right here is just fine, I think. We can get the big Christmas tree in the background. And do call me Abigail." The two ladies chitchatted for a minute while Daniel set up the shot.

"Okay, ready when y'all are," Daniel announced. Abigail began her description of the big Twelve Days of Christmas promotion.

"This fabulous contest will benefit the Tuscaloosa Children's Home, along with other worthwhile charities here in town," she explained.

"How does it work?" Dallas asked.

"Well, we're staging a sort of themed scavenger hunt where people will have to track down specific items that represent the twelve days of Christmas. Our new talk show host, Annabelle, who hosts a segment called *Saved by the Belle* every day at noon, will be giving out clues. We ask that no one really bring us live animals here to the station," she said with a laugh, "but something that represents the days themselves. We've hidden those items all over town. The person who can gather all the twelve days wins an iPad. To enter, anyone can fill out the form online and make a small donation. Remember, all proceeds will go to the Tuscaloosa Children's Home, a wonderful organization."

"Well, this is just terrific," Dallas said, forcing a smile. "Anything else you'd like to add?"

"That's all for now. Just stay tuned to WTAL and WRCT for updates," Abigail finished.

Dallas wrapped up the story and thanked Abigail for her time. "I'm so happy your news director agreed to partner with

us on this. It gives us tremendous visibility," Abigail said as
Daniel began to pack up the cords.

Suddenly Dallas realized that her news director had also
set up her new job directing the play. Was he using *her* to do
all the station's charity work? Especially when there were
bigger, higher profile stories she *should* be spending her time
on? Maybe he didn't want her to get the anchor seat after all.
She'd always thought Mike liked her, but if that were true,
why would he do this to her? It felt as if she was being sabotaged. All charity work. Every single story, except the one
about the missing Baby Jesus statue, was about charities. Not
a single lead story had been assigned to her since Thanksgiv-
ing, now that she thought about it. She would most definitely
bring this up with Mike this afternoon at their meeting.

"Thanks again, Ms. Harper. I'm sure we'll be back for a
follow-up story next week to check in on how it's all developing. Good luck with the contest," Dallas said as she turned
to walk out.

Just then, Daniel shouted, "Good Lord almighty, do ya'll
know there are three chickens on the front porch?"

"Oh, no. That didn't take very long at all, did it? I was so
afraid of this." Abigail sighed. She stepped out in front of them,
nearly tripping over the animals, one taking flight right into
the mansion.

"Y'all, please, you have to take these chickens outta here,"
she shouted to the skinny man in overalls.

"This here is the three French hens. That count for somethin'?"

Abigail lunged after the birds, shaking her hands wildly
and shooing them off the porch. "This is gonna be a long two
weeks," she said, smiling at Dallas before making her way over
to re-explain the rules of the contest to her visitor.

"Good luck," Dallas responded, a bit surprised at how sweet

Abigail seemed to be, even when chasing chickens around a porch. Dallas wasn't used to that. People who were close to Lewis and Vivi didn't usually smile at Dallas. But Abigail and her sister didn't seem to know anything about her history with the little clique from her past. The sisters had just moved here from Tennessee. Dallas kinda liked that fact. She had never had a girlfriend. Too many people in town knew what her mother had done, abandoning one child for the sake of the other; they knew about Dallas's woman-lovin' father and his tarnished reputation and they assumed she'd be just the same. When her relationship with Blake hadn't panned out either, people mostly assumed Dallas was to blame, since everyone thought Blake was perfect. Truthfully, Dallas had never had a chance to prove to herself that she could even have a girlfriend. She flashed Abigail a real smile as she turned toward the news van, the possibility of a new friendship cheering her mood.

Dallas practiced her speech to Mike all the way back to the station. Why would he be trying to hurt her chances for the anchor seat? She couldn't even fathom an answer. As they pulled into a parking spot, she took a deep breath, ready for the confrontation. Well, the *meeting*. But now she had an agenda. She was determined to get to the bottom of this latest possible sabotage and find herself a lead story to cover. Dallas always had a bit of a chip on her shoulder, always assumed someone was out to get her. Maybe this time she was right.

6

Dallas jumped out of the news van, walking at a steady clip to the newsroom to find Mike. She was early for their meeting and could see he was in with someone else. She paced outside his window.

Her tenacity and focus had always been strong suits. She certainly never gave up on anything she wanted. That drive and bulldog mentality hadn't always benefited her, though. In fact, it had been one of the problems back when her mother had abandoned her. She just couldn't give up on her brother. She was a fighter. That's why she wrote all those letters to him that first year. But eventually, she realized he would never answer her, so she gave up trying to contact him. But she tried as hard as she could to hold what was left of her family together, even at fifteen she thought she could fix it all. That never-give-up attitude was always her innate personality.

Those traits helped her enormously as a reporter, though, and were much of the reason she'd been as successful as she

had been so early in her career. She would do whatever it took
to get a story—and that had never been truer than it was now.
She'd fight Mike on this if she had to, but she really hoped it
wouldn't come to that.

Dallas went to her desk to wait on Mike. She thumbed
through the message notes that had been left on her desk. At
the top of the pile was another one from her mother.

I need to see you.

She sighed and put it in her drawer. Dallas got out her cal-
endar, looking over the next few days. Some of her stories had
already been assigned. Obviously, if they had already been assigned, they were just fluff. No breaking news. No lead stories.

Mike emerged from his office and nodded his head to Dallas. He would see her now. She straightened her spine and gave
her long hair a toss, ready to go after what she wanted and get
her questions answered.

"Hey, Dallas," Mike said, shutting the door after her. "Come
on in and have a seat."

Dallas sat down and crossed her long tan legs. She had on
a cream-colored shift dress that hit above her knees and tall,
knee-high boots with spiky high heels in nude leather. Since
Mike had been the one to schedule the meeting, she had to
sit through whatever he had to say before she could dig in and
ask him why he was sabotaging her. But she knew she'd better rephrase that before she actually said it, for fear of sounding too accusatory. She braced herself for Mike's comments.

"Dallas, I need to talk to you about yesterday."

Here it comes.

"I wanted to call you in here to thank you."

Wait…what?

"I know this whole directing thing is really out of your
comfort zone, especially since you have a lot on your plate

competing for the anchor chair. So thanks for agreeing to do the play." Mike leaned back in his swivel chair and smiled.

Dallas didn't know what to think. She tried to smile, to look gracious, but she was instantly suspicious. It was her nature not to trust.

"Sure, Mike. No problem. I mean…I knew I had to do it. It's fine." Dallas really didn't know what to say. She really didn't have any idea how she was going to bring up the topic of being shoved into all the fluff pieces lately, especially after the unexpected praise. The timing seemed off, but waiting was not something Dallas did very well, especially when it came to questions about her career. With no other plan available to her, she dived right in.

"Mike, I've been wondering about something.… Lately, I seem to be coverin' a lot of…charity-based stories, you know? I just sorta miss having something more challenging. I miss the excitement of the leads." There. It was out there and she'd used that honey method that had come to serve her so well. She batted her long lashes and uncrossed her legs, leaning forward toward Mike.

"Oh, I don't know. I think you're doing the same amount of leads as all the reporters here. And you know everyone is doing lots of charity stories right now. It's just that time of year."

Dallas wasn't buying it. She leaned back in her chair and shifted position so that her skirt inched up a little higher on her thigh. She had Mike's attention.

"Look, Mike," she began, "it's no secret between me and you that I want that anchor seat. I just wanna make sure I'm on the right track to get it."

"Don't worry, Dallas. It's all good. Now look, I gotta get to another meeting downtown, but I did want you to know I appreciate you doing that play. Now, take care and get outta here."

He winked at her as they both stood, her towering over the short, rather chubby news director in her five-inch boots. She wasn't satisfied but went on back to her desk anyway. Her phone was ringing as she approached. Any call could be a lead to something big, so she hurried to the ringing phone.

"Dallas Dubois," she answered.

"Please don't hang up again." LouAnn was on the other end of the line.

"Mother, I told you now is a bad time," Dallas said, shocked at her persistence.

"I just want to see you, that's all. It's been too long. Please." LouAnn sounded desperate.

"Yes, it has been a really long time. And that was most certainly not my choice. You can't wait twenty years and expect that we'll just pick up where we left off. Now I have a job to do. Please don't call me again." And she hung up.

There it was again. That lump in her throat. It was choking her. Daniel must have seen the emotional call from his edit bay, because he was now making his way toward her.

"Hey, you okay?" he whispered, almost nervously.

"No, not really. But I will be. I just need a minute."

"What's going on? Did Mike have a problem with the Baby Jesus story?"

"No, it's nothing about Mike. It's private."

"Well, I'm here if you need me. I hate seein' you sad, ya know?"

Dallas knew Daniel had a good heart, but if she had to work with him on a daily basis, there was no way she could let her guard down in front of him. Business was business and she had to keep it that way.

"I'm fine, Daniel. Don't worry. Just the time of year...all that sentimental stuff. And then, you know, the fact that two reporters will be let go in a few weeks. I guess I just let it get to me, but I'm fine now."

"Aw, Dallas, they would never let you go. I mean, after all that fantastic election coverage and that *Find Lewis* campaign you launched last spring, you're a famous reporter. Come on, you know that," he reminded her.

She smiled a weak smile as she reached for a tissue. Not to dab her eyes, but to blot her lipstick. She had managed to swallow that lump and move past the moment with the help of Daniel, although she would never admit she needed anyone.

Christmastime or not, she had grown used to going it alone. And she wasn't fixin' to change that for anyone—not for Mike, not for Daniel and especially not for a long-absentee mother.

L ate that afternoon, Dallas and Daniel wrapped up the editing on the Twelve Days of Christmas story they'd shot that morning, then she grabbed her coat to head to the Bama Theatre for another rehearsal. The weather had turned bitter cold, which was totally abnormal for Tuscaloosa in mid-December. It was normally mild in Tuscaloosa, but this time of year the weather could be unpredictable. A freak snowstorm one day, then the next, sunny and sixty degrees. The current drop in temperature had Dallas bundled up beyond recognition—something she really didn't like.

She parked in the front of the theater and made her way inside. Just as she entered the lobby, she heard her name mentioned from around the corner in the auditorium. Cal was talking to Betty Ann, the choir director. Dallas turned her back so they wouldn't see she was there and listened.

"Oh, Cal. Give her a chance. I think she'll figure it out," Betty Ann was reasoning.

"I'm not so sure," Cal shot back. "I have known this woman most of my life, and I'm telling you, she never changes. She's probably the worst choice we could make for a director replacement. She'll scare those poor kids to death and they'll quit."

Dallas bristled at that. Maybe she was a bit standoffish, but scary? Come on!

"Well, I think that's just a tad harsh," Betty Ann said. "Now, don't you? She's a media professional, which I would say makes her quite qualified—more than you or me, at least. And I know the board checked with her news director, and the TV station is fully behind her. Don't judge her too quickly, okay? Let's give her another chance."

"I guess we don't have a choice," Cal said. "But I'm watching out for those kids. They're my priority. Some of them from the foster home don't have a soul in the world to protect or support them. I'm not gonna be able to just stand back and watch her make demands they can't meet, or talk down to them and make 'em feel worse about themselves."

Dallas thrust her nose in the air and rounded the corner, surprising them both.

"Good afternoon," she said as she walked quickly right by them.

Both of them stood, bug-eyed, likely wondering if she'd heard them. Betty Ann made a quick exit down the theater side aisle as Cal headed to the sound booth upstairs.

"Okay, children take your places," Dallas said as she removed her long coat and warm gloves, throwing them on a theater seat and climbing the stairs to the stage. "We don't have any time to waste today." She clapped her hands together and got right to work, directing them to their positions for the first scene. *Better to make this successful than to fail in front of everyone,* she thought. *Nobody really thinks I can do this, so I'll just have to prove them wrong.* Plus, she knew Cal was listening to everything up there in the booth, as if he was God, so she was more determined than ever to show him just what she was capable of.

"Wait, Ms. Dubois," Betty Ann broke in. "The children are still in choir practice right now. You're a bit early."

"Well, can't they practice the songs second today instead of first?"

"Well, no, not really."

"And why would that be?" Dallas demanded impatiently.

"Some of the children only come for the choir practice. Once we're finished, they can go on home while the rest of the children stay for play rehearsal. It won't be long, okay?" Betty Ann didn't wait for an answer. She began to round the children up and head them down the hall off stage left to the choir room.

"Wait. Wait, please. Now, I'm a little confused. Am I the director or are you the director, Ms. Betty Ann?"

"Well, of course you are in charge," replied Betty Ann, stunned. "But this is what works best for the children, Ms. Dubois. Is this a problem for you?" Her voice was almost sickly sweet, and she was smiling back at Dallas as if she could take her down with one little flick of the wrist. Betty Ann was an old-school Southern belle, schooled in the way of all good Southern women who smiled while they were ripping your head off, slowly. Or choking you with their string of pearls. It took quite a woman to intimidate Dallas, but suddenly she wasn't so sure she was up for a fight.

"Of course not, but I just wanted to be clear so I know my responsibilities," Dallas said, backing down. The whole take-charge attitude wasn't really working at the moment.

"Wonderful. I knew I could count on you," Betty Ann said, grinning as she took the children on to the choir room.

With the children off the stage, Dallas wandered around the set. It was precious, really, with little candy-cane streetlights and fake snow atop all the rooflines. A life-size gingerbread house sat in the corner, complete with Twizzler candies and gumdrop trimmings. Dallas was lost in the memories of her early childhood, where she stood singing on that very stage in a long-ago Christmastime production. She smiled briefly, softening in her recollection.

The set was actually too perfect—since when Dallas took her next step, she lost her footing on the stairs down the trap door, which was concealed by a carefully arranged pile of fake snow. Unable to steady herself, she fell right to the bottom, twisting her ankle on the way down. She was in a lot of pain, but still she was thankful that no one was around to see her in an embarrassed heap at the bottom of the stairs, her cream-colored dress dirty with dark marks and shoe prints from the wooden stage steps.

She tried to get up, but her ankle was hurt terribly. Suddenly, she heard someone walking across the stage. She thought it must be Cal and hurriedly tried to get up again. He couldn't see her like this. She'd managed to shift only slightly to the side when she looked up to notice a cute little pudgy boy was standing at the top of the steps looking down at her. His mop of dark curly hair hung loosely around blue eyes that stared down at her.

"Ms. Dubois, are you okay? Do you need help?" he asked.

"No, I'm fine," she said dismissively, her cheeks aflame. "Just go back to class. What are you doing out here anyway?" She hated feeling even remotely vulnerable and wasn't sure she'd ever be able to break that habit, even when the most adorable little boy was looking into her eyes.

"I was going to the potty and I saw you fall down," he said. Just then, Cal appeared next to him.

"Need some help?" he asked with a smirk.

"No, actually, I'm fine. Now, both of you just go. Really. I'm fine."

"Well, are you plannin' on stayin' there long? The kids'll be back here pretty soon to get started," Cal said with his hands on his hips.

"Yes. Go. Really." She winced as she tried to pull herself up, regretting the five-inch boots that, she admitted to herself, weren't exactly the proper footwear for directing a children's play.

"Go! Both of you." She winced again.

"Come on, don't be so stubborn. Can you just let me help you?" But Cal didn't wait for a response. He skipped down the stairs and slipped his arm under hers and his other arm around her waist and helped her up. He was inches from her face. This was the very position she had promised herself to never be in again. The one she'd found herself in at the hospital when she'd been covering the birth of baby Tallulah. It was that dangerous spot that made her unable to think. Made her heart quicken and her palms sweat. His gray-green eyes fixed on hers, she could feel his breath on her face.

It didn't seem to matter that they really didn't get along; being that close stirred something inside her, made her feel a spark. And by the look in his eyes, she bet he felt it, too.

But she couldn't even begin to think about that right now. Instead, she pushed away from him and began dusting herself off. She moved toward the stairs and tentatively climbed to the top, moving slowly on her tender ankle.

Cal followed closely behind her, and the little boy was still waiting on stage when she made it to the top. He reached out a small hand to Dallas, but she only shook her head.

"Thanks, but I'm fine. Go on back to class, uhm…" She didn't know the child's name yet.

"Tristan," he smiled sweetly. "Tristan Brooks is my name."

"Well, go back to choir, Tristan. Now."

"Ms. Dubois," he said, "Why don't you like us?"

Dallas stopped fixing herself and stood in the silence. Cal looked at her with his eyebrows raised, apparently as interested in her answer as Tristan. She swallowed hard and cleared her throat, but before she could answer, the little boy ran off, disappearing into the darkness off stage. She gave herself a final dust-off, then smiled a forced grin at Cal and limped off to the ladies' room.

In the bathroom, she sat down on an antique couch by the makeup mirrors and took off her boots. Her right ankle looked bruised and a tad swollen. She stood on it with all her weight. It hurt, but she decided it was just twisted. It felt good to be barefoot on the cold tile floor.

Then a knock.

"Hey, Dallas. The kids are coming back." It was Cal. Was he worried about her?

"Okay, I'll be right there,"

"Can you walk?" he asked through the door.

"I most certainly can." She couldn't help her tone—it came out snippy before she could even think about it. "Uh, thanks, though," she added.

"Sure." She could hear him walk away.

Her palms were still sweaty. Her heart was still jumping. If there would never be anything between them, she was going to have to learn to tone down her reactions to him along with everything else. As hard as she tried, she couldn't shake that image of his face so close to hers.

8

Dallas arrived back at her place that evening and turned on the fireplace. It was a gas fireplace, so all you had to do was click on a switch and the flame appeared like magic. She had set up her little Christmas tree, the same one she had used for the past several years, in the corner next to the front window where the little twinkling lights could be seen from the street—though nothing would compete with the glaring monstrosity that was her neighbor's decorations. She changed into some comfortable clothes, poured herself a glass of wine and flicked on the TV. Then she sank into the couch with a bag of frozen peas from the freezer on her swollen ankle.

Wilhelmina snuggled up next to her fuzzy socks, eventually creeping up to Dallas's lap. The two of them sat together watching her favorite Christmas channel—Hallmark movies. You couldn't beat those at Christmastime.

Alone in her house, Dallas let her walls come down. With her precious cat asleep on her lap, she felt safe and at peace from the frantic life she lived outside. She could take a break from the façade she constructed in front of the public. Here, she didn't have to be tough or abrasive, cold or stoic. In the safe confines of her home, she was soft and romantic and longed for closeness. But she didn't trust anyone with that side of her anymore. Not anyone but Wilhelmina. She sat comfortably, dozing early.

It was barely 7:30 p.m. when she heard a knock on the door, followed by giggling. What would a bunch of kids want with her? She moved Wilhelmina to the side, pushed the blanket off and hobbled awkwardly to the door. When she opened it, she was greeted by a chorus of young voices.

"You're a mean one, Mrs. Grinch…" the kids sang.

Well, isn't this sweet, she thought, wondering when caroling had become so cruel.

The kids continued to sing their own version of the famous Grinch song, personalizing it just for Dallas. She was not amused. Some of the faces she recognized as a few of the older kids from the play, and she was a little shocked that they'd be brave enough to play this kind of prank. Instead of laughing and being in on the joke, she rolled her eyes and slammed the door on them, remembering exactly why she had never been a fan of kids to begin with.

She scooped up Wilhelmina and limped to her bedroom. Her cell phone rang just as she'd sat down, so she reached across her bed and fumbled through her bag to find it.

"Hello?"

"Hey, it's just me," Daniel said on the other line. "We gotta set up early. That Dickens thing is all day, so you want me to swing by and just pick you up?"

"Sure, that'd be great. Thanks." She was starting to think she might actually like Daniel, that they might be able to get along, after all.

"Well, this way you won't have to drive your car, and I can just drop you off when it's over," he explained.

"Awesome. I really appreciate it. Parking for that thing is gonna be just awful. So, thanks again."

"No problemo," he said. "See ya at eight sharp."

"Okay, good night."

"Night."

Dallas smiled as she turned over in her bed. Daniel was slowly becoming a friend. And for once, she decided she was going to allow that. She was glad he hadn't been around to witness her great escape down the trap door stairs. All she could think of was how mortified she had been today with Cal and Tristan staring down at her.

It bothered her even more because it was Cal. Part of her wanted to appear perfect to him, to prove to him she was something special. Make him see just what he was missing. The same part of her wanted to prove something to her mother, to everyone, to show them that she *was* something, and weren't they just sorry that they weren't in her circle? But the trouble was, she had been pushing everyone away for so long that no one was even in her immediate circle to care. She had locked everyone out.

Quit it, she scolded herself. This was not the time to sulk over what she didn't have. Instead, she needed to keep her eye on the prize. She needed to get the anchor spot and remain employed. Blaming the wine and lack of dinner for making her feel gloomy, she gingerly got to her feet and stumbled into the kitchen looking for something to eat.

Dallas had another secret that no one knew, and she'd never let anyone know this deep, dark part of herself. It was embarrassing, since so much of her life had been about competition—though not necessarily when it came to the basic skills of living.

Dallas had a huge problem when it came to blissful domesticity. She'd never learned to cook. Anything. She couldn't bake something from a box. Somehow she even managed to burn noodles. And it didn't stop there—she couldn't iron, let alone sew on a button. She was a disaster as a homemaker. Her secret dream was to marry someone rich enough that those things just wouldn't matter.

But until she could learn to let someone in, to trust someone enough to even consider marriage, her best friend would continue to be her microwave.

After a quick frozen dinner, she fed Wilhelmina and turned in early. She promised herself to go talk to those idiot neighbors before tomorrow night. Their Christmas lights were shining like the Las Vegas strip and she did need her beauty sleep, after all. Tomorrow was a big day. Dixie Dickens was the big story and she had finally been assigned the lead. She just hoped Cal wouldn't be there to throw her off.

9

Dallas awoke excited. It was her first lead story in two weeks and she was ready. Dixie Dickens was a wonderful Christmas festival held every year. It was a time when the whole city was full of holiday excitement. Dallas and Daniel made their way downtown and parked in front of the old bank building near the city clock.

Every business and storefront was decked out for a Victorian Christmas. People were showing up in droves in period costumes. Long, velvet, cranberry-colored dresses, huge brimmed hats, tuxes with tails, white spats over black shiny shoes. Men wore tall top hats, offering their arm to the ladies. Costumed carolers strolled along the downtown streets.

The streetlights were wrapped in garland and topped with deep red velvet bows. Stands for hot cider and warm cocoa were set up along the sidewalks and down near the river. Tiny white lights were strung across the main street with huge wreaths draped right in the middle. Downtown historic sites would be open for candlelight tours as soon as dusk fell.

And at the end of the street, Father Christmas awaited the children who would anxiously stand in line for a chance to whisper their sugarplum wishes in his ear.

All of the romance of the Victorian period was alive and made Dallas feel better just being at the event. Even *she* was excited, if a tad nervous. It was the big story in town that day, and she knew Cal and the entire gang would be milling around somewhere.

"Let's set up near the downtown Christmas tree first," Dallas said.

"Perfect. I was thinking the same thing," Daniel agreed as he began to unload the van and set up the camera. "People won't start to arrive till the afternoon, and the lights won't come on till dusk."

"I was thinking I might like to do my stand-up tonight in front of the bagpipe parade. It'll have great visuals and natural sound and they'll be just far enough away" Dallas said. She was always a pro. Born to do the job she was doing. And she was a natural on camera, too.

The mood was light as she made her way around the area, taking a few notes and watching the shops set out their stands and put their candles in the windows. Her ankle was still a bit swollen but feeling much better. She'd decided to wear her three-inch heels today to play it safe. And she didn't have to worry about a rehearsal tonight because the children from the choir were actually downtown marching in the evening parade.

The mayor would also be here making the rounds tonight. Kitty, Dallas's former stepmother and Blake's mother, was practically engaged to him, so she'd likely be at his side. They had been fused at the hip since late June and that made Dallas cringe a little.

Her relationship with Kitty wasn't so bad. She had been married to Dallas's dad for about ten years, starting just before Dallas had been sent to live with them. During that time, Kitty had tried to be a mother or at least a friend to Dallas, but she hadn't actually spoken to Kitty since Vivi's wedding back in September. It wasn't really Kitty who was making her so nervous, though—it was her daughter, Blake, who would also be at the festival tonight.

Dallas worked hard that day, talking to many different merchants and making sure she was covering the event as thoroughly as she could. Late afternoon came, and she and Daniel sat in the satellite van to package the story, editing all the interviews and extra footage into the video that would run just before Dallas did the live stand-up to close the segment. She'd be the lead story tonight on the six o'clock news, and that was in just a couple of hours.

"I'm heading out for some hot chocolate. Want anything?" she asked Daniel.

"Yeah, I'll take a hot cider."

"Okay, be back in a few." Dallas slipped out of the news van and into the cold night air.

Dusk was falling, and the clear cold winter air helped create a magnificent sunset over the Warrior River. Vibrant orange and turquoise illuminated the evening sky like a painting, casting a warm glow over downtown Tuscaloosa, now awash in the evening's blush. In moments, the twinkling lights appeared, sprinkled over downtown like decorations on a cake.

Dallas walked over to the hot chocolate house and got in line. The closed-off streets were starting to fill up with families.

"Hey, aren't you Dallas Dubois? I recognize you from TV," said the young woman at the window.

"Oh," Dallas said with a practiced smile. "Yep, it's me, in person." She loved being recognized. "I'll take a hot chocolate and an apple cider, please."

"Comin' right up." The girl disappeared to the side and returned with the warm drinks. "That'll be two dollars."

"Thanks so much," Dallas said as she handed the money to the girl.

"Would you mind if I have your autograph?" she asked Dallas. "My momma will just die when she sees it."

"Sure," Dallas replied, basking in the attention. She set the cups down on the counter and took a pen from the girl and signed her order pad.

"Oh, thank you, Ms. Dubois. This is so awesome."

"No problem," she said, picking up her drinks again and turning around.

"Yes, Ms. Dubois, I'd love to get your autograph, too."

Cal was standing right behind her, a look of sarcastic admiration on his face, and the surprise had her stumbling back, her warm drinks sloshing onto her winter-white Calvin Klein coat.

"Oh, no! Look at this mess," she cried. "And I have a live shot in an hour."

"Oh, crap. I'm so sorry. I really didn't mean to scare you like that." Cal did look genuinely sorry as he grabbed handfuls of napkins from the stand to help her clean up. He had a young man with him, his oldest nephew, Justin, there for the night. Justin was a freshman at Alabama. He looked enthralled to meet the star news reporter, even though she was currently splattered with a little hot chocolate.

"This is my nephew, Justin," Cal said, offering her the napkins once she'd put down her cups. "He's a freshman at Alabama. Justin, this is Dallas Dubois."

"Wow. Nice to meet you, ma'am. I love watching you

on TV," the boy said, looking a little starstruck. She knew it wasn't typical for the younger crowed to be familiar with local TV reporters, aside from maybe the anchors since they appeared on air nightly, but her Barbie-doll looks had garnered her more than a few male fans from the around town.

Dallas was busy trying to dab herself off before the stains set in, but she stuck her hand out to give Justin's a shake.

"Yes, uhm… Hi, Justin, nice to meet you, too." She gave a tight smile and then went back to the mess on her coat.

"Let me help you," Cal said. And before she could say no, he was trying to wipe off the hot chocolate, too, patting the collar of her coat, his face in that dangerous place again, much too close to her own.

"Don't worry, Cal, it's fine. I've gotta go. These are gettin' cold and Daniel is waiting."

She grabbed the drinks and headed back to the news van in a hurry.

"So, Uncle Cal. Your friend is pretty hot," Justin said as they walked back to Vivi and Lewis. "Why don't you ask her out?"

"No way, kiddo. I've known that woman my whole life and she is nothing but bad news." Then he laughed. "No pun intended."

"I think I'd sacrifice the headline for her," Justin teased. "She's easily the hottest reporter Tuscaloosa has ever had."

"Yeah, but she's also incredibly full of herself. No room for me and all that hairspray in my little car."

They laughed and rejoined the others curbside, waiting for the parade to begin.

Dallas positioned herself on the street corner where the bagpipe parade would march right behind her as she did her live stand-up. Everything was in place and ready to go. For a quick fix, she'd taken her scarf out of her coat and let it hang over the chocolate spatters so no one could see her little accident. Dallas was nothing if not resourceful.

The top of the newscast was playing in her earpiece, and she could hear the anchors introduce her. Daniel pointed and, giving her the signal, she was on.

"Good evening, Tuscaloosa. We are live at Dixie Dickens Downtown where we have traveled back to the lush and lovely times of the storybook Victorian era. So many Tuscaloosans are braving the chilly temperatures to be out here tonight just to have a chance to immerse themselves in the days of Charles Dickens and Tiny Tim."

That was the toss to her packaged story, which was now playing while she waited for the engineers to toss it back to her for her live stand-up. Dallas could hear the bagpipes approaching from down the street. It was all going just as she'd planned.

Just then, the children's choir rounded the street corner singing "I'll Be Home For Christmas" as they came up behind her in front of the bagpipes. She turned, recognizing the little faces as those from the Christmas play she was directing, and Betty Ann was walking backward in front of them, directing.

As Dallas watched them, her eyes locked with little Tristan, who had been there when she'd fallen down the stairs. She was suddenly caught in the memory of what he'd asked her: *Why don't you like us?* The question shook her even more now as the children sang the song that reminded her of the days when her own childhood was happy, when she'd had her older brother and her mother home with her for Christmas. Behind Tristan she recognized one of the older children who'd caroled cruelly on her doorstep the night before. Behind the choir, Kitty and the mayor walked happily, arm in arm, waving merrily at the gathered crowds.

A knot began to form in her stomach. It was as if the town had planned this—to parade all the uncomfortable moments she'd been dealing with lately in front of her right before she was meant to be live on TV.

Dallas was fixin' to hit overload when she turned and saw Lewis and Vivi, Blake and Sonny, all standing and laughing with Cal. In that very second, the engineers threw the shot back to her. Between the cute little boy, the song, the thought of being Mrs. Grinch and seeing the Cal clique, it was just too much for her.

Daniel signaled her to go. "You're on...."

"We are live in downtown Tuscaloosa...."

She could feel all the eyes searing her like laser beams. She locked gazes with Blake, who smiled at her. Dallas took that as a dare, assuming Blake meant, *Go on, I dare you to finish the broadcast under all this pressure.*

"So come on out and join us...um... Yes, we are live at the, uh, Dixie Dickens...."

She looked at Cal. Of course he could tell she was having trouble, but he didn't smile back, and she took that as a vote of no confidence. It was her first live shot in weeks, yet suddenly, every single insecurity Dallas had ever had hit her all at once in this one important moment. The anchor seat hung in the balance. And Dallas was blowing it. In front of everyone.

"Dallas Dubois...good night." She didn't even utter the station call letters. Totally embarrassed, she tossed her microphone to Daniel and ran off into the darkness. This was the first major mistake she had ever made on live TV. Well, unless you counted a few weeks ago when she'd told all of Tuscaloosa she hated children, but she had covered herself on that one, so it didn't count. This time, there was no way to hide her blundering.

Everyone heard her stutter. The Cal clique watched her run off. Anyone who'd had the TV on tonight would have seen her fail miserably—including Mike, her station manager. Dallas couldn't imagine how this night could get any worse.

Blake felt terrible as she watched Dallas make a quick exit through the commotion of the parade. Even after everything she and Dallas had been through over the years, Blake still wanted her to succeed. She placed her hand on her burgeoning belly, her other hand held tightly by the love of her life, police chief Sonny Bartholomew. It hadn't been an easy road to find this kind of happiness, to find the love and the family she'd always hoped for. She knew Dallas must be searching for the same thing, even if she wasn't exactly the warmest person Blake knew.

Suddenly Blake was struck with the memory of a certain beauty pageant when she and her best friend, Vivi, had covered Dallas's sparkly dress with itching powder. Dallas had been driving them crazy with her bad attitude and downright meanness, so they'd thought a little public humiliation might put her in her place. But once the plan was in effect, Blake regretted having gone so far. She'd felt so bad when they found Dallas sitting in the wings of the stage, sixteen years old, itching and crying and all alone. Dallas didn't have a mother to come backstage and tend to her, they'd realized. And Blake was supposed to have been her family.

In a split second, Blake knew she had a once-in-a-lifetime chance to fix that. To make up for that awful trick and to take some responsibility. She kissed Sonny on the cheek and said, "I'll be right back," then she darted off into the darkness after Dallas.

Eventually she found her sitting on a dark street corner behind the courthouse, and she was crying. Dallas never cried in front of anyone, Blake knew. Not ever. She had buried her face in her knees, and didn't see Blake approaching until she was right in front of her. Blake knelt down on one knee.

"Dallas. It's okay. Really." She barely knew what to say, with all their history of bad blood.

"Oh, perfect," Dallas groaned. "Blake, just get out of here. Leave me alone."

"Please, let me talk to you. I promise I am being for real. Listen to me, it's all okay."

"What do you know about it? Anyway, I can't trust *you*. You've lived for this moment!" Dallas was furious, her cheeks wet with tears but her eyes blazing with anger. "You've always wanted to see how hard I can fall. So, go ahead and have your laugh. You've been out to get me my whole life. I'm sure you and your friends are just delighted with that display back there. Just get the hell outta here."

"Dallas, I'm not going anywhere. I can be just as stubborn as you. I'm a lawyer, remember?"

"How could I forget?" Dallas rolled her eyes. "You've been bragging about that since graduation day."

"What I mean is, we're a lot alike, Dallas. Strong and determined. And no matter what happened out there tonight, you are a wonderful reporter."

Dallas's mouth hung open. Her brows were bent. She looked utterly stunned to hear that statement from her archenemy.

"You are." Blake was looking Dallas right in the eyes as she spoke, and she meant every word that she said. Blake had been through some huge changes recently—her divorce from political-minded Harry, finding Sonny, her high-school sweetheart and true love, and now she was carrying Sonny's baby. She had matured since those days when all she and Dallas could do was bicker. She was genuine and sincere in her words to Dallas, and she just hoped Dallas would be able to see that.

"I know it seemed rough out there," Blake continued, "but you did better than you think. Honestly, it just looked like those damn bagpipes were too freakin' loud and you couldn't hear yourself think. That's all. You were great, and I bet no one will even think twice about that. Don't worry about it anymore. You need to get out there and enjoy this party now."

"Blake, I don't know why you're doing this. Is this just some way to mock me?" Dallas seemed worn down but hopeful.

"No…not at all. I just wanted you to know you're good at this. I know we've never been all that nice to each other, and I'm really sorry about that. We've both made mistakes, but, listen, I want to put all that in the past, okay?"

"Sure, I mean…I guess." Dallas took a tissue from her coat

pocket and wiped the tears from her cheeks. "I still have no idea why in the world you are doin' this."

"I'm doing it 'cause it's time. That's all. It was overdue." Blake reached over and squeezed Dallas's cold hand and smiled a confident smile. "Now, go have some fun. I'll see you later." And Blake walked away.

Dallas stood alone on the dark street corner. What the hell had just happened? She felt her head swimming as she tried to process everything. Something was stirring inside her that she hadn't felt in a very long time. Even though she had messed up her report, even though everything seemed to be hitting her at once, and her job—heck, her happiness—was on the line, something inside her felt really good. It was a feeling she hadn't felt since childhood. It was a sense of hope, and she held on to it as tightly as she could.

Dallas walked slowly back to the news van, and Daniel hugged her as soon as she stepped up into the back.

"You were fine, ya know?" he said softly. "Besides, nobody really heard anything, those freakin' bagpipers were so loud," he added, laughing. She knew it was obvious that she'd been crying, and he was trying to lighten the mood. He knew she put so much pressure on herself, and the bubble had burst tonight. At least in her eyes.

Dallas sat in the passenger seat and buckled up. "Let's just head back, okay? I need to go home." She had to reconcile to herself that tonight's performance didn't do anything to help her shot at the anchor seat. And she had to try to wrap her mind around the idea of Blake and…friendship? Even the thought of that was too crazy to process.

"You sure you don't wanna go back to the station?"

"No, I really need to get off this ankle." She gave him a small smile. She was tired. And she really didn't want to face anyone at WTAL. She just wanted to get home to Wilhelmina, where she felt safe. Where everything still made sense.

Daniel let Dallas out in front of her house, and she made her way up to the front porch. It was dark. She had forgotten to leave the light on, and her few Christmas lights weren't on any sort of automatic timer. The neighbor's Times Square lights were glaring, as usual, so she used them to find her way up the stairs of her front porch and fumbled to put her key in the front door. Out of the shadows of the porch, a figure approached her.

"Dallas?" The person reached for her arm, and Dallas nearly jumped out of her skin.

"I'm sorry to show up like this," the woman said softly. "I didn't mean to scare you, but I really needed to see you. And since you wouldn't return my calls, I had to come here."

"Mother!" Dallas had to take this in a minute. She hadn't seen her mother in so many years and, looking at her now, she realized she would have hardly recognized her on the street. "You shouldn't have come here," she said as she opened her front door and flicked on the porch light, all of the Christmas lights coming on at the same time.

"Please, let me come in. It's freezing out here."

"Fine," Dallas said after a slight pause. "But you can't stay long. I have an early meeting tomorrow and I just got back from work." She allowed her mother inside. LouAnn looked frail. She was certainly not aging well. She was already a small woman, but she had withered over the years. Her dry gray hair was unruly, sticking out from under her knitted winter hat.

Dallas took her coat and hat, hanging them on a hook by the door before leading her mother into the living room. They sat awkwardly at opposite ends of the couch, both of them silent for a few moments.

Eventually, LouAnn spoke. "Dallas, I want you to know I think it's time we all get together this year, you know, for Christmas."

"Really? You think it's time? Why not last year? Why not twenty years ago, Mother?"

"Look, I know you're still angry…"

"Angry? Is *that* all you think I am? Let me clue you in. I'm infuriated. I'm appalled. I want nothing to do with you. Ever! You left me. You chose Houston over me—something no proper mother would ever even consider. I'm not just angry, Mother. I'm alone! And it's because of you and your inability to take responsibilities. I was your daughter and you abandoned me. I'm not sure why you think you can turn up on my doorstep after twenty years of silence and think we're gonna have a nice little chat. It's laughable, really. Now, thank you very much for this little surprise visit, but I want you to go."

"Would it have been better if I had chosen you? Is that what you wanted?"

"Oh, mother, you are such a piece of work. What kind of mother *chooses?* No, you shouldn't have chosen either of us. You were the parent. It was your job to hold the family together, not tear us apart…don't you think?"

"I was wrong, Dallas. Please, just…"

"You have to leave now. I have nothing else to say to you."

"Your brother wants to see you, too. We need you to forgive us." LouAnn was breaking down.

"Me? Forgive y'all? Really? I was a child! I was fourteen years old and I begged for forgiveness—from both of you. I wrote letters and wondered where my family was, what I'd done that was so bad my family would throw me away. You treated me like garbage. Just threw me out like trash. And when I asked to come home, or for you to come to my graduations or any other events in my life, both of you flat-out ignored me and never even wrote me back," Dallas was shaking with years of pent-up rage and sadness, tears spilling down her cheeks.

"I'm sorry. I was so wrong," LouAnn pleaded, sobbing.

"I lost my home, my friends and, most of all, my family. And what have you done since then to make things better? Did you answer my letters? Ever even call to check on me? Ever try to say you were so sorry that you threw me away and missed every single life event for the last twenty years? Or even apologize properly to show that you really wanted me back in your life? Nothing. Nothing at all. You just show up out of the blue and you think...what? That it will be as though all these years hadn't passed? As if you'd been here all along? No, Mother. There's too much water under the bridge. Please, just go, okay?" Dallas stood and went to the door, holding out her mother's things in one hand and opening the door with the other.

LouAnn cried quietly as she zipped up her coat and turned to the door.

"Please, Dallas. Just think about it."

Dallas didn't answer her. LouAnn walked out slowly, her head down, and Dallas locked the door behind her. She went to her bedroom and closed the door. Falling across her bed, she suddenly felt as if she was fourteen all over again. All the deep buried pain engulfed her and she cried herself to sleep.

11

"Hey, Blake, am I bothering you? It's Dallas."

Dallas still wasn't sure how she'd mustered up the courage to pick up the phone and call Blake, but she'd decided it was time to try her hand at trusting someone. She still questioned the entire conversation she'd had with Blake the night before, but she was going to try accepting Blake's offer of reconciliation. It was an experiment in hope—and Dallas felt she sure could use some of that right about now. Still, it was weird that the person she'd picked for this test was Blake, her oldest enemy. But she had known her longer than anyone else in her present life, and to Dallas, something felt right about it.

"Dallas! Hey. No, not at all. Feeling better?"

It was a huge relief to hear Blake was still friendly. Dallas braced herself and carried on. "Um, yeah, a bit better. I wanted to call to thank you for...that talk we had last night. And also, I was wondering something."

"Sure, what can I do for ya?" Blake asked.

"Well, I remember you spent a lot of time in the theater when we were growing up and, I don't know if you heard, but I'm directing the Christmas play right now and I could use some advice." There. Whew. She took a deep breath. She'd done it. Taken the first step. She was actually reaching out to someone, and it felt...okay. *I can do this,* she thought.

Blake responded without hesitation. "Sure, I'd love to help out. I was on the stage so much, I think Kitty would have loved if I had just become an actor instead of a lawyer. But they're basically the same thing," she laughed.

"Kitty would have loved whatever you did," Dallas said, recalling all the unconditional love showered on Blake by her mother. "Well, great! So...um...do you think you can meet me for lunch today? I just need a little direction." Dallas laughed at herself. "Yeah, a little direction for the director."

"Sure. I'm wide-open for lunch. Where ya wanna go?"

"I love Fifteenth Street Diner."

"Oh, me, too. Okay. See you there in, like, an hour?"

"Sounds great. See you then." Dallas hung up and leaned back in her chair. *Wow. Blake might turn into a friend,* she thought. *What planet am I on?*

During a Tuscaloosa winter, you never know what you're gonna get. The crisp, cold December air had turned milder, with temperatures in the mid fifties and bright sunshine. The surprises in the weather seemed to reflect Dallas's life right now: something new at every turn.

"Hey, Blake," Dallas said as she slid into the crimson vinyl booth at the fifties-style diner.

"Hey, Dallas. I've already ordered our drinks. I remember how you loved your sweet tea as a girl, so I just assumed..."

"Yeah...still the same. Thanks." Dallas liked that Blake had remembered such a small detail. Already she felt at ease.

Was she being a fool? She and the one person who had been her nemesis as long as she could remember were sitting down together for lunch. She studied Blake's face and mannerisms carefully as she talked, looking for signs that this might not be real. That she was somehow being tricked or mocked. But she never picked up anything but genuine happiness. Sonny had certainly brought out the best in Blake. Maybe being in love was everything the fairy tales said.

Blake looked exactly how you'd expect a Southern beauty pageant winner to look—long dark hair that fell loosely around her ample breasts, gorgeous light blue-green eyes, flawlessly tanned skin. But she wasn't as tall as Dallas. Dallas was about five foot eight in bare feet. Blake stood only about five foot four and now that she was pregnant, she was almost always in flats. Dallas towered over her in her usual five-inch heels.

"So," Dallas began, but it wasn't easy after all these years. "I, uh, wanted to say thanks again for last night. I mean that was really nice of you and all."

"Hey, no biggie. I mean, I'm fixin' to be a mother pretty soon, and all that anger just isn't good for anybody, ya know? Especially a new baby. I mean all that crap in the past is just stupid. We were teenagers and now we're adults. There's no reason we should carry on like rivals anymore."

Blake was surprisingly down-to-earth. Where the hell had that huge ego of hers gone to? It wasn't the apocalypse, but it sure felt as if the world was totally off its axis.

"It's a surprise to hear you say this, I have to say, Blake."

"I know," Blake said a little sadly. "We've held on to these grudges for a lot of years. But, seriously, I'm just tired. Keeping up all that attitude is just exhausting, really. I want to apologize for all the awful things I did when we were young. I was terrible back then, I see that now. I really want to clear the air."

"Well, I appreciate that so much. But I wanted to say that

I'm sorry, too. For back when we were teenagers, sure. But…"
Dallas hesitated, unsure of how exactly to explain. "I guess
I'm most sorry for what I've done as an adult. I mean, all that
sneaking around with the camera trying to catch some news
about you and Sonny sneaking around—I was completely out
of line to try to use that against you. And then, my God…
what happened with Harry that day…"

Dallas felt her cheeks blazing as she remembered that awful
afternoon with Blake's now-ex-husband. He had been in the
middle of his run for senate, and Dallas had hoped to benefit from his connections. She had basically thrown herself
at him that particular day in his backyard—and Blake had
walked in right at the worst moment. Dallas was ashamed to
even think about it.

"Oh, Blake, I'm just totally embarrassed about all that. I
hope you can understand how sorry I am. Most of the time,
I'm just thinking about work and how to make sure I can keep
my job or…well, sometimes I don't make the best decisions
about how to do that."

"Hey, you know what?" Blake said, and Dallas was surprised to realize she was smiling. "You actually did me a favor.
Truth is, you weren't the only one I caught him with. Anyway, it's all said and done now. I want to be married to the
kind of man who wouldn't cheat—even when tempted with
a woman like you! You're the ultimate fantasy girl, and poor
Harry just couldn't live up to the test. Besides, he's not my
husband anymore."

"I haven't even begun to forgive myself over that, so I'm
just…I can't believe that you would. We've been against each
other so long that it just doesn't feel real to be sittin' here with
you and actually havin' a nice talk."

"It's real for me. I kinda always felt in the back of my head that maybe I'm the one who started this twenty-year tug-of-war, anyway."

"What do ya mean?"

"You know, way back when Vivi and I sabotaged your dress with itching powder."

"Oh, I think I remember that." Dallas smiled, raising her eyebrows at Blake.

"I'm really sorry about that awful trick and, well, I just need to bring this baby into the world when I don't have any anger or hate. And Sonny completes me in a way I never knew possible so that…all this stuff just seems ridiculous now." She smiled wistfully, resting her hand on her five-month baby bump.

"He always did love you, Blake. Since you guys started dating back in high school. I guess everybody knew that but you."

Blake smiled wistfully. "Now, tell me all about this Christmas play. Sounds like a hoot," Blake said, smiling.

The waitress came back with their drinks and took their orders. Dallas ordered the chunky vegetable beef soup and a side of fried green tomatoes.

"Oh, I love their fried green tomatoes! Best in town. I'll just have the same," Blake said, smiling at the waitress.

Blake was so confident and she had a beautiful pregnant glow. Dallas thought the pregnancy hormones might be holding the real Blake hostage. Like the happy drunk, she was the happy pregnant lady.

"Yes, the play," Dallas said. "Well, I'm pinch-hitting this one. The director got the flu bug, and they called my news director and asked if I would step in, since we always try to do a lot of community service this time of year. Mike said yes before he actually asked me."

"That's awful. Did you even wanna do it?"

"Me? Direct a play with kids? Come on, Blake. Not that much has changed," she replied with a smirk. "So, no. Not

really. But Mike said it was part of station *policy* to do chari-
table work this month, and I guess I was next on the list."

"So, what did you need my help with?"

"Well, the show is in less than two weeks, and some of these
kids have no idea what their lines are yet. They're either reading straight from the book or else they need me to say their
lines from the wings."

"Oh, my. That's no way to put on a show. But luckily,
you've come to the right place," Blake answered. "I directed
little kids as a college project eons ago. You have to gain their
trust first. Let them know you're on their side and that you're
there for them. Then all they wanna do is please you, so they
try very hard."

Dallas realized she had been going about this all wrong.
"Threatening them with kicking them out of the show might
be a little too harsh then, huh?"

Blake burst out laughing. "Ya think?"

"I guess I'll try this new approach today. They're having so
much trouble. At first I was so irritated by the whole thing,
especially since I hadn't even signed up for it. But then…"
Dallas had felt such a whirlwind of emotions after being confronted by her mother. She had suddenly remembered what
it was like to be the powerless child at the mercy of the adults
around you—and how awful it was to be cast off by them.
The memories had helped her realize how the kids from the
play must feel around her when she hollered at them or flat-
out ignored them. But she wasn't sure she was ready to share
all that with Blake. This friendship thing was still very new
and very fragile. "Well, anyway…something made me realize that maybe I was the one being difficult, not them. They
seem scared," Dallas explained.

"Well, they probably are, a little. They loved Mrs. Fairbanks. She had been their director for a month before she got

sick. Plus, she's been the director of that theater forever. And they probably don't watch the news, so they have no idea who you are."

Ouch. That hurt Dallas's ego for a second. But she realized Blake was probably right.

"You do have a point."

The waitress returned to set the plate of fried green tomatoes between them and refill Dallas's sweet tea. They sat and chatted for over an hour, laughing and apologizing and making up for lost time. It didn't seem real, and yet, at the same time, it felt so genuine and honest. It was good to clear the air. It was good to be *real* for a change. To not have that firewall so thick and impenetrable. It was a new feeling for Dallas, but one she really wanted to get used to. She was even looking forward to rehearsal that night.

"Thanks so much for all the advice, Blake," she said, sipping the last of her tea.

"Hey, no problem, anytime. I like to be needed. It's my business, you know?" Blake got out her wallet to pay.

"No. Let me. I asked you here," Dallas said.

"Get it next time. It's fine." Blake laid down the cash and a generous tip as they got up to leave.

"Dallas," Blake said. "I have an idea. If you need any help with anything for this play, like sets or costumes maybe, Vivi is a fantastic seamstress and I'm pretty good with the sets, too. I mean, I don't want to intrude or anything, but I was just thinkin' out loud. In case there was anything we could do."

"That would be great." Dallas swallowed hard at the thought of spending time with Vivi. Blake was one thing—even at their worst, Blake had somehow been a bit above all the pettiness. But Vivi had never liked her. She had never liked Vivi either, but Vivi had a fiery redheaded temper and a mouthful of opinions, and she spoke her mind about everything. She wasn't sure a happy reunion was in store for them.

"Okay. Just holler when you need us." And with that, Blake jumped in her new little BMW and peeled out of the lot.

Dallas felt as if she was caught in an alternate universe, but the truth was she liked this new planet a little better. She decided she would try to get the kids at the theater to like her. Maybe then they would do a little better—and make her look like a better director. After the screw-up on live TV the night before, she would take any good PR she could get. Who knew? Directing might be a good back-up career.

Dallas was just pulling into the lot at WTAL when Daniel came running out.

"Don't go in. Get in the news van," Daniel said as he headed to the van with the camera.

Great, she thought. *I was so bad that Mike doesn't even want to see me.* "What's up?" she asked, shutting her car door and jumping into the van.

"Miss Peaches Shelby got some more pictures of her Baby Jesus statue in the mail today, and Mike wants you to do another story. He told me to call you and let you know, but here you are." Daniel was smiling. "And he never even said a word about last night. Maybe he's just gonna drop it."

"Oh, I wish." Dallas clicked her seat belt as Daniel left the parking lot. You'd think the pope had just arrived, the way he sped to Peaches's house.

He ripped into her driveway, Miss Peaches coming out the front door as she heard them, her hand full of pictures.

"Ms. Shelby, thanks so much for calling," Dallas said as she approached her. "I hear you got some news in the mail today."

"Thank y'all for comin' back out. I wanna get this solved and my Baby Jesus found and back in his manger. Here are the pictures I got today." She handed the pictures to Dallas.

Peaches was a small woman, thin, with soft, white hair. She had been the librarian at the high school before she'd retired last year. Dallas had always liked her. She was sweet, always wearing her pearl necklace and little pearl earrings, too. Ms. Peaches was eager for Dallas to see the new batch of pictures.

"Here's the one they took at the president's mansion on campus, and here's one from the stadium. I swear they got my statue on the grand tour of the entire University of Alabama."

"Did they send a note? Any clues other than the pictures?" Dallas asked.

"Just this note, but I can't make anything of it," she said, handing the piece of paper to Dallas.

Don't miss the next installment of "Where in the World Is Baby Jesus!" Alabama has certainly been blessed.

"I think it could be a clue," Dallas said, handing the note and the photos back to Peaches. "I think the police should see it." A missing nativity statue wasn't exactly a high-priority crime, but if she could get this case police attention, she could make it a bigger news story.

"You know what, Ms. Dubois? I think you may be right."

Dallas smiled at her. "Be sure to let the police know. And keep me posted, too. We'll find your statue. I know it. We'll do a big story on it, too. Your manger scene will be famous."

"I sure do hope so. My Greg gave me that manger scene before he passed away three Christmases ago. He was so proud of it. He always wanted a big manger scene for the yard and he finally got it." She paused and looked at Dallas. "It's important to me—even if it is just plastic."

Dallas did her stand-up for the camera and then said good-bye to Peaches, jumping into the van with Daniel.

"I gotta hurry and voice this story. I have rehearsal in just a few," she said as she closed her door.

"No problemo," Daniel said. "Have you talked to Mike at all today?"

"Nope, and it will be just fine with me if I don't."

"Come on, you're not still worried about last night, are you?"

"Of course I am," she said seriously. "But it's too late to change it now. I just hope I'll still have a job in two weeks."

"I promise you it was no big deal. Let's go back and watch the tape from last night. I'll show you it didn't look half as bad as you think."

"No, thanks, I'll pass. I'm not sure I can bear it."

"Have it your way," he said.

Back at the station, Dallas and Daniel were sitting in the edit bay working on the story when Mike popped in.

"Dallas, can I see you in my office?"

Mike Maddox wasn't one to mince words. He was short and round, with a full head of graying hair. He always wore his bright, colorful dress shirts tucked in tight and his ties a tad too short. He was matter-of-fact and didn't usually play games. So Dallas was worried when he asked to see her. She knew that her performance at Dixie Dickens had not been anywhere near on par for her. Yes, she had been having a strange time of things lately, but she still knew she was a damn good reporter. That fact was never in question.

Being part of television news was all Dallas could ever remember wanting to do. It had been her dream since she was a teenager. Yes, okay, she loved the limelight. That's what had drawn her to cheerleading from the time she was in middle school. And, Lord, every beauty pageant under the sun had pulled her in like ants to a picnic.

But she had a knack for digging up a story like few others, and her real talent was live television—usually. She knew in her heart she was the best choice for that anchor seat, and even if she had screwed it up a little last night, she wasn't going down without a fight. That was just her nature. Mike once told her he'd hired her because she had tenacity to spare. She could get down, as she had been the last week, but she never stayed there for long.

Maybe a preemptive strike would be best when dealing with Mike.

"Have a seat, Dallas."

"Mike, I apologize for last night, I know it wasn't my best," she blurted out before her butt even hit the chair.

"What?" He looked at her with his brows clenched.

"That stand-up last night was ridiculous. I mean, those bagpipers were so loud, the kinfolk in Scotland could hear 'em." She laughed a nervous laugh.

"Dallas, that's not why I called you in here."

"Oh, okay. What's up?"

"I just wanted to let you know that the announcement for the anchor replacement has been moved up. Jill McIntyre is leaving us sooner than we thought."

"Oh, so…when will it be?"

"December twenty-third. Jill needs to be out before Christmas, so I've brought each reporter in today to let them know personally that while I was hoping we could get everyone through the holidays without any job losses, we won't be able to do it."

"So, two of us will lose our jobs right before Christmas," Dallas said, just to verify the awful news she was hearing.

"Yes, I'm really sorry. It's going to be a tough decision. All of y'all are very good at what you do."

Dallas swallowed and tried to digest this information. "Okay, well, I'd really like another live shot. At least one before you make your decision, if I can get it," she said.

"I know. Everyone would. I'll do what I can to give everybody a fair shot. Now, get back to work. I know you have that play to do."

Dallas forced a grin and stood up, smoothing down her pants. She shook Mike's hand and left his office. Yes, she did have the play on her very full plate. How could she handle the kids this afternoon after getting news like that? She felt miserable again, not exactly the best mood to try the "friendly" technique she'd been planning on.

Dallas popped by her desk on the way to the edit bay to check her email. At the top of the list was an email from Callahan Enterprises. They were a pretty big deal in town, though all Dallas knew of them was that they were the supplier of the food at the Alabama home football games. She clicked on the message.

Ms. Dubois,
It has come to our attention that you have been covering the story of the missing baby Jesus decoration. We want you to know that we have gained information and believe we know who is responsible. Please do not phone us here. This is a private message and if anyone here finds out I have written you it could jeopardize my job. Please await further instructions.
Thank you,
Deep Throat

Dallas was skeptical. A source about a small-time prank? From a company as big as Callahan Enterprises? She wanted to keep getting messages, though, so she decided to play along and just see what these clowns had to say. Maybe someone had hacked Callahan Enterprises and was playing a joke. She decided she would only tell Daniel for the moment.

Back in the edit bay, she and Daniel went back to work on the missing Baby Jesus story.

"I have no idea who it's really from. I think at this point I'm gonna wait and see," she said after telling him about the note.

"Good idea. You know, this could be a story in itself," Daniel said. "Let's just see what they say next."

"The only thing is, if Callahan Enterprises has been hacked, we should probably let them know."

"Well, you know Cal Hollingsworth is a computer genius. He could get to the bottom of—"

"No way," Dallas interrupted him. "I don't want him over here digging in my email. I'll wait and see if I get another message for now."

Daniel smiled and went back to work on the story for the six o'clock news. Dallas went over the script she had written, and they got ready to lay the voice track down, but she was still in competition mode after that meeting with Mike, and her wheels were spinning. She was feeling ambitious and ready to compete. *No more whining,* she told herself.

"Daniel, why don't we expand this story?"

"What do you mean 'expand?'"

"I want to take this story to the citizens of Tuscaloosa. I think we need to hear what they think about someone stealing a Baby Jesus decoration right here in our town during Christmas. I want to get the community element—you know, a town banding together and all that. I'll talk to Mike and try to make this happen for tomorrow."

"I love it," he agreed. "Now, let's lay down your voice tracks for this story and get you to rehearsal."

14

Dallas arrived at the Bama Theatre right on time. With less than two weeks before opening night, she knew there was no time to waste. In a cruel twist of fate, the day of the Christmas play would be the same day Dallas would be finding out about the anchor position. Well, it would most definitely be an event for the record books. But Dallas figured that if she could just make it to Christmas, she'd be able to conquer anything in the future. The struggles she was facing were just more in a long line of battles she'd had to overcome. And she was ready.

She pulled into a back lot near the theater this time and went in through the stage doors. Choir practice was just ending, and Betty Ann had let the children go for a quick bathroom break. The doors slammed behind Dallas when she walked in.

Betty Ann looked up. "Oh, Dallas, it's you. That scared the daylights outta me."

"Oh, sorry about that," she apologized. "Those doors are so heavy."

"That parade yesterday was something, huh? What did you think of our kids?"

"I...yes, I loved the parade," Dallas said, putting on her best smile.

"Those kids just loved it. For some of these precious little things, singing in that parade and this play will be the highlight of their Christmas. Those poor children living in the home—well, they just don't have anybody to love 'em on Christmas mornin' the way the rest of us do."

Dallas thought for a second. She took in a deep breath. She knew how that felt. Daniel had asked her several weeks ago to come spend Christmas with him and his family, his mom and two brothers, but Dallas hadn't confirmed. It was such an intimate family holiday, and while she liked Daniel more and more each day, she still didn't think they were close enough for her to intrude on his private life.

"I know it, Betty Ann. That must be so hard for them."

"So, yes, they were singing to beat the band last night. And isn't that little Tristan just precious, with those big blue eyes? I'm happy he still has his mom and dad."

"But what about Sara Grace Griffin? I remember her name 'cause she was the first to let me know just where I stood with her."

"Yeah, she is definitely outspoken," Betty Ann said with a laugh. "She's one of the kids in foster care. This will be her first Christmas in the system, actually. Her mom died quite unexpectedly last winter and she never knew her dad. There was no one else to take responsibility—no family or friends. They moved around a lot, I gather, and hadn't really put down roots."

Dallas had always lived in Tuscaloosa, but she knew what

it was like to not feel connected to anyone, to never really belong. "Well, I'm trying to learn everyone's names. I think I know all of two so far," Dallas said, embarrassed. "I'll keep working on it. I hope they can learn to trust me a little."

"Oh, honey, they just wanna be loved. Every single one of 'em. Kids are easy if you know that secret."

Just then, the kids burst through the big doors from the bathroom area and started jumping around and hollering on the stage.

"Children, settle down now, Ms. Dubois is here for rehearsal. Those of you who have solos will be singing today with your music from the speakers. I am not going to play the piano for you anymore. Mr. Cal will be giving you the signal from the booth."

Dallas looked up and there he was. He waved to the children when Betty Ann mentioned his name. Dallas turned to the children.

"Okay, y'all," she began, clapping her hands together and trying to seem as warm and approachable as she could. "I have an idea. First, why don't y'all call me Ms. Dallas instead of Ms. Dubois? You know like how you say Miss Betty Ann's name? Or Mr. Cal's name?"

"I like that," Sara Grace piped up from the group.

"Great, then we have a deal. Now, let's take our places, everyone. We're gonna start from the top."

All the kids got right into their spots, from the old toyshop to the big gingerbread house. As they began to run through their lines, Dallas was impressed at how well everything was going. There was a glitch here and there, but nothing too much for Dallas to handle. And the kids seemed to be really responding to her new attitude. She was thankful children didn't seem to hold grudges, that they were quick to forgive.

Sleigh Bells was all about one little town in Dickens-era

America celebrating Christmas. In the end, a manger scene would be revealed to the audience with real live animals up on the stage. It was only one lamb and one donkey, but that was enough to fill the children with anticipation.

Just before intermission, Sara Grace had a solo. She would be singing the song that had been haunting Dallas so much this year. The first few notes of "I'll Be Home for Christmas," began, and Sara Grace stepped forward to center stage. She had her microphone in place, clipped to her little red dress. She looked up at Cal, and he nodded for her to begin.

Dallas stood in the wings watching this pretty little blonde girl sing softly, her eyes big and round. She looked a little scared. Dallas found herself pulling for her, crossing her fingers that her performance would go smoothly, even if it were just a rehearsal.

As she began to sing, her lovely little voice carried beautifully across the theater.

"…and presents on the tree…" she sang.

Then she missed a word. She cleared her throat as the music kept going. Then she missed a phrase. Her face reddened and she was clenching her hands nervously. Dallas could see it was too much for her. She stood there, alone, center-stage, visibly beginning to tremble as the music continued from the speakers. Then a sob choked from her throat, and she began crying in place on the stage.

Dallas couldn't take it. She knew exactly how Sara Grace felt.

She and Betty Ann moved toward her, but when they made eye contact, Betty Ann stepped back. Dallas wanted to be the one to comfort the child, and Betty Ann must have sensed that because she gave her an encouraging smile.

Dallas walked onstage from the wings, motioning to Cal to cut the music as she walked toward Sara Grace.

"Sweetheart, it's okay," Dallas said softly.

The little girl continued to sob, sitting on the floor now with her head in her hands.

Dallas removed her high heels and sat on the bare wooden stage next to Sara Grace, reaching over and pulling the tiny child into her lap. She rocked her back and forth, and continued to console her, caressing her blond hair.

"Sara Grace, it's okay, baby. You sing so pretty. I wish I had a voice like yours."

Sara Grace looked up at her and gave a shy smile.

"Now, tell Miss Dallas what's wrong. You sounded just wonderful. Was it because you forgot a word?"

"No, ma'am. It's just…" She hiccupped back another cry, tears spilling from her gorgeous green eyes.

"It's okay, baby. You can tell me."

"It's just… It's just I was missing my mommy, so…I forgot, that's all. And since she's gone, I won't have anyone here to watch me sing next week." Her little lips quivered as she tried to hold herself together.

"You know what? I know just how you feel," Dallas said gently. "I didn't have my mommy to watch me when I was on stage either. And it made me very sad, too. I understand just how scary that feels. But listen to me, sweetheart, you know what? I'll be right there on the big night." Dallas gestured toward the wings. "I will definitely be watching you, and I won't leave you, so you can just look right over your shoulder if you get scared, and I'll be there, listening to you and smiling at you, okay?"

"Promise me?" Sara Grace looked up at her with such sweetness and innocence, and Dallas's heart was breaking for her.

"I promise you, baby. I'll be right there."

This was raw Dallas. The Dallas without all the armor.

She'd spent so much time defending herself, bracing herself for disappointment and learning that she'd always have to fight for what she wanted—nothing came easy. Yet, when confronted with this vulnerable little girl, she felt all those walls quickly and easily melting away. As she sat there rocking Sara Grace, she realized how much they were the same. Both tough and outspoken on the outside, but just needing love and someone to believe in them on the inside. Sara Grace had begun to develop her own armor, and Dallas was thankful to see she may have shown up in the nick of time.

The theater was silent, but when she saw Cal making his way down to the stage, she realized that the mic had been on the whole time and that he had likely heard their whole conversation.

She stood up and called practice to an end for the day. The children scurried around gathering their things, and Betty Ann gave Dallas a confident smile.

Dallas walked backstage to get her purse. Cal met her in the wings, his look soft and sweet as opposed to his usual sour expression. She looked up at him, since in her bare feet he towered over her.

"Hey," he said simply.

"Hey," she said.

"I just wanted to say…um, what you did back there, for Sara Grace, that was pretty great."

Dallas closed her eyes and exhaled. She wasn't sure what she'd been expecting, but it wasn't compliments from the man who'd nicknamed her the Ice Queen. "Thanks." She couldn't muster any more words.

"I want to apologize," he said, stuffing his hands in his pockets.

"For what?"

"For the way I've been acting. I mean, I think maybe I misjudged you."

She smiled but didn't trust herself to say anything. Her emotions were running way too close to the surface to trust herself to speak.

"Seriously. I guess I don't know you as well as I thought I did," he said. "I should've known that a lot can change between college and now, but I didn't really give you much of a chance."

"Don't worry about it, Cal. Really." She felt the flare-up again, but this time it didn't bother her quite so much.

"Sara Grace is one of my favorite kids here," he said. "You did a really good thing with her."

"Thanks."

"Listen, I'm gonna run across the street and get some hot chocolate. I think I owe you one after making you spill yours last night. Wanna join me?"

Dallas felt her heart skip a beat. *Oh, my goodness.* Being asked out by Cal was her teenaged fantasy come true. Part of her thought it might be smart to quit while she was ahead. She'd won over Blake, the kids, Betty Ann and now Cal... maybe she should just head home and call it a night. But before her mind could make any decisions, her heart jumped in and took the lead.

"Sure, let me just grab my heels."

Dallas was a nervous wreck—her heart racing so fast she was sure Cal could see it under her blouse. They walked across the street in the evening air, with the sun setting and a December chill creeping in. The little diner, Glory Bound, was warm and small. They grabbed a table in the corner.

"So, um, this is really nice, Cal. Thanks for asking me over here." This awkwardness she felt was completely new to her. Dallas was the kind of woman whom men gravitated to, and she had always known how to act around them. What to say, how to smile, how to cross her legs just so to get their attention. Yet with Cal, she felt like a teenager all over again.

"I like to admit it when I've been wrong. It's a habit of mine." He glanced up shyly and smiled.

"Well, I forgive you. I'm sure I don't help my reputation with some of my actions anyway."

Owning up to bad behavior? That was another first for Dallas.

She thought about her most recent relationship with Dan *the man* Donohugh, Harry Heart's campaign manager. That was one hundred percent a relationship of convenience. For both of them. She'd rubbed up on Dan so he would give her all the top information on Harry's campaign, using him to leverage her career. He had been doing the same, though. Having a beautiful woman on your arm was great, but having a direct media contact for the politician you were supporting was even better.

But the relationship eventually ended, fading away after the November election once they'd found that their usefulness to each other had expired. Her experience with true love was limited to exactly one relationship during college. But that hadn't lasted—the guy had left her because she was so busy being awesome, or trying to be, that she hadn't paid enough attention to how awesome he was. That was the closest to romantic love Dallas had ever been, but it had been so fleeting that she hadn't really had much time to really *feel* it.

Oh, she had been married three times, but those didn't really count as far as true love was concerned. She'd never experienced really being *head over heels* in love. The kind of love you live for. That all-encompassing "I can't live without you" sort of love. All of her marriages had been purely to help her career or to get some money that would help her career. And they had only wanted Dallas as arm candy—a trophy wife to parade around at office parties and corporate events. Every marriage had lasted less than a year, each of them used as a step up a ladder to career fame. She wasn't exactly proud of that, but she hadn't chosen anyone who had real feelings for her anyway. No hearts had been broken when it was time to part ways, so she'd always just considered those relationships as mutual business transactions. One of the best "deals" she'd made was to keep the name from her last marriage. *Dubois* had some star quality to it.

But after all these years, Dallas longed for some real closeness, something more intimate and substantial, something more like love. But she was an awkward person when it came to being real. And that thick firewall she had built up sure didn't help any. But holding Sara Grace tonight had changed her somehow. It had felt like a revelation, like a new beginning. And most of all, it had felt like such a relief.

"I wanted to tell you, Cal, I really appreciate what you said…about being wrong about me. Coming from you, that really means something."

"Well, it's just the way I was raised, ya know? If you're wrong, say it and clear the air."

He was sweet, Dallas thought, noticing a glint in his eyes when he looked at her. He had a shyness to him that she found endearing. These were things she had actually never even paid attention to before. Over all the years she had known him and had a crush on him, she'd never gotten past that gorgeous hair and that delicious body.

"Tell me a little about them, I mean about your family, Cal. All I know is your dad played football at Alabama, just like you." She was surprised that she genuinely wanted to know. Plus, she was a reporter at heart, so the questions were bubbling up anyway. And it kept him sitting across from her a little longer.

"Yeah, well, my dad and even my granddad and both my uncles played for Alabama. Both of my older brothers played, too. I guess it runs in the blood. I'm the only one, though, that got my doctorate, and I'm definitely the only computer geek in the family," he said, smiling at her. "Tell me about your family."

Oh, God, she wasn't ready for that. She didn't want to say

too much, since all of this with him was so new, and she was afraid it might scare him off. She swallowed hard, feeling her anxiety take over.

"Oh, you know, nothing special," she said nonchalantly. "My dad was a businessman," she added. It was the first thing that came to mind that she wasn't ashamed of admitting.

"You mean nobody else was a broadcaster?" he said with a grin. He had one dimple on the left cheek, and she noticed she could only see it when he smiled a certain way. She had never seen him smile like this before.

"No, just me."

Just then, a young woman came up to their little table.

"Aren't you that TV reporter? I just love your work," she gushed. Then, "Ohmygosh! And you're our old quarterback. Hollingsworth, right? I was such a fan. I used to keep your picture up in my locker."

Both of them smiled.

"Oh, my lord, I'd just love to get autographs! Do y'all mind?" she asked.

"No, sweetheart, of course not," Dallas said. She was in her element now. She reached up and took the paper and pen from the woman and signed her name, then handed them both over to Cal.

"Oh, I dunno, I might need some liniment for my old crippled hands, you know, since I'm the *old* quarterback," he teased.

Dallas laughed. She wished she had gotten to know him better when they were younger. Cal signed his name and put his old number down, 15, then handed the paper back to the young woman.

"Thanks so much. This is awesome! Oh…are y'all… together? Did I just interrupt your date?" She cringed a little with embarrassment.

Cal and Dallas sat still, looking at each other, then at the girl, then back to each other's eyes.

"Um," Dallas tried to fill the dead air. It was a habit. "Well…we're old friends."

Cal looked up at the girl and smiled. "Yes. Old friends."

16

Dallas's head was spinning as she unlocked her front door. Cal was swirling around in her mind. The smile remained on her face involuntarily that night, even while she was falling sleep. Maybe she could have the fairy tale she had dreamed of as a little girl. At least the handsome prince part. But Dallas's fairy tale went beyond catching her dream man— it also included a dream career, being a respected news anchor.

The next morning, Wilhelmina woke her by licking her nose with her warm, sandpapery tongue.

"Good morning, pretty girl," Dallas said, sliding her hand down the kitty's back. She made a sleepy wobble to the kitchen, fed Wilhelmina, then poured herself a hot cup of coffee from the auto-timed coffeemaker on the counter. She may not have been a domestic goddess, but at least she could make coffee.

Her little, two-bedroom house was sweet, and it suited her perfectly. Though it was in an older part of town near the campus, it was really smack-dab in the center of things, close to the TV station, campus and downtown. It didn't take her long to get anywhere, just in case she was called out on a story.

Her cozy little kitchen was well appointed with all the appliances, but most of them were older models. She had never turned on the oven once since she'd moved in, and the stove scared her because the older model was gas, and the pilot light was out. She'd have to stick a match to the burner to light the eye, and there was no way that was gonna happen. So she stuck to the microwave.

The walls in this room were a creamy yellow, and the Formica countertops were a buttery pastel. Over the little porcelain sink was a nice-size window that overlooked the small but fertile backyard. Crabapple tress, a weeping willow and a couple of mimosa trees were scattered around the lot. One giant magnolia tree kept watch over the little backyard from the far left corner. In the springtime the yard was fragrant and lovely. There was a tiny, screened-in back porch just off the back door, and Dallas could sit out there on warmer mornings and watch the birds and butterflies chase each other.

But not today. Temperatures were back down in the low forties and dropping. An ice storm was predicted for later that night. She dressed in a thick scarf and her heavy winter-white coat, then headed out to work, her warm coffee cup refilled on the way out.

She arrived at work to a flurry of activity in the newsroom.

"Hey, Daniel," she called when she spotted him amongst the chaos. "I hear ice is predicted for tonight. Guess that'll be the lead."

"Nope, the lead is that every single store from here to Birmingham is sold outta milk and bread," he said, laughing, as he walked over to her desk. "Why is it that with any winter storm, everybody thinks milk and bread is the hunker-down cure?"

"Been that way as long as I can remember. People are crazy. Hey, you think we can cover that expansion of the Baby Jesus story today?"

"Sounds good to me. There's Mike. Go ask him."

Dallas told Mike what she had in mind, but he had other things for her on his agenda.

"How 'bout you get out there and take the lead on the storm today?"

Dallas was thrilled. "Sure! Absolutely." She felt like Rudolph during that Christmas Eve blizzard. *Ready, Santa!*

"What's the angle you're thinking about?" she asked.

"The usual. All the milk and bread from here to Georgia are sold out already. Then do the stand-up from Walmart or someplace where they're cleaned out."

"Perfect." She turned to find Daniel when she suddenly remembered there was another play rehearsal scheduled for that evening. She was stuck between a rock and a hard place. There was no way she was gonna miss an opportunity to make up for the last two live shots she had screwed up, but she also had an important obligation to the kids. She was just starting to break the ice with them, and it would be a major setback to disappoint them now.

And then, of course, there was the ice she was breaking with Cal.

Dallas knew she could find a way through this.

"Daniel, you gotta help me. I have rehearsal, and Mike's forgotten and given me the lead. I'm supposed to be at the theater from four to six today. What can we do?"

Daniel closed his eyes for a minute to think. She could see the minute the idea hit him. "We shoot the package. I park the live truck in front of the Bama Theatre and when you're done with rehearsal, you race out and we do the stand-up. Easy."

"Oh, Daniel, you're a lifesaver! Thank you." Then she remembered Mike said do the stand-up in front of a store where they would be sold out of milk and bread. She wasn't sure how to pull that off, but she didn't dare mention it to Mike. He'd just throw the lead story to someone else. No, she'd just figure it out.

Dallas finally sat down at her desk to get organized for the day. Her messages stacked high, she began sifting through them.

Dallas, I'm sorry about the other night. Please reconsider.

Her mother again. She crumpled it up and threw it in the trash. A few more, one from Abigail Harper at the radio station.

The scavenger hunt has suddenly heated up. Looks like we will have a winner. Wondering if we can announce the iPad recipient the night of the children's Christmas play?

Dallas thought about it. It sounded like a perfect idea, since both broadcast organizations were raising money for the Tuscaloosa Children's Home. She'd call Abigail and tell her. Maybe she'd even set up a story about it. Looked as if the twenty-third was gearing up to be the quite the day.

The next message stopped her cold.

I had a nice time last night. Let's try it again sometime.

It was from Cal. She took a deep breath and smiled, pressing the note to her chest. No, she thought, there was no way in hell she was missing play practice, even for the lead story.

17

Dallas and Daniel ran all over town with their mic and camera. Sure enough, every store, from Walmart to the Zippy Marts, was selling out of milk and bread as if it was the end of the world. Daniel shot the B-roll, and Dallas interviewed the frantic shoppers. It hardly ever got cold enough in Alabama for an ice storm, at least not in West Central Alabama. Snow was a rarity—maybe once a season, if at all. So this was huge. Everyone was getting ready to hunker down.

Once they got all the footage they needed, Daniel and Dallas sped back to the station to package the story. It was pretty routine, so it didn't take long. Dallas had gotten word from the theater board that rehearsal was still a go, since the ice storm was not expected to arrive till after suppertime, so after they finished with their edits, they sneaked out of WTAL and headed to the Bama. They had to be extra careful. In the TV news business, days like this—where there was a lot going on and everybody was crazy busy—were called

A news days. A little old ice storm could create an A news day in Tuscaloosa.

Daniel pulled up to the front entrance of the theater.

"Thanks for the ride, Daniel. And remember, don't be late," Dallas said, jumping out of the news van.

"I know. I'm gonna call Mike and tell him we left early to set up. That should keep him from asking questions."

"Great idea! What would I do without you?" She smiled and shut the door and ran inside the lobby of the grand old theater. Cal was just rounding the corner from the steps up to the booth, and she nearly knocked him down.

"Hey, Ms. TV star, slow it down. I'll have to sign you up for linebacker tryouts if you don't."

"Sorry about that. It's so windy out there. Just trying to get in before I get frostbite."

"Well, it's sure warm in here. No coat necessary." He moved a step closer. "May I?" he offered as he helped her take her coat off.

She was taken aback for a second. Dallas had actually never encountered a real Southern gentleman. In fact, she couldn't remember a man ever once helping her off with her coat. Seriously, not even once. He was close to her, his hands slipping beneath the collar as he stood behind her. She could feel him touching her hair. She could smell his Burberry cologne. She inhaled, trying to hold on to the moment.

"There you go. I'll just hang it up over there in the coat-check room, okay?" He walked away with her winter-white coat over his arm. She was sure he must have said something, but she was too intoxicated by him to know what it was, so she just offered an, "Uh-huh."

"Did you get my message?" he asked. "The one I left at the TV station?"

"Oh, yes, I did. That was really sweet."

"Well," he asked, "whatya think?"

"About what?" she asked.

"About going out again, like maybe tonight after rehearsal?" He looked almost boyish with that tousled hair and adorable dimple. "I felt a little silly leaving a message at the station, but I didn't even have your cell number."

"Oh, well, lemme give it to you right now"

He slipped his cell from his back pocket, and she recited the number.

"Great, so...how about tonight? Don't make me beg." He winked at her.

"Yes, yes, that would be wonderful. Let's do it after rehearsal today."

"Do it?" he said with a laugh.

Dallas immediately blushed. "I just meant...you know, grab a bite."

"A bite? Sounds good to me. Is there a special place?"

"For what?" She enjoyed flirting back. And instead of the usual awkwardness, this playful chatting with Cal was starting to feel natural.

"You know, for where you like to be bitten?"

She gave him a coquettish smile. "Very funny. I'll go wherever you like. Just make it someplace warm."

"My pleasure." He looked at his watch. "Kids will be ready soon. I better go set up. I'll catch you after practice." He turned to head upstairs to the sound booth.

As Dallas turned around to go to the stage, some of the children greeted her in the lobby.

"Eww, they love each other," one of the boys taunted. The other kids chimed in with giggling and cooing.

"Miss Dallas and Mr. Cal sittin' in a tree, k-i-s-s-i-n-g..." they began to chant as Dallas tuned beet-red.

"Okay, now, back to the stage you go," Dallas said, clapping her hands together.

Sara Grace hung back and walked down the aisle to the stage next to Dallas. Without saying a word, Sara Grace had slipped her little hand into Dallas's. She looked down at the little girl and smiled, locking eyes with her and giving her hand a squeeze. The bond had formed. And for both, it was a good thing.

"Okay, Sara Grace," Dallas said as they got to the stage. "Now remember, I'll be right there in the wings. You're gonna nail that solo today. I can just feel it."

"Me, too, Miss Dallas," Sara Grace said, grinning at her new best friend.

The rehearsal got under way, the children moving through their lines, showing a huge improvement from when Dallas had first started working with them. That is, until the two little boys doing the puppet show in the toyshop scene lost it.

Corey, the student production assistant, ran over to break it up.

"You two need to stop right now. Come on!" he demanded, then realized the two weren't yelling but laughing as they roughhoused.

"Jay, Christopher, cut it out," Corey shouted over the laughter. Before he could stop the horseplay, Corey yelped in pain.

Christopher had chomped down with his nutcracker, right on Corey's crotch.

Betty Ann leaned in and whispered to Dallas, "He thinks that nutcracker is actually a *nut*cracker!" They snickered quietly as Corey struggled with the brawling boys. "I can't, for the life of me, get him to stop tryin' to bite everybody in sight." Betty Ann sighed and then headed straight to the bent-over Corey and helped him off stage.

"Christopher and Jay, get over here," Dallas called. "I need you both to sit out for a few minutes." Dallas showed them to the side of the stage.

"Now, look, we have to perform this show for lots of people very soon. We have to be serious. I'm gonna keep the puppets for today, and if you guys decide to work really hard, tomorrow I will give them back."

"Okay, we're sorry, Miss Dallas," Jay said.

How could she stay upset at faces that cute? Jay had almost white-blond hair and sky-blue eyes, and Christopher had red hair and a freckled little nose. She was truly falling in love with these kids. There was still a handful she had yet to learn the names of, but she was trying.

Sara Grace's solo was next and Cal started the music. Dallas stood in the wings just back enough so Sara Grace could see her out of the corner of her eye.

"I'll be home for Christmas. You can count on me..." she began. It was such a special song, as both Dallas and Sara Grace weren't really sure what *home* meant anymore.

The song continued, and then Sara Grace missed a word. She looked immediately over her shoulder, and just as promised, Dallas was right there, smiling at her and moving her mouth with the words of the song. Sara Grace swallowed, then sang like she had never sung before, belting out the Christmas melody as if she was on Broadway. Dallas noticed the change. Sara Grace now knew for sure that there was at least one person who believed in her.

When she finished, loud and clear, the auditorium erupted, all the children cheering, and Betty Ann walked over at a clip, clapping hard. Dallas met Betty Ann center stage, and both of them hugged an emotional and exuberant Sara Grace.

"I did it," she gushed.

"Yes, you did, sweetheart, and it was awesome! I'm so proud of you!" Dallas said.

She looked up to the sound booth, where Cal was standing and whistling down at Sara Grace. It was a moment none of them would ever forget.

It was nearly six o'clock when rehearsal ended, and Dallas knew there was no chance she'd be able to make it to any Walmart in time.

"Y'all follow me up to the lobby. I've got some exciting news to tell you," Dallas announced to the children as she led them up the aisle to the front of the theater.

"Now, listen," she said, addressing the group of children. "I have to go outside and be on TV for my job. I need you all to stay with Mr. Cal and Miss Betty Ann. Y'all can watch me right through the front windows," she told them as she grabbed her coat from the coat check in the front lobby. She could see Daniel waiting outside.

The skies had grown dark, and little ice crystals had formed in the bare trees on the sidewalk. She had absolutely no idea how she would explain to Mike the fact that she wasn't in front of a grocery store, emptied of all its bread and milk, but she decided not to worry about that. She was on a high since Sara Grace's performance. It had been a breakthrough day at the theater, in more ways than one.

All the kids stayed inside, looking out the lobby windows to watch their director do her thing. Cal stood to the side, watching from behind the glass doors. Corey stood with Betty Ann, far enough away from Jay and Christopher to be out of their biting reach.

Dallas slipped on her cream-colored fuzzy gloves and her deep-pink wool scarf as she walked over to pop her head inside the news van.

"Hey, Daniel. Practice ran a tad late, so I guess we'll just have to go live from here," she said.

"How are we gonna tie the grocery shortage in with the Bama?"

"Well, I don't know yet. I'm workin' on it." Dallas was anxious, but she had learned over the years not to let it show. She positioned her earpiece and stood in front of the Bama Theatre waiting on her cue. She heard the top of the newscast roll in her ear. The toss came and she winged it.

"Good evening, Jill and Dave. I'm here live in downtown Tuscaloosa, and the streets are desolate, empty of the usual Friday night traffic. Restaurants have closed early tonight as everyone prepares for the impending ice storm." The toss to the packaged story went smoothly. The footage lasted about a minute and a half. Dallas had just that much time to come up with a plan to tie in the milk and bread part of the story, when a flake drifted down in front of her. It began snowing.

The children, seeing the snowfall, burst through the doors and began trying to catch it on their tongues. Betty Ann, Corey and Cal followed them out to the sidewalk. The engineers tossed it back to Dallas, and Daniel pointed to her. She was on.

"Instead of ice, looks like snow is on the menu for tonight. And with no school already tomorrow, seems like the kids will have something wonderful and white to fill their Saturday morning." Daniel got a wide shot of the kids playing in the first flakes.

"Don't forget to join us in less than two weeks right here at the Bama Theatre for the holiday production of *Sleigh Bells,* our children's Christmas play benefiting the Children's Home of Tuscaloosa. All of these little ones will be on stage to entertain you. Have a safe and warm night, Tuscaloosa, and have fun building those snowmen tomorrow. For WTAL, I'm Dallas Dubois."

It was perfect. Daniel gave her the thumbs up and said, "Okay, we're clear."

Dallas removed her earpiece and leaned down and hugged Tristan and Sara Grace.

"C'mere kids," she said, hugging them all at once. She looked like Julie Andrews and the Von Trapp kids as they all laughed and chased the falling snowflakes together. "You were all great!" Don't forget to watch tonight at ten o'clock so you can see yourselves on TV. I'm sure they will show this again."

"They most certainly will. That was one lucky break! The timing of the kids and the snow was a miracle. Best stand-up ever," Daniel gushed, then hugged her.

Cal approached the group around Dallas. "Nice work, Ms. Reporter." Dallas reached out and received his hug. "Or maybe it's Ms. Emmy Winner now. That was pretty impeccable timing, I'd have to say."

"Thanks. Sometimes timing is everything."

Before everyone got too wet and snowy, Dallas and Betty Ann rounded the kids up and got them back inside. Parents' cars had begun to form a line outside. The children who were going back to the center for the night were picked up by their bus, and Corey and Betty Ann got the rest of them to their heated cars as fast as they could so they could all get home before the roads got too bad.

As Betty Ann and Corey headed to the stage to get their things, Cal hung back with Dallas.

"Probably a bad idea to drive on the roads right now," he said with a shy smile.

"Yeah, it looks really dangerous already," she replied. She knew full well she could hitch a ride with Daniel. He had a big satellite truck outfitted for all kinds of weather. But she'd already nailed her live shot, and Cal was warming her more than any old car heater could at the moment, so she ran outside and let Daniel know she had a few things to do at the theater and told him he could go on.

"Okay, if you're sure," he said with his eyebrows up, looking at Cal.

"I'm positive."

18

Betty Ann locked up, and she and Corey walked out the side doors together. The Bama Theatre was built as a replica of Davanzati Place in Florence, Italy, with the night sky painted above complete with twinkling little stars. With all the lights dimmed, it became a magical place.

Dallas stood at the base of the aisle, up next to the stage. Cal was right in front of her.

"I guess that's a yes to my earlier question," he said.

"Which one?" she asked.

"If you'd like to try going out again." He grinned, moving closer.

"I think so, Mr. Football Star. Seems like we're sorta trapped here."

"*Old* Mr. Football Star." He laughed. They were inches apart in the amber-lit auditorium, and Dallas's heart was beating so fast it felt as if it was buzzing.

"You were great today. It was fun watching you do your thing."

"Thanks. I do love my job," she said, allowing him in her space.

"Well, that was obvious. You shine, especially when you're live with that camera pointed at you."

"That's my favorite thing, going live." She hesitated for a minute, her thoughts snapping back to the anchor job she longed for, so close now and yet still just out of reach. In that position, she'd be going live all the time, every night on the six and ten. She wondered if she should tell Cal.

The snow was really coming down now. Any longer and they both might get stuck there overnight. *What a delicious idea,* Dallas thought.

"I've got an idea," Cal said. "I'll be right back." He turned and dashed up the curved staircase to the sound booth. Before she knew it, she heard an old mix of soft Christmas music begin to play over the speakers, an overture they'd be using as the audience arrived.

Dallas was sitting on the stage in the middle of the Victorian Christmas set when Cal arrived with a bottle of wine and cups. The music started as he sat down next to her.

"Luckily I happened to have this on hand—it was gift from one of the board members as a thank-you for volunteering. Now seems like the perfect time to open it. How's about we toast to that great news report you just did?"

Dallas was melting. Romance was something she'd only ever read about in books. All she had ever known to do in her adult life was to wrap her long arms and legs around her potential prey and get what she wanted. She had never been courted. But Cal was clearly a Southern gentleman, through and through.

He handed her a paper cup filled with a deep red merlot,

and they toasted. Dallas really wanted to get to know him but was careful not to be too pushy, taking off her reporter's hat and putting aside her list of questions.

Cal began the conversation. "I want you to know that this is unexpected for me. I mean, of course I always thought you were beautiful, but I had no idea…you know…about the real you, I guess."

Dallas loved that *beautiful* comment. It was one thing to be *hot* or *sexy,* but to be called beautiful was much more rare and special.

"Me, too," she answered. "I mean, I just always thought you were pretty arrogant." She blurted that out before she could stop herself.

He started laughing.

"Sorry, I didn't mean…"

"No, it's okay. I thought you were an egomaniac."

Now they were both laughing.

"But, now I see a little more," he added.

"Do you like what you see?" she flirted, lowering her chin and batting her long lashes.

"Oh, I think you'll do," he teased.

She dropped her mouth open and popped him on the knee.

"I'm just kiddin'. I think it's pretty obvious, don't you?" Cal asked.

"Yeah, I guess so," she said. The flirting continued, and they were halfway through the bottle of wine when Cal asked her about her family. Dallas held back. *Still not time,* she thought. But she allowed him in a tiny bit.

"Well, my mom had me go live with my dad when I was only fourteen. She wanted to be a famous singer, and she decided to suddenly pursue that." Dallas decided that sounded a lot better than actually sharing the whole family feud story with him. She was always so ashamed of it. And LouAnn did want to be a singer at one time so it didn't really feel like a lie to leave it at that.

"So, she just left you?" he asked.

"Yeah. That's when Blake and I became stepsisters."

"I kinda remember that, actually, from back in high school. Lewis and I were best friends, so I knew Blake pretty well since she and Vivi were so tight. Lewis always had a crush on that redhead."

"I'm sure Blake had all kinds of nice, sweet things to say about me then." She smirked, hoping that would lighten the mood. But Cal was focused on hearing more about her life.

"It must have been hard without your mom," he said. "Where is she now?"

"In town, actually. I just saw her the other night." Well, that wasn't a lie either. She had demanded LouAnn leave her house immediately, but she didn't have to tell him that part. She was enjoying the happiness she felt with Cal, and she didn't want to give that up by delving into the dark parts of her life right now.

He smiled at her and scooched closer. The Christmas music was still playing.

Cal reached over and laid his big hand over hers. It felt so warm. He folded his fingers around hers.

"May I have this dance?" he asked. She was at a point of no return. She found herself standing before she even knew it.

"Why, of course, sir." She loved the way he wooed her. It reminded her of *Gone with the Wind*. They slipped their arms around each other. He was still much taller than she was, even though she wore stilettos that day. He pulled her close, his chest pressed up against hers. She was nearly breathless, being this close to him, and she could feel his breath on her cheek.

They swayed under the tiny star lights, his one hand clasping hers out to the side, his other hand resting on the small of her back, old-fashioned-like.

She reveled in the moment. A teenaged fantasy she was actually *living*. The star football player and class scholar was actually holding her in his arms.

Suddenly he stopped moving. "Wait here just one second," he said, running over to the wings of the stage. After a moment, she found herself standing under hundreds of tiny snowflakes, floating down from the theater catwalk. Cal quickly joined her in the snowfall, wrapping her in his embrace as the music continued.

"Nice touch. Do you do this for all the girls?"

"Only the ones who've proven me wrong." He breathed in her skin. They were both in a quiet state of learning each other's touch for the first time. As they talked, they kept up the exploring.

"And only those who I know won't mind helping me reload the snow machine."

Dallas giggled into his neck. She laid her head into the crook under his cheek, and he bent down to press his cheek against hers. He smelled delicious and felt powerful and protective. This was new, too: a protective man. She was lost in her real-life fairy tale.

Then *that* song came on.

Dallas had all of her walls down. Vulnerable and open, she kept moving to "I'll Be Home for Christmas." She tried with all her might not to, but the tears began to flow.

Cal could tell she was suddenly emotional.

"You okay, sweetie?"

"Yeah, this song just brings back memories, that's all."

"It's okay now. You're here with me." He pulled her in tighter. As the song continued, tears streamed down her face. Cal gently placed his fingertips under her chin, lifting her face, and pressed his warm soft lips to hers. A tingle of heat shot through her, relaxing her all over. She kept her face lifted and he kissed her again, sweetly and slowly, tasting her until the song was over. She loved feeling his face all over hers.

"Maybe now that song will stir a better memory." He kissed her on her tear-streaked cheek, cupping her face in his hand. He gently drew his thumb across her bottom lip.

"I'm listening to anything you wanna tell me," he said.

"Tell you what?" she asked, closing her eyes as he held her face in those perfect quarterback hands.

"About that memory. I'm here. No pushing. Just know whatever it is, it's okay."

"Thanks, Cal. I'll be okay. It's really nothing. That was just always my favorite song, that's all." She smiled as she wiped her face. She just wasn't ready.

"It's good little Sara Grace is singing it then," he said with a grin. "Dallas, this has been really nice. Let me drive you home. I don't want you to drive in this stuff."

"Oh, Cal, that's okay," she started, but then she recalled her car wasn't there at the theater. "On second thought, I left my car at the station. Wanna give me a ride back?"

"Love to. I'll need payment for that, though, you know. It's a little treacherous out there."

"Oh, no, here it comes. I knew you'd show your true colors eventually."

"What?" he said playfully. "I mean, I *am* risking my life."

"Fine, what's my fare?"

"A little more of what I just received will work. I really liked that form of payment." He grinned that grin where she could only see one dimple. He had her in a way no one ever had. She found him endearing from head to toe.

They walked out into the frigid air, a few flurries still flying around as they walked to Cal's car. Cal drove a vintage

Porsche 911. It still had the original leather interior, in perfect mint condition. He walked around to her door, slipping his hand under hers to pull the door handle. She sat down inside, looking up at him. She had been put into the chariot.

"Nice car," Dallas said as she buckled up.

"Thanks. It was my dad's."

"Wow. What did your dad do? I mean besides play football."

"He just loved cars. Collected them after he retired. He gave me this one as a gift when I got my doctorate."

She could tell that Cal might have a few secrets of his own. She knew his dad must have had to do more than play college football to raise a family and own a collection of fine cars. But she decided not to push. Cal would open up whenever he was ready to tell her more.

He started the car and they drove out into the empty streets of downtown Tuscaloosa headed to the station. Dallas felt something roll under her feet. She reached down and picked up a toy drummer.

"What's this?" she asked.

"Oh, nothing," Cal answered. "Just something for that scavenger hunt."

"Oh, are you trying to win the iPad?"

"Well, just really playing along for fun."

Cal looked straight ahead, smiling but not offering a bit more information on the subject.

Dallas was comfortable in the leather seats, the heater warming the air and Cal warming her hand. He looked at her every now and then as he drove, squeezing her hand.

"Why don't I just drop you at home? That way you won't be out in this tonight. The roads are already starting to freeze."

"I don't work tomorrow. I'm sure all this stuff'll be gone by the afternoon and I'll need my car. I'll be okay."

"I know what. I'll drive you home for now, and then tomorrow I'll come get you and we can go get your car together when this weather's cleared. How does that sound?"

Dallas calculated. But it didn't take her long. This way, she'd get to see him tomorrow.

"Okay, that would be great, Cal, as long as you're sure you don't mind?" She smiled.

"My pleasure."

She directed him to her house, and they were there in ten minutes, even with the icy roads. Cal pulled up in front, the little accumulation of snow crunching under his tires. Dallas reached to unbuckle her seat belt, but Cal's hand was suddenly on top of hers.

"Wait a second there, Miss. I do believe you owe me payment for this ride," he teased, leaning in toward her.

"Oh, I'm happy to pay in full."

Cal leaned over and pulled her in for a deeper kiss than the last. She placed her hands over his ears and returned the kiss just as passionately, moving her hands through all his thick golden hair. They kissed in the car until the windows were fogged.

"I have to say, I was never so wrong in my entire life about someone as I was about you. And I'm really happy about that," he said as he kept kissing her. She was basking in all his attention. Their chemistry was on fire. It was obvious to Dallas that Cal was feeling pretty excited about her, too.

Cal opened his door and got out, walking around to Dallas's side. He opened her door and offered his hand. He walked her to the front door, the Times Square lights across the street glaring in their eyes.

"Gosh, think your neighbors wanna be noticed?"

"I know, I've been meaning to get over there to tell them to turn it down a little. But they're like this for every holiday.

The man is a Civil War reenactor, so in the spring, they even shoot off a fake cannon."

"You gotta be kiddin'!" Cal shook his head. "Yeah, well thank God the reenactments don't occur in the winter, or you'd be deaf *and* blind."

Dallas burst out laughing. She liked his sense of humor and that it was always right there, just under the surface.

He lingered at the doorway, kissing her a long, sweet good-bye. "So, what time tomorrow?" he asked.

"Let's shoot for noon. This stuff will be half gone by then," she answered breathlessly.

"I'll call you, but not too early. Don't wanna wake a sleeping beauty."

"Why not? Isn't that what Prince Charming always does?"

19

All the snow had disappeared by Saturday afternoon, and she and Cal had spent the weekend getting to know each other even better. Monday morning came before she knew it, and she arrived at work ready to see Mike and hear his thoughts on her improv stand-up from the Friday night live shot.

Mike met her in the hallway before she even had a chance to get to her desk. "Can you come in here, Dallas. I want you to see something."

Dallas followed him into his office, still in her coat. He hit the remote control and her live report, package and all, popped on. She stood there watching herself. But she also watched Mike's face. He grimaced as she talked first of empty milk and bread aisles, then suddenly went to the stand-up where she was surrounded with kids. They didn't really go together, and what had seemed like a work of art in the moment now appeared to be the last-minute mash up that it was.

"So tell me," he said, "did you order the snow, on cue? I mean you *were* at a theater?"

"Um, well…Daniel and I couldn't really get to a grocery store because—" she began, but then decided the truth was better. Mike was the one who'd asked her to direct the play in the first place, so she figured he'd have to at least be glad she was trying to follow his instructions. "The thing is that I had play rehearsal last night, but I didn't want to give up the lead story either. So I made the decision to do both." She was nervous but certainly didn't come across that way. She smiled confidently.

"Well, it may be the smartest decision of your career," he said looking at her proudly.

That was not at all the reaction she was expecting. "Really? Oh, Mike, I'm happy you liked it."

"All those kids, the freshly falling snow and then you threw in that tie-in to our charity Christmas production! I mean, it was pretty quick thinking, live and really in the moment. And it worked like a charm. Good job." He patted her shoulder as he walked past her into the newsroom.

Daniel had come up behind her and stood in the doorway, listening. He knew he would be as much to blame if Mike was gonna reprimand her, and he was by her side, thick or thin. She was just starting to realize that.

"Can you freakin' believe this?" Daniel high-fived her.

"I know! Oh, my God, I was fixin' to have a heart attack when he played that footage. I had no idea what I was gonna say," she confided.

"You'd never have known it…cool as a cucumber," he said.

Dallas walked back to her desk, taking off her coat and throwing it across her chair, Daniel following behind her.

"So, what's on tap today?" she asked.

"I think Mike liked your idea to expand the Peaches–Baby

Jesus story. I heard the producers bring it up in the news meeting. He's suggested we go out and get a few man-on-the-street interviews to get the community involved in the story."

She was glad to hear that. Opening her email to see what had come up over the weekend, she found another message from Callahan Enterprises. When she clicked on the message, it looked like a poem.

Ms. Dubois,
Baby Jesus is getting quite a tour.
Find the statue next at Ten Hoor.

Ten Hoor was a building on campus, Dallas remembered. "Let's run over to the campus," she told Daniel. "I need to check something out. I think it could be worthwhile."

They drove through the campus and parked at Ten Hoor Hall, running around the front of the building and inside the main great hall at the entryway. Nothing.

"I don't understand," she said as they headed back to the news van. Then her cell rang. It was Ms. Peaches Shelby.

"Ms. Dubois, I'm so sorry to bother you on your cell phone, but I got another picture in the mail today, and my little statue was at a building on campus. I thought you might want to know."

"Of course, Ms. Shelby. The building wouldn't happen to be Ten Hoor, would it?"

"How in the world did you know?"

"Let's just say I got a message myself today. Somebody's sure up to something. Thanks, Ms. Shelby. I'll be in touch."

She hung up and told Daniel what was going on.

"I think it's time to get the computer genius on the case." Dallas liked the sound of that.

"Fine, I'll check in with Cal later on. Right now, let's get on over to Walmart and get this man-on-the-street thing done and filed for tonight."

"Great. I wanna hear just what Tuscaloosa thinks of that missing statue."

Dallas checked her cell phone for messages as they walked. She was striding confidently, her recently cleaned coattails flying behind her with her big, crimson, knockoff Prada bag securely on her shoulder. Things seemed to finally be coming up Dallas. She was feeling as if she had a good shot at that anchor job after Mike's reaction to her Friday-night report, and Cal was becoming someone she truly cared about.

She glanced at her phone. Cal had sent a text.

Hey, baby. I think we should make dinner together tonight. You?

She sent a text back. You want ME for dinner?

A text came back instantly. Yes! Perfect idea. You can be the platter and I will lay the food out all over you. Yum.

She smiled to herself and kept walking, picturing the dinner table they could set.

She and Cal learned pretty quickly that they were both very sexually flirtatious. Experimental. They hadn't actually slept together yet, but they'd spent the weekend exploring and learning each other's buttons...so to speak. It had been fun to go out on a couple of real dates. She wasn't used to dating. Dallas was starting to trust a man. And for Cal, he was learning just who Dallas really was.

Both of them were very smart. Everyone knew Cal was really brilliant. That was common knowledge among those who knew him, at the university and in his circle of friends. But Dallas was now proving just how smart and quick she was, neither of which were exactly part of her reputation. And in the same way that she was surprising Cal, it was quite the surprise for Dallas to see how the usually quiet and reserved Cal could be playful, fun and quite the tease. From the…experimenting they had done, she also had a good feeling he'd be a perfect match in bed. They seemed to be on the same page in every chapter of the book.

"To the usual spot?" Daniel asked her as they reached the van, opening the door to the driver's seat and snapping her back from thoughts of Cal.

"Sounds good to me. Let's go." She jumped into her seat and buckled up as she continued to scroll down her phone.

Then she stopped cold. A voice mail from her mother.

She hit Skip.

Nothing would get her down today. She had waited a long time to get back to this point. It had been at least a month since things had been going this well at work. Maybe longer. *No, I won't deal with her today,* she thought. Besides, if her brother was part of this whole reunion idea, as her mother had said, why didn't he try to reach her? She had a pretty good feeling it was just something LouAnn had said in an attempt to get her way. Not exactly surprising behavior, but still disappointing.

Dallas recalled how over the first few years after the family split up, she had tried over and over to reach out to her brother, only to be rejected each time. She remembered going to sleep at night, just fourteen years old, wondering what she'd done that was so awful that the brother she truly loved so much, the man she completely idolized and looked up to, could throw her to the side like trash that didn't matter.

If he really did want this, too, why hadn't he as much as sent a text? That question began to bother her.

The truth was, when she'd been sent away, it was having been rejected by her brother that had hurt her more than her mother. Without their dad around, they'd bonded even more, knowing they'd stick together as siblings no matter what their parents did. They had felt like a team. So, when Houston had turned on her, she'd felt as though she'd never trust another person again. Houston breaking his word was what had shaped her into that tough, cold Ice Queen for the rest of her life. It had made her feel as if she didn't matter that much to men. Her defenses were always up when it came to anyone, but men especially. At least her mother had been honest. She'd felt she had to choose and so she had. But Houston? He'd led Dallas to believe he'd always be there for her, and then he'd simply walked away. She'd taken that to mean that she wasn't the sort of girl worth loving for who she was. She figured if Houston could abandon her, then anyone could. So she didn't value herself when it came to men. Instead, she'd learned to use her sexuality to get what she wanted from them.

But with Cal, it was already different. He had told her he loved watching her work. He liked all of her tenacity and talent. And more than anything, he thought she was smart and treated her that way. Sure, he also showed he was attracted to her, that he desired her, but she could tell it wasn't the only thing that kept him around. Reminding herself of that got her confidence up. She shook the bad thoughts away as they drove into the hilly Walmart parking lot.

They arrived at Walmart to get the man-on-the-street interviews. Daniel set up in the parking lot as Dallas began to grab anyone interested in being on camera.

"Good morning, ma'am. Could we ask you a few questions regarding the Baby Jesus statue that's been popping up around town?" she asked a chubby woman with a buggy overflowing with Christmas toys.

"Yes, I think it's just totally awful. I mean, the nerve of those people to take the Savior straight outta the manger. I hope they catch those sons-a-bitches and fry 'em in hell."

Dallas cringed, but she knew better than most that crude people got the most news play. "That's awfully harsh. Don't you think it also seems un-Christmassy to feel so full of revenge?" Dallas asked, quickly pushing the mic back to the woman's lips. She was hoping for a response, and, boy, did she ever get one.

"Ma'am, this here is the sweet Baby Jesus we're talkin' 'bout. He has been stolen—stolen, I tell you—straight from his manger and taken on some damn joyride by a buncha hoodlums with no respect. If they don't get punished for this, there is no justice!" She gave a quick jerk of her head and pushed her buggy up the hill to her car.

"That was intense," Daniel said.

"Yep. Just the kind of reaction that'll get everyone riled up." Dallas smiled. "I knew the people would side with Miss Peaches, though I guess I hadn't expected anything so extreme. We'll get the town behind her and get to the bottom of this."

Dallas interviewed several more very upset people, the last one sewing it up for everyone.

"Tuscaloosa is, for the most part, a very Christian town," the older man explained. "It's one thing to play childish pranks, but this just ain't funny. No siree bobtail, it sure ain't when you mess with Baby Jesus."

"And there you have it," Dallas said to the camera. "We are close to finding the statue stolen from the front yard of Miss Peaches Shelby, and more evidence has turned up today. It looks to me like whoever has the Baby Jesus will be in quite a bit of trouble when they're found, if the city of Tuscaloosa has anything to say about it. I'm Dallas Dubois for WTAL News."

"That's a wrap. I think you're on a roll," Daniel said.

"Let's hope."

Dallas walked over to the van and helped Daniel roll up the

mic cable. They got in the car to go grab some lunch before heading back to the station.

"Daniel, I've been thinking. I haven't said this before, but maybe I wasn't as nice to you as I could have been sometimes."

Daniel almost drove right over the curb leaving the Walmart parking lot. Apologizing wasn't something Dallas was known for, and it was obviously surprising.

"Well, you had your moments…"

"I just wanted to say that you've been a good friend and I do apologize if I was…well, bitchy."

They both laughed, Daniel a little more loudly than Dallas.

"I wasn't *that* bad, now, was I?" she said, feigning disbelief.

"Well, let's just say you were a little more Wicked Witch of the West than Glinda the Good Witch."

"Okay, well, I said I was sorry and I meant it," she said.

She looked out the window as Daniel drove. All of these changes were feeling pretty good, but that call from her mother was bothering her like a just-bitten tongue—she tried to ignore it, but it kept getting in her way. She decided to send a text. She wasn't even sure if her mother got text messages, but she figured it would at least ease her guilt.

Mother, no time till January.

That was it. She slipped her phone back into the inside pocket of her purse.

A minute later, her phone jingled with a text message. *Damn.*

Please. It's time to stop this.

Ugh! That was the very one thing Dallas could not stand. Her mother saying it was time. Time! As though all those years when Dallas thought it was time didn't matter now that LouAnn was ready. As though Dallas was supposed to stay away and raise herself till the queen decided it was time to get the family back together. No, this was not gonna work, she thought. *I'll decide when it's time.* And maybe that time would be never.

She ignored the message and dropped the cell back into her purse. What had she done by sending a text to her mother? That woman would be texting her now day and night.

Sure enough, her cell phone rang. She glanced at the caller ID and thanked God when she saw that it was Mike.

"Hey, can y'all get over to the Brooks Mansion?" he asked.

"Sure, what's up?"

"They have a developing story over there, and we need to get some footage, maybe a story for the ten o'clock. Can you make it?"

"You mean I'll get a story on both the six and ten tonight? Absolutely," she said, as excited as if she'd won the lottery.

Mike gave her the details, and they drove straight over to the Brooks Mansion.

As they entered the beautiful circular drive, they couldn't believe their eyes. There were animals running and *flying* all over the place, and Lewis, Abigail…and Cal were all out chasing them.

20

"Holy shit, what is this?" Daniel asked, slamming the van into Park and leaping out to grab the camera.

"Looks like this little scavenger hunt has taken on a life of its own!" Dallas said as she jumped out.

"Grab that goose!" Lewis shouted as he ran by.

"My God, why would anyone bring you a goose?" Dallas shouted over all the commotion.

"Not *a* goose, *six* geese—a-layin'!" Abigail explained, lunging toward a swan.

"Don't tell me," Daniel said. "You've also got seven swans a-swimming?"

"I never realized how many specimens of fowl are actually in that song until now," Cal said, running after a hen.

"I guess that was a French hen," Daniel joked.

Dallas laughed at him. "What are you doing here?" she asked Cal.

"The university is on winter break and my best friend called me for help. Where else would I be?"

As the men continued to round up the animals, taking them around back to an outbuilding that had once been used as an outdoor kitchen for the old working plantation, Dallas interviewed Abigail for the news.

"I'm warning you, Tuscaloosa, if we get even one more animal here at WRCT, we will end this contest without a winner. We are not a zoo and have no room for all these birds. We asked that you bring us the *replicas* of the decorations of the Twelve Days of Christmas by following the clues online. From now on, if anyone brings a live animal to the Brooks Mansion, they will be disqualified." Abigail's hair was a mess, her jacket unbuttoned and her blouse halfway untucked. She looked exasperated and you just knew she meant every single word she said.

"Remember," Dallas said in the wrap-up, "this scavenger hunt benefits the Children's Home of Tuscaloosa, and all donations and fees will be given directly to that foundation as part of our Home for the Holidays charity event. An iPad goes to the person who can gather all twelve of the Christmas decorations hidden around Tuscaloosa—none of which are live animals. I'm Dallas Dubois for WTAL."

Cal had come around front to watch as Dallas did her stand-up. She'd seen him standing on the front porch with his hands in his pockets, smiling at her as she worked. He approached her now as Abigail excused herself to go pull herself together.

"That was pretty good," he said, impressed.

"What was?"

"You got that shout-out for the charity in again. I love that."

"It's the least I could do. I mean, we're all involved this year."

"Well, you're great at this. I mean it. You really are." He leaned in and kissed her, long and slow since no one was paying any attention. The heat from her body sent a shiver through him as she melted into him, and he pulled her small, curvy body in close. They'd thought they were alone.

About that second, Daniel and Lewis rounded the corner from the back and got an eyeful. Cal hadn't told Lewis anything about this new relationship yet. He knew how Lewis would feel, considering their history, and there was no doubt he'd tell Vivi. Then she'd tell Blake. Cal had hoped he'd have a chance to let Lewis know what Dallas was really like. Especially how gentle she had been with Sara Grace. But, well, now it was pretty much out there.

"Hey, y'all," Dallas said, and Cal could hear how suddenly nervous and uncomfortable she'd become. She cleared her throat. "We…uh…didn't know you were there."

"No kiddin'," Lewis said, his eyebrows up.

"Dallas was just telling me how happy she was that she would have a story on both the six and ten tonight," Cal said, trying to boost her up.

"She sure looks ecstatic," Lewis said, smirking and nodding.

"Well, I was just congratulating her," Cal continued.

"I'd love to see what you'd do to her if she won an Emmy," Daniel joked.

Cal and Dallas moved apart and let daylight between them.

"Well, I was going to tell you later, Lewis, but seems later is now," Cal said.

Lewis laughed. "I think I might have a slight inkling as to what you're gonna say."

"Dallas and I are seeing each other."

"Well, you must need glasses, Cal, since you need to be eyeball to eyeball to see her."

Everyone laughed.

"Well, I guess congratulations are in order. It's about time.

I mean, it was sure no secret the huge crush he had on you in high school," Lewis said.

Cal was relieved that Lewis wasn't going to say anything snide. He'd only just gotten used to Dallas's soft side, and the last thing he wanted was for Lewis—or anyone else—to force her walls back up.

"What? *He* had a crush on *me?*" Dallas exclaimed. "I think you have me mistaken for another girl."

"Uh, nope. I was his best friend. I think I would know."

Dallas looked at Cal. She was so adorable when she was surprised like that. She looked so vulnerable, as though she had no idea just how amazing she was and how lucky he felt to be dating her.

"Is it true, Cal? You had a crush on *me?*"

"Yep. It's true," he said, blushing.

"Oh, he thought you were so full of yourself, too," Lewis chimed in. "It was weird. He would be insane with lust for you one minute, and then say he couldn't stand you at the same time."

"I know just how he felt," Dallas said, and she smiled, easing Cal's embarrassment. *All this time, Cal and I were suffering from the exact same allergy,* Dallas thought to herself.

"Whada y'all say we get inside and have some hot chocolate and get warmed up?" Lewis suggested. "We got all those damn birds locked up safe for now. I know a man that has a farm already willin' to come get 'em, so we can relax for now."

"Sounds good to me, but I think these two are pretty warm already," Daniel said, winking at Cal and leading the way up the porch steps into the mansion.

Cal hung back and grabbed Lewis aside. "Hey, keep this to yourself for now. I know there's been some bad blood between Vivi and Dallas over the years. The truth is, she's really soft under all that hairspray and I don't want her to get hurt.

I wanna wait for just the right time to let everyone in on the fact that I'm seein' her. Okay?"

"Hey, man, no prob. Lips are sealed till you decide." Lewis smiled at Cal. He slapped his back as a show of solidarity and they joined everyone else in the mansion.

After work, Dallas met Cal at her house. He brought over some groceries to cook her dinner. Thank God, she thought. She didn't yet want him to know about her massive lack of domestic talent. He brought linguini and all the ingredients for fresh marinara sauce and, of course, a great bottle of wine.

"Hey, baby," he said, leaning in for a kiss, one arm holding the bag of groceries and the other arm reaching around Dallas, pulling her in.

"Mmm, you smell good enough to eat," she purred. She knew how to turn on the sex kitten when she wanted to. Cal could dish it back though.

"I thought that's what I was doing to you tonight.... Didn't somebody volunteer to be my platter earlier?"

"I did, but I'll need my dessert, too," she said, winking at him as she closed the door to the dropping temperatures behind him.

Dallas was excited. She knew how to sell her sexuality, but she had always been hungry for something deeper, something more meaningful. Cal was the first man to even come close to that possibility.

Courting was something Cal clearly knew how to do. His parents had been married for more than fifty years, he'd told her. They had one of those romances you dreamed about, a rare story, but Cal wanted that, too. He'd told her about his two older brothers, who were both married with kids. He'd also told her that he wanted to make sure he chose right so he would only have to choose once, which was why he still hadn't married.

Dallas had a feeling she was a huge risk for him. She was sure if any of his friends even had an inkling of him seeing Dallas, they'd certainly shake him and tell him he was nuts. Three times married and she had a reputation. She just hoped he would trust his instincts

"Okay, let's see, how do ya turn this thing on?" he asked as he tried to get the stove on.

"I think the pilot light's out," Dallas said, as though it had only just happened. "Be careful"

"How 'bout the oven? I wanted to stick the bread in," he asked, fiddling with all the knobs.

"Hmm, not sure…" Dallas reluctantly admitted.

"So, I'm guessing it's never been turned on, at least not by you, huh?" He smiled at her.

"Um, well, it's a lot of trouble to cook for just me," she justified.

"I know what you mean," Cal said. "I'm the same."

Dallas had wriggled out of that one. Now she just prayed he didn't need to iron anything.

"Oh, I meant to talk to you about this earlier. I might need you to run by the station soon and check on something for me.

I'm getting some strange emails that I was hoping you might be able to track for me," she said, changing the subject quickly.

"No problem, baby. I'll take care of that for you." Cal waved it off as if it was nothing for him to help her out. Well, he was a genius with computers.

Pretty soon, Cal had noodles boiling and the marinara simmering. And before they knew it, dinner and good conversation had melted into the late hours of the night. Cal poured them both a glass of Chianti.

"Let's go sit by the fire," Cal said, taking the lead.

Dallas had changed into soft charcoal-gray yoga pants and a deep V-neck navy sweater. She was padding around in her favorite fuzzy socks. She could tell that Cal loved seeing her like this even more than the overly made-up reporter in five-inch heels who everyone always saw. She was much more real— approachable and soft.

It was true that when Dallas got home each night, she shut her world outside off and brushed all that Aqua Net out of her golden blond hair. It felt wonderful to finally share that side of her with someone other than Wilhelmina. She sat down on the pillows Cal had grabbed from the couch and settled in next to him on the floor.

"Thanks for cooking me dinner," she said.

"My pleasure. I like to cook, especially Italian. At home, I never get the chance to because it's just me."

"Well, you can cook for me anytime," she said leaning back into him.

Cal took a handful of her hair and pushed it around her shoulder, exposing the back of her neck to him. He pressed his lips to her skin, sending a chill down both of her arms. She held her hair up, allowing him to nibble the rest of her neck. He traveled his tongue toward her collarbone, kissing the hollows under her jawline, then back up behind her ear.

She rolled her head around, intoxicated by the scent of him and the feeling of his tender mouth on her bare skin. He touched her shoulders, massaging them under his strong hands, then dropped them to her waist, sneaking under her sweater with his gentle fingertips, dragging his hands up her back. She laid back completely as he held her in his arms. He bent over her, kissing her softly at first and then with much more passion. She opened her mouth and let him in.

Dallas wrapped her arms up around Cal's neck, as he gently put her head down on a crimson satin pillow, her long hair trailing down either side. He stopped kissing her only for a moment to look deeply into her eyes.

Slipping the tips of his fingers under her sweater, he began to walk his fingertips up her abdomen to her lacy demi bra, cupping her breasts. She giggled, revealing her ticklish spot, and he flashed that single dimple in response. He slipped her bra down until her full, round breasts spilled out into his waiting hands, and he took his time kissing her nipples and tasting her flesh while she lost herself in his slow, focused attention.

He took off his shirt, then lifted her sweater over her head as she rose from the pillow, sliding her hands over his hard, muscular back. While she was up, her arms around him, he unhooked her bra and let the coral-colored lacy garment drop to the floor. Cal stretched out on top of her, her breasts pressed against his rigid nipples, his tongue traveling into the hollows of her neck.

Dallas was nervous. This was a place she normally felt very comfortable. But tonight she was vulnerable. Cal looked into her eyes where other men usually focused on the rest of her. And his slow attention to detail threw her off guard.

Her husbands had all been so different from each other, but none of them had been very sophisticated. She had married Bobby Lawless right out of high school. He was an amateur race car driver, and he'd wanted Dallas to move to Talladega. His mother, Jolene, owned a beauty shop and had tried constantly to get Dallas to drop out of school and go to cosmetology training. That marriage had lasted ten whole months.

Her second marriage had been to a much older man. Clearly, Dallas had been looking to fill the daddy role. She'd thought she had hit the double jackpot with her sugar daddy till she'd found out one day he was a gambling criminal on the run. How she'd managed to stay in school had been a miracle. That marriage had only been eight months.

Then came that cute LSU boy. Bryan Dubois. He was from the sticks but was a great football player. She'd married him right after she'd finally graduated with her broadcast journalism degree. Everything had been all great and hunky-dory for a while—till she'd found out he liked other women on the side. Lots of other women. She'd divorced him after only eleven months but kept his last name, thinking it made her sound like a TV star.

Cal was unlike any of them. In fact, she had never even met anyone like him. He seemed to want to please her. To be thoughtful. Of course, she would naturally have a ton of trouble trusting this sweet Southern gentleman. Dallas was used to being on top, so to speak, used to using her gorgeous long legs and ample bosom to get a man to do whatever she wanted.

But Cal didn't need to be bribed. He *liked* her. Maybe she had never stopped her hectic career-driven life long enough to see what a man could give her when he actually liked *her,* not just the idea of getting into her lacy panties. Oh, of course Cal was totally turned on by her. He was a man, after all. But he had a way she wasn't used to, and she became hungry for his way as the night wore on.

Dallas had never been slowly devoured. She had to learn how to allow herself to be loved like this: to be free in her mind. Most important, to relax and stop trying to impress him. It was hard for her, but little by little she let go.

"Are you scared?" Cal asked, stopping once again to look at her. "You're trembling."

"I am?"

"Listen, honey, we don't have to do anything if you're not ready."

"No, it's not that. I just, well…I've never done it this way before."

"Whadya mean?"

Dallas exhaled her breath into his neck as she snuggled into him. "I mean, I've never gone this slow, never had someone pay so much attention to how things felt to me."

"Well, making you feel good is my main goal here," he said softly into her skin.

"Well, you do know how to pay attention to all the details. I do like your way." She smiled, trying to shake off the insecurities.

"I just want you to relax and know I'm happy, too," he said, kissing her. "Trust me, there's nothing I'd rather be doing than taking my time to explore every inch of your beautiful body."

Cal picked up where he'd left off, tasting her breasts just as Wilhelmina jumped up onto the small of his back and began kneading the waistband of his jeans.

They both let out a laugh, and it worked as a relief to the tension building between them.

"Wilhelmina! Get off him. He's mine," Dallas said, giggling and shooing her off her lover.

"It's okay. I love cats," he said, reaching over to pet the kitty as she stepped off his back.

"Really? Me, too. I'm more of a cat person than a dog person, but I just love all animals," she said.

"We always had several pets when I was growing up." He

paused and moved to her side to lie next to her. "Did you have pets when you were little?" he asked.

Dallas stiffened. It was automatic reflex when anyone ever asked her about her past.

"Um, no. My mom was allergic." She couldn't think of anything else to say.

"Hey, it's okay." He comforted her, pressing her into him tightly, somehow sensing that she needed it. "You know you can tell me anything. And I'm here whenever you're ready to talk. I can tell something's bothering you more than your mom's allergy."

She gave him a small smile and exhaled quickly. She had never ever told anyone the whole sordid story of her family. Sure, her husbands and a few others over the years knew she was estranged from her mother. The closer few even knew she had a brother and was estranged from him, too. But no one ever knew of the intense pain she felt at the loss of him. She guarded that bit of information. If anyone knew, she might look vulnerable, and she didn't want anyone to interpret that as weakness.

She sat up and reached for her sweater. The mood was broken as the ghosts of her lost family hovered overhead. The fire crackled in the fireplace, but suddenly Dallas was cold. She pushed her hair from her face. Cal sat up, stroking her shoulder. She could tell he was nervous she was pushing him away, that he had taken it too far.

Dallas swallowed hard. She looked into the fire, then at the twinkling lights on her Christmas tree. Then she looked into Cal's gorgeous eyes. He looked so open and so lovingly concerned. She knew it was time to finally tear down the last of the bricks in the firewall.

22

"What is it, babe?" Cal asked, trying to soothe her. "I don't wanna upset you, sweetheart. Really, we can just drop it."

"No, Cal. It's okay. There are some things I want to tell you. It's just…"

"If you're not ready, I understand." He moved around her to be in front of her. He wanted to make sure she could see his sincerity. He looked right into her eyes, which were beginning to brim with tears. He wanted to make her pain go away, but without knowing what was causing it, he had no idea where to begin.

"No, Cal, I *am* ready. It's just really hard, that's all. I want you to know. I *need* you to know everything."

He sat cross-legged in front of her, grabbing his dark green crew neck sweater and white T-shirt and slipping them back on, ready to catch whatever was coming his way.

With the fire blazing behind his back, Dallas began her story.

Cal held her trembling hands as she went through all the details. He could see how tough this was for her, how raw her feelings were, though it had been so many years since everything had fallen apart. She had never told her painful story before. She had never trusted anyone with her most intimate secrets, the ones she kept buried and hidden so deeply. She had never trusted anyone with all of her pain, and Cal felt both honored and humbled. When she finished, she inhaled a fresh breath and looked into Cal's eyes.

"I tried for a really long time to get Houston to talk to me, to make him see my letters so he would know I just missed him so much. Nothing else mattered to me but to just have him back. It was all I wanted for so long. But the years went by, and he never wrote to me or tried to contact me, and I guess I just let the anger and hurt feelings consume me."

"Oh, baby, I'm so sorry. But I get it. I understand you so much more now."

"I've...just missed him so much. I needed him so much growing up, and suddenly he wasn't there anymore. I would need to ask his advice, and I would have to remember he wasn't around to give it. He was my biggest cheerleader, my support, my very best friend. How could he just throw me away? Didn't he miss me, too?" She laid her head over on Cal's shoulder, weeping.

Cal felt closer to her. He could feel her pain within his own body, a pain she had never been able to let go. Until now, he hoped.

"I thought he loved me as much as I loved him, but I realized I was wrong."

Dallas wept in his arms. She wept for the family that she lost, the teenage years that had been destroyed by loneliness and self-doubt. For the guilt that consumed her for thinking it was all her fault: that somehow she had run her brother off and was being punished for the rest of her life because of it.

But her secret had fallen into capable, strong and gentle hands. For the first time in her life, he would give her a safe place to fall. He held her, rocking her, kissing her head and caressing her hair.

"I didn't want to burden you with any of this," she apologized. "I mean it's my family, my life, and I've been strong and pushed right through it. I don't know what it was about you, about tonight, that just broke the dam. But I guess I'm happy you know now. You're the only one that knows everything," she told him as he continued to hold her in front of the fire.

"Oh, baby, I'm so glad you trusted me." Cal reached over and placed his fingers underneath her hair, behind her ear and his thumb on her cheek, wiping her tears away. He leaned over and kissed her on the cheek, then pressed his lips to her quivering mouth.

"It's okay. You're with me. I feel like I understand every single thing about you now. All of it makes sense. I'm just so sad that you even went through any of this. It's so awful."

"It's okay, really. It was a long time ago."

But Cal didn't buy the tough-girl act. Clearly it wasn't okay; that was obvious from how emotional even talking about her family made her. "Have either of them tried to contact you since? I mean I'm sure you'd have a thing or two to say to them."

"Neither of them ever tried to contact me. Ever. It's been like twenty years or so and I haven't even heard a peep. Graduations, pageants—they didn't show up to a single event. Didn't even send a card." Dallas sat up and wiped her face with her sleeves. "Until last week."

"What happened last week?" Cal asked.

"My mother called me, and then she showed up here. I told

her I was too busy right now with the play, but that was just because I had no idea how I was supposed to even begin to talk to her after all this time."

"Oh, my God," Cal said, shocked. "You're right, though. I mean, what do you say to a mother who walks in after twenty years of silence?"

"I had nothing to say. It took my breath away. I was so angry and I just wanted to yell at her. I'm not ready to have any kind of productive conversation."

"Well, it should be all on your terms, that's for sure."

"Right now, I just want to lie here a little longer with you if that's okay."

"That's what I'm here for, baby. I want to be here for you, to hold you."

Dallas snuggled into Cal's chest, both of them lying back on the pillows until she fell asleep. In the wee hours, Cal slipped from under her and knelt down next to her. He scooped her up and carried her in his strong arms to her bed. He thought about leaving a note for her, but decided it might make her think he'd gotten too wary to carry the burdens she'd let go of last night. Then he thought he would lie next to her in bed, but she hadn't actually invited him to stay the night, and he didn't want her to assume he'd take advantage of her when she was this vulnerable. Cal valued the trust she had placed in him too much. He would protect that, no matter what.

So in true Cal form, he made a sleepy wobble back to her couch, covered himself with a crimson plaid blanket and fell asleep. He simply wanted to be there for her when she woke up.

23

Dallas woke with the sunlight streaming across her face. It took her a minute to put all the fragments of memories together from the night before. She knew she hadn't fallen asleep in bed. She stretched her legs out, realizing she was still in her clothes. She rubbed her puffy eyes, her makeup all but gone. Wilhelmina stretched across the pillow next to her, where she almost always spent the night.

She realized Cal must have carried her to her bed.

He was nowhere in sight, and from the look of the bed, he hadn't climbed in with her. She swung her feet around and touched her polished toes to the wooden floor and stumbled to the kitchen, still in a haze. She made her way down the short hallway. And there he was, still asleep on the couch. He was bunched up, his long body not quite fitting end to end.

Cal looked adorable, his messy hair hanging over his eyes. The blanket scrunched up under his whiskery chin. She had to stop to let this moment sink in. He wasn't in her bed. He hadn't left a note. He hadn't tried to sleep with her when the moment hadn't been right. He'd simply taken care of her.

She seriously couldn't remember a single moment like this in her entire life. She stepped quietly over to him and leaned down and kissed his cheek. He stirred only a little, then opened his sleepy eyes.

"Hey, sleepyhead," she whispered as he turned over.

"Hey, you sleep okay? How are you feeling this morning?" He sat up, letting the blanket drop as he rubbed his eyes. Dallas sat down next to him and snuggled up against his shoulder.

"I'm good," she said. "I'm actually really good." She was smiling up at him. "But I'm sure you didn't sleep very well out here."

"Oh, it was fine. I can sleep anywhere. I used to bunk with a bunch of sweaty football players, remember? I can literally sleep standing up." He leaned over and kissed the top of her head. "Don't you have to work today?"

"Yeah. It's a big day, too, so I gotta get in the shower."

"Okay, why don't you go get ready so you're not late, and I'll fix us something quick for breakfast? Got any oatmeal?"

She had instant oatmeal that mixed with water and popped into the microwave. She hoped that would be okay. "Yeah, in the cabinet, left of the fridge. Are you sure? I mean, I don't want to keep you either," she said.

"I'm out for winter break, remember? I've already turned in all the final grades, so I'm a free man till January."

"Okay, if you're sure."

"Positive." He started to stand up when Dallas grabbed his arm.

"Cal?"

"Yes, baby?"

"I wanted to say thanks...."

"I haven't even made the oatmeal yet." He winked at her.

"No, for last night," she said. "I hope it wasn't too much

for you. I mean, I know it wasn't really where the night was heading but... Anyway, just thanks."

"No one made me stay," he said, looking deeply into her eyes. "I wanted to be here. I needed to know everything if we're gonna take this any deeper."

Were they? The thought made her heart jump.

"We have to totally trust each other, right?" Cal continued. "We can't possibly be each other's person if we don't. When I said I was here for you last night, I meant it. Nobody tied me up...although we can think about that for later." He laughed and put his head to hers. "Now, go get dressed."

Dallas smiled and kissed him before getting up and making her way to the shower. She suddenly wanted to tell him she loved him. Did she? She couldn't bring herself to say it. Not yet. But he had certainly proven himself beyond any shadow of a doubt to her.

I must've fallen down the rabbit hole and this is all a dream, she thought, turning on the hot water. Where had he been all her life? Then she remembered. He had always been right there, looking at her from across the high school cafeteria, then from across the quad at the university. But she had been too busy running from him. Running from anything that might hurt her again.

Maybe it was time to stop all the running.

It was coming down to the wire at the station, and the announcement about the new anchor position was on everyone's lips. Dallas tossed her coat across her chair and walked up the corridor to find Daniel when she saw Mike talking and laughing with Courtney James, and she immediately felt that twinge of insecurity.

Courtney was newer to the team, an outsider from somewhere in north Alabama. Barely out of college. She was smart and pretty, and she was also in the running for the anchor position. Dallas had way more experience, and she certainly knew her hometown of Tuscaloosa better than this new girl, but seeing Courtney on such good terms with Mike still made her feel uncomfortable. Oh, she certainly didn't mind a little competition—as long as she stayed on top.

"Hey, Mike. Hey, Courtney," she said greeting both of them as she approached. "What's on tap for today?"

"Morning, Dallas. Good job last night," Mike said. She felt

a boost of confidence at being complimented in front of her competition. And she was certainly dressed the part in her bright Christmassy red lipstick and her pearls.

"Oh, thanks. It was hilarious out there with all those birds running crazy." She brushed off the compliment as if it was nothing, as though she pulled off lead stories with ease all the time.

"Yes, that was one of the *funnier* stories last night," Courtney said smugly. "So now, about that story on the crime spree near Skyland," Courtney continued, turning to face Mike. "Did you want me to take that today?" She tossed Dallas a quick smirk, then returned her attention to Mike.

This was like an episode of *The Bachelor*—all the girls trying to impress one man.

"Sure, that sounds like a good one. It'll be the lead, so be on time," he said.

"Of course." Courtney swung her long dark locks and prissed away.

Ugh, that witch. She's trying to slip in and get what should be mine, Dallas thought. As she stood there, fuming, it occurred to her that she hadn't yet been given a story about anything near as serious as a crime spree. Even the leads she had taken seemed fluff stories in comparison, and she was really starting to get sick of it. Her anxiety about staying on top was getting to her—again.

"Mike, I was thinking…" she began, searching her mind for bits of news that had been floating around the station. "You know that robbery suspect from the Piggly Wiggly case? I think I can get an angle on him."

"No, that's okay, we got Dave Harley out on that one already," Mike replied distractedly. He had a clipboard and pen in hand, and was paying more attention to his notes than to Dallas.

"Well how 'bout that woman who murdered her husband? Isn't her trial coming up?" she pushed.

"Yep, covered. Look, you got a really full plate already, and you're helping us tremendously with the constant coverage from our charity partners, the theater and the radio station. So don't worry about taking on even more, Dallas. I'm tellin' ya, it's fine."

"Okay, thanks." She pasted on her best fake smile and headed to the edit bays to find Daniel.

What is wrong with me? she thought. *I just had the best night of my life, finally finding someone who I can totally trust, maybe even love, and then I come here and feel crazy again.*

She decided to try and focus on the good. Today she was covering the preparation for the annual Tuscaloosa Christmas parade. All the floats were being decorated, and the lineup and particulars were being put in order. Dallas would be riding in this parade herself on the station's float, right behind the mayor's float. The parade was set for Friday night, just a few days away.

Dallas and Daniel went straight to work when they hit the parade site, interviewing both workers and bystanders, watching the whole thing take shape. People were saying this might be the best parade on record. With a ton of excellent footage and some great interview material, they packed up and headed to Taco Casa for a quick drive-through lunch.

Dallas started worrying—and that was usually not a good thing when she was so anxious. She'd get so nervous, she'd come up with far-fetched, sometimes ridiculous, scenarios. This time, she was thinking, as she had been for months, about the anchor seat. What if they put Courtney on the same float with her and Courtney pushed her off? It was an insane thought, but Dallas couldn't help imagining the absolute worst-case scenarios.

"What are you so stinkin' quiet about?" Daniel asked on the drive over.

"I don't know. I just worry, that's all."

"Let me guess, about the anchor job?"

"Well, they're gonna be announcing soon, and I haven't had a real meaty story to compete with."

"Excuuuuse me, missy, but who had the lead during the entire senatorial campaign? Live shots nearly every single night? And who had billboards from here to Mississippi when Lewis Heart went missing last spring? I think you are the queen of the lead—and queen of the live shot, if you ask me. They're not gonna base their decision on just the couple of weeks leading up to the announcement. You have an entire career of amazing work behind you, and *that's* what you're using to compete. Maybe Mike's just tryin' to give the others a fighting chance."

"Well, I don't want them to have a fighting chance," she said with a playful laugh. He was right, of course. And she was pretty glad she had such a great friend in her corner to keep her sane whenever she started to go off track.

"You're good, Dallas. Everyone knows this stuff comes so naturally to you. You have a definite gift when it comes to live television. Don't keep sweatin' it."

Dallas exhaled. "You're right. Okay, I know I'm being crazy."

"I bet it's the hunger talking. Let's eat. I'm starved." Daniel pulled up to the window and ordered.

After lunch was over, Daniel and Dallas went back to WTAL to package the story on the parade. She recorded her voice-over and checked in with Mike, then headed out to the theater. The clouds had rolled in, and the darkness had invaded the rare December sunshine they'd had today. Sleet was expected before midnight.

She was only a few minutes early, but the stage was still empty, so she figured Betty Ann must be running late with the kids today. As she made her way down the aisle, she could hear a piano playing, but it wasn't the usual Christmas songs from choir practice. The music was darkly beautiful, dramatic and played with such intensity. Dallas followed the sound, which came from down the hallway near the star dressing room. She came upon the beautiful grand piano, with her precious Cal sitting there playing the classical piece Pachelbel's *Canon in D.* Dallas stood still, careful not to interrupt him, and listened. Her heart was melting. This was definitely her dream man. Was there anything he couldn't do?

He was gorgeous, even wearing tiny rectangle-shaped, wire-framed glasses she had never seen him in before.

He finished the song and pushed the hair back from his eyes. He was in partial darkness and still didn't see her there. She broke into spontaneous applause. He looked over to her and smiled.

"How long have you been there?" he asked.

"Long enough to know your secret," she smiled, walking over to him.

"Aww, I'm embarrassed," he said.

Dear God, he is adorable, she thought. She was falling hard. "No, silly. Don't be. It was my number-one wish that my dream man would play the piano."

"Number one? Really?"

"Okay, maybe number two—or three. But it was on my list. I loved hearing you play. I had no idea you played at all— especially not that well." She moved to stand behind him as he sat on the bench, pressing herself against his back and drap-ing her arms around his neck and shoulders.

"Now you have to play for me all the time," she said playfully, caressing his chest from behind.

"Anything that pleases the lady." He kissed her hand and clasped his fingers through hers.

He turned around on the seat, his legs spread, catching her in between them. He placed his hands on her hips, kissing her stomach, feeling the curve of her body. Then he stood to hold her properly. His hands moved from her hips to her ribs, just below her breasts. He kissed her passionately in the darkness, running his hands up her body, then dropping them down her backside, squeezing her butt on arrival. If it hadn't been time for the kids to arrive, that grand piano would have served as more than musical entertainment. In fact, it would have given entertainment a whole new meaning.

They heard the kids laughing and wanted to make sure they weren't the subjects of *their* entertainment this time, so they pulled away from each other before they were seen.

"Whadya wanna do tonight?" he asked as he slipped in one last kiss.

"I'm up for anything," she said.

"Okay, I'll think of something fun and let you know after practice," he said, taking a risk and squeezing her ass one more time.

"Ooh, a surprise. I love surprises. And you've already given me one by playing the piano." She tiptoed up to him and bit his earlobe, gently giving it a tug, then walked back down the hallway past the dressing room to the stage, thinking of nothing but Cal and his promise of a surprise.

Rehearsal began, and the children were enthusiastic. It was just a little over a week until the show, and the excitement was bubbling over. They started at the top.

"Okay, kiddos, this is going to be what we call the run-throughs. It's time to practice the whole show straight through from start to finish, just like we'd do on the big day."

The kids clapped and shouted, excitement buzzing through them.

"When is the donkey coming?" Tristan asked wide-eyed.

"Not till the real show, sweetheart," Dallas answered back, grinning. "Now, let's get going."

The children took their places, and Cal began the music from his booth—just as Courtney James and her cameraman walked in. Dallas caught them from her peripheral vision and lost her breath—and nearly her lunch. *What is she doing here? Mike didn't tell me about this,* she thought angrily. She saw the red light on the camera flick on and knew she was being taped.

Dallas kept directing the kids as they moved around the stage, eventually catching the attention of Betty Ann.

"Take this for a second. I've got a fly to swat." Dallas turned and went down to the audience seats.

"Can I help you with something? You seem to have lost your way. No crime to report of in here."

"Hello, Dallas. Love the shoes." Dallas had finally given in to the appeal of flats when working with the kids, so Courtney towered over her in her high heels.

"I wasn't told you'd be doing a story on the theater today. This is kinda my storyline, you know?" Dallas felt suddenly protective of the charity tie-ins she had created for the TV station, now that someone else was barging into her territory.

"Oh, I'm not here to cover the theater or even the kids. *You* are the story."

"What? Me? That's ridiculous." Dallas said, confused.

"Mike wants a story on how one of our own is directing this year's charity Christmas play," Courtney said as if she was being made to clean toilets.

"Seriously? *I'm* the story?"

"God, for the hundredth time, yes. You."

Courtney was looking as though she had to pick cotton in the heat of July. Clearly she just wanted this punishment over with, and Dallas was brimming with satisfaction. Competitiveness was in her blood, and this could definitely be counted as a win.

"Well, how wonderful," she said, accentuating her Southern drawl. "Just one second while I get myself together." She turned, slinging her long blond hair behind one shoulder and sauntering up the stairs and backstage. After a few short moments, she emerged in her blazer and high heels for the interview.

"Okay, now what would you like to ask me?"

She loved this—being the center of attention and getting one up on the competition at the same time.

"First of all, how *ever* did you get this unusual assignment?" Courtney asked almost scornfully.

"Well, I was originally going to be the celebrity emcee for the production, when suddenly the director, poor Miss Fairbanks, got the flu bug. I had been here for most of the rehearsals already, so I was the obvious choice, I suppose."

"Uh-huh. Well, do tell, how's it going?"

"Fantastic, so far! The children are wonderful, and I think we're going to have a heck of a show."

"And how do you like directing? I mean, could it be the start of an entirely new career for you?"

Dallas was expecting some sort of curveball from Courtney, but she took it all in stride. "Oh, don't get me wrong, I love having this opportunity, but TV news is in my blood. *Nothing* could tear me away from my day job." Dallas smiled her perfect, superstar smile.

"Okay, that's all we need," Courtney said abruptly, turning away from Dallas and back to her cameraman. "Kevin, lets get some B roll."

"I'll go get my directing shoes on and meet y'all on stage," Dallas said. She knew it was making the very driven Courtney crazy to have to do a story on her, so she was even more effervescent than usual.

"Okay, children, listen up," Dallas said, making her way back on stage. "Miss James is here, and she will be taping some of this for us to see on TV tonight."

The children went nuts, their already sky-high enthusiasm now pushed over the top. Kevin's camera rolled.

"Okay, let's calm down and show 'em what we do best," Dallas said to the kids, but they barely heard her as they bounced around the stage.

"Listen to Miss Dallas, y'all," Betty Ann called as she tried to round up the kids. She and Dallas were chasing a few of the children, trying to get things under control, but the camera kept rolling, Courtney smirking and taking notes.

Chris and Jay got out the nutcracker puppets before Dallas could stop them, and they hopped around the stage biting anyone nearby. Chris climbed on top of the gingerbread house hollering, "Look, I'm Santa!" Then he tried to squeeze into the chimney, breaking the roof in half. A few of the smaller children had begun to fling the fake snow around the stage, one of them tripping on her own feet, taking down a string of lights as she tried to catch her balance.

Dallas was mortified—her carefully orchestrated interview now a joke next to the catastrophe happening on stage.

"Getting all this, Kevin?" Courtney said with a laugh as she flung her long dark hair back toward a cringing Dallas.

"Every single thing," Kevin answered.

"Looks like you're running a zoo instead of a play, Dallas. Maybe you were right. Better not lose your day job."

Just when Dallas was feeling the last ounce of confidence drift away, Prince Charming came to the rescue. Cal could see what was going on from the booth, and in an effort to get things under control he turned on the music for Sara Grace's solo. The kids recognized the music and stopped what they were doing to return to their seats. They all knew it was time for Sara Grace to sing, and since it was one of the highlights of the play, the kids always enjoyed watching with full attention.

Meanwhile, Sara Grace heard her cue and approached center stage.

She sang her best that day, soaring with the voice of an angel and the stage presence of a Broadway star. Even Courtney was moved, Dallas could tell, since she stood mesmerized by Sara Grace's voice.

When she finished, Sara Grace ran straight to Dallas and hugged her, not letting go.

"That was beautiful, sweetie pie. I'm just so proud of you." Dallas bent down in a genuine moment and looked Sara Grace in the eyes. Dallas looked up at Cal, who was standing up now, with his arms folded. He was looking down, grinning at her.

Kevin was taping everything. This was good for everyone. Cal and Sara Grace had saved the day for Dallas. And since this would make great television for tonight's newscast—emotional stories always won out over most things—Dallas knew Courtney would use it, even if she didn't want to.

"Thanks, I think we have everything," Courtney said. "Tell the kids to watch the six o'clock if they'd like to see themselves on TV." She and Kevin turned to walk back up the aisle. Dallas knew Courtney could have that story edited any way she wanted, and the kids had given her some pretty decent footage if she wanted to make Dallas look bad. She thought about calling Mike and letting him know they'd had a slight incident, but she didn't want to draw any more attention to it. She hoped Courtney would just put the focus on Sara Grace.

Then she realized she had a much bigger problem to worry about. Her eyes wandered to the stage, taking in the little town in disarray, especially the gingerbread house. In all their excitement, the kids had all but destroyed some of the set, the gingerbread house crumpled and unusable now. Dallas wasn't sure how she'd get everything back into shape in time for the big performance.

Then she remembered something. Blake had told her at lunch the other day that she was great with set design. With help from Blake and the production assistant, Corey, she was sure they could put the house and the rest of it back together again in time for the show.

In that moment, Dallas realized it was most definitely true: she *had* fallen down the rabbit hole. She was calling Blake O'Hara Heart for help.

26

Rehearsal ended, and Dallas made a beeline to her cell phone. She had become consumed with thoughts about this call for the entire practice. Blake had been open and genuine with her during their lunch last week, so Dallas wasn't worried about that. It was the timing. With the play quickly approaching, she'd need help right away.

She reached for the cell in her leather faux Hermès bag.

"Hey, Blake. It's me, Dallas."

"Oh, hey. How are you?" Dallas was relieved by the cheery tone of Blake's voice.

"Great, and you?"

"Just peachy. Gettin' as big as the side of a barn, but, hey, my boy's gonna be a football star, I'm sure, 'cause of the way he kicks all the time."

"Oh, my gosh. You already know it's a boy?"

"Yep, we just found out yesterday."

"That's wonderful. I bet Sonny is thrilled. Congratulations."

"Thanks! So, what's up?"

"Well, I'm calling because I have a quick question for ya. How would you feel about helping me fix a gingerbread house?"

"Sure, I love those little houses. So adorable—and delicious."

Dallas couldn't help but laugh. "Yeah, well, it's…a little bigger than what you might expect."

"How big?"

"Life-size," Dallas replied. "It's part of the set for the Christmas play."

"Oh, my word. What happened to it?"

"One of the kids sat on it during practice and fell through the roof, trying to be Santa Claus," Dallas explained.

Blake burst out laughing. "Sorry, sorry—I know that must have you feeling pretty stressed. Of course I can help. I did so much set design in college, it'll be a snap. I'll create a new roof and y'all can stick it right on."

Dallas felt the weight drop from her shoulders. "Works for me," she said happily.

"How 'bout you come by Vivi's on Saturday? We can have lunch and fix it together. She's got plenty of space there."

Spending an afternoon with Vivi wasn't exactly Dallas's idea of a good time, but she wasn't about to argue now. "Oh, that's great. I'll be there. Noon sound okay?"

"Perfect. Now let me tell you the supplies we'll need and you can bring them."

Dallas fumbled for a pen in her bag as Blake rattled off a list.

"Okay, got it," Dallas said, writing the last of the items down.

"I'll call Vivi and we'll see you then."

Was Dallas joining the Sassy Belle clique? She'd heard Blake talking about their little club back in high school. She and

Vivi had called themselves the Sassy Belles, their motto being, "Classy, sassy and a tad smart-assy." She'd been jealous of their friendship for as long as she could remember, and every time she'd heard Blake refer to a woman as a Sassy Belle, she'd felt a twinge of longing to be part of that circle of tight-knit women. She also knew they'd sworn never to invite her in. But here she was, being invited to Vivi's. Maybe things were going to change.

Cal approached her just as she was hanging up.

"You handled that surprise visit well," he said.

"Ya think? I'm not so sure."

"Who was that woman anyway? I don't remember seeing her on the news."

"She's new. She didn't even go to Alabama. I have no idea why in the world Mike hired her."

"Surely not everyone there in the newsroom went to Bama," Cal teased her.

"No, but any reporter who wants to be an anchor in Tuscaloosa should at least be *from* here. That way the locals love her and she's involved in the community."

"Uh-huh, like you." Cal waggled his eyebrows at her, and she had to laugh.

"Well, of course."

"I've been thinking about tonight. Wanna come to my house for a change?"

It was an offer she was dying to take him up on. To see Cal in his man cave made her stir from top to bottom.

"I do, but I need to go out and get some supplies to fix this gingerbread house. Tonight's the only night that looks open with the parade coming up in a couple of days and rehearsals going overtime. Blake is gonna help me get things repaired, and she gave me the list of things she'll need."

"You're working *with* Blake? After all these years, that comes as a pretty big surprise."

"I know—and Vivi's gonna help, too, it sounds like. I can't believe it myself."

"Well those two are fused at the hip, so if you get one, you get both. What a huge change. I mean, y'all are all three gonna work *together* on something."

"Yep. Wonders never cease. Kitty always said that."

"I've always liked her. What was that like to live in her house?" Cal asked.

"Well, she sure loved Blake. That woman lived for her daughter. She tried to be nice to me, too, while I was there but…I was pretty angry back then, so I did a lot of things that got me negative attention. I know Kitty was trying, but I was always so jealous of everything Blake had with her."

"That's understandable. I know you had to be pretty mad at your own mom, especially when you had Kitty to compare her against."

"I was. Still am. But I'm working on it. It's just gonna take me a really long time."

"What about Houston?"

"What about him? He knows where to find me if he wanted to talk. And after nearly twenty years with me begging him to even write me a note, I really have nothing left to say to him."

"I don't blame you. If he really wanted to make up, he could reach out."

Dallas wanted desperately to change the subject. "Hey, wanna run by the craft store with me on our way to your house?" Dallas asked.

"Sounds good to me. Let's take my car," he said, helping her gather her things.

"Oh, and before I forget to mention it, thanks so much for

stepping in today with that music. You were a lifesaver," she said, smiling at him.

"I saw the mess you were in, and I couldn't think of anything else to do. I know all the kids sit down and hush the minute they hear the song, and we needed them to sit down and hush." He snaked his arm snuggly around her waist and pulled her into him, kissing her temple. "Now, let's go get this stuff bought and get to my house."

"Yeah," Dallas said, giving him a coy smile, "so I can get the chance thank you properly."

Cal pulled into a spot at the art supply store. It took him at least ten minutes to find one; since it was less than two weeks till Christmas, everybody and their brother seemed to be there.

"We need to hurry so I can get home in time to watch Courtney's story," Dallas said. "I just hope she shows the best of us, and not the mayhem that broke loose."

"All right, let's get in and get out," Cal said.

The aisles were crowded with Christmas decorations, from garland to plastic statues, nearly falling from the piled-high stacks. Dallas and Cal could barely get down some of the aisles shuffling sideways.

"Hey, have you heard from Ms. Shelby lately?" Cal asked. The little plastic manger scenes reminded him of Dallas's ongoing story.

Dallas was impressed that he had been watching her segments.

"Yes, actually. I got a message from her late today. I'm

going back for a follow-up next week. She's started working with the police. The whole thing has become quite a puzzle. They've had that poor Baby Jesus all over campus."

"You never can tell with frat brothers," Cal said.

"You speak from experience, do you?" Dallas chided.

"Well, you know. That was a while ago."

"Yeah, a *long* while, according to your most recent fan, old quarterback," she teased him.

They made their way through the aisles of candy canes, fake Christmas trees and window candles, all the way back to the items Blake had listed.

"Gosh, this stuff is all so big, it's barely gonna fit in the buggy."

"I'd say I'd get you another one, but I think they're all out. We got the last one," Cal said, trying to help her fit it all in.

Just then, two of the kids from the play spotted her and came racing over, both of them grabbing her around her waist in a hug. "Ms. Dallas, what are you doing here?"

"Hey, y'all," Dallas said. She was still having so much trouble with remembering everyone's names. "I'm buying stuff to fix the gingerbread house for the set. What're y'all doin' here?"

"Mommy and Daddy needed some more decorations for our school party," the little girl informed her. "Daddy, this is our new director."

Dallas turned around to greet the children's dad, and she nearly passed out when she suddenly found herself standing eye to eye with her brother, Houston. She couldn't speak. Her mouth dropped open. Her gut clenched as if she had been pushed from a skyscraper. The moment seemed to be going in slow-motion.

"Dallas?" Houston said, clearly stunned himself. He didn't seem to know what to say either.

No words of any kind, on paper or otherwise, had passed

back and forth between them for twenty years. Dallas wrote to him, but she never got any response at all. Now she felt stuck. She wanted to hit him, beat him senseless for never answering a single note. She also wanted to hug him and hold him as if she would never let go. Instead she just stood there. Silent.

"Hey, I'm Cal Hollingsworth." Cal pushed in, breaking the awkward silence. He shook Houston's hand.

"Oh, um, sorry, yes. This is Cal, the sound director for the play," Dallas said, still in shock. She swallowed hard. "Cal, this is…Houston. My brother."

She saw Cal's eyes widen for a brief moment in surprise, but he pulled it together quickly and smiled stiffly at Houston.

"I'm sorry I haven't learned your names yet," Dallas said, bending down to the young children. All this time, she'd had a niece and nephew, and she'd never even known. It was even more ridiculous that she'd been spending time with them during rehearsals with absolutely no idea that they were actually related.

"I'm Anna Beth and this is my brother, Austin," the little girl announced.

Just then a woman approached whom Dallas didn't recognize. She was young, a redhead with blue eyes, medium height and willowy. Really pretty. She looked a bit younger than Houston, who had aged and grown a tad heavy.

This was definitely not Eleanor—the woman Houston had broken up the family for.

"Hey, I'm Amy. It's so nice to meet you. So, you're the new director?" she asked, having missed the part about her and Houston being siblings.

"Yes, nice to meet you, too," Dallas managed. She looked at Houston, expecting him to jump in and make the proper introduction, but he just stood there silently, his face pale and his lips drawn into a tight, thin line.

After another moment of uncomfortable silence, Dallas decided it was time to cut and run. "Well, it was nice running into you," she said. "So nice to meet you, Amy." With that, she turned and bolted out of the store, completely forgetting about her cart full of supplies, and nearly knocking over a big plastic Santa.

Dallas ran straight to Cal's car without looking back, pulling angrily at the locked door until she heard the beep of Cal hitting the auto-unlock for her. She jumped in, slamming the door. Cal was close behind her, climbing into the driver's seat as Dallas burst into tears right there in the parking lot.

"It's okay, baby, it's okay." Cal reached across the armrest and pulled her toward him.

"I hate that son of a bitch. I hate him. He just stood there like an asshole. What the hell is wrong with him? He's not even human."

"Why didn't you say something? Call him out?" Cal asked.

"I couldn't. All the words were stuck. I mean, my God, that was my niece and nephew standing there. I see them nearly every stinkin' day, and I don't even know them. Oh, Cal…" Dallas sobbed and bent her face over into her lap, all that anger and sadness flooding out of her once again.

"Do you want to try again? I mean, I can go in and get him and bring him out here."

"No. I can't. Not right now. He can never see me like this and know how much he hurt me."

"Well, I wanna tell him myself. He needs to know, Dallas. Is that the woman? The one you were telling me about?"

"No. He obviously got some sense somewhere along the line and married an actual lady. Why didn't he even try to contact me then? I mean, he wasn't with Eleanor anymore, which was the whole reason everything fell apart. He got a new girlfriend and even *then* he didn't try to reach out to me. And now I find out I've been teaching my niece and nephew and didn't even know it." She continued to cry it all out as Cal leaned over to catch her broken heart.

"Let's just get outta here for now, baby. We can come back later for the supplies."

He started the car and turned on the heater, driving Dallas to her favorite spot for comfort food: Taco Casa. This was not the time for a romantic evening at his place, Cal decided. He wanted to get her somewhere she felt safe and comfortable, so after picking up something from the drive-through, Cal made his way back to Dallas's little house by the campus.

She had calmed a little by the time Cal got her home. He took her inside with her sack of burritos and sweet tea. She looked as if she had just witnessed a death in the family. Her mascara was smeared down her cheeks and her face was pale. Her lipstick was wiped away. Her hair was disheveled. She kicked her shoes off and padded barefoot into the kitchen, Wilhelmina jumping up on the little corner table waiting to be greeted.

"Okay, let's get some food in you. You'll feel better in just a minute," Cal assured her. In the Deep South, food solved all kinds of problems, at least for a moment.

Dallas sat down at the table, her head in her hands. "Why didn't he even say anything? I don't get it. I mean, Cal, am I really so awful? He wouldn't even introduce me to his family as his sister. I must be an embarrassment to him."

"Aw, baby, no. Of course not. It's not you."

But there was nothing more Cal could say. They sat quietly in her cozy kitchen and ate their Taco Casa food, petting a purring Wilhelmina. When they finished, Cal grabbed the bags and wrappers and cleaned up.

"I'm gonna jump in the shower real quick," Dallas said. "Will you stay?"

"Of course, sweetheart. Just go relax."

She smiled and pushed her messy hair from her face, walking back to her bedroom. Cal heard the water turn on. He sat down on the couch, trying to think of what to say when she came back out. He wanted to have a solution ready. He was a typical man. He wanted to fix things for her. Instead of just listening for the rest of the night, he decided he would come up with some suggestions to get this issue resolved. He was pretty distraught himself after seeing what this encounter did to her at the store. Plus, he knew she would still have to see her niece and nephew at rehearsal over the next little while. If she didn't find a way to handle this, she'd be an emotional wreck by the night of the performance. He sat patiently on the couch petting Wilhelmina and thinking of what to say.

After a while, Dallas emerged from the bedroom in her white spalike robe. Her freshly scrubbed face looked sweet, but sad, so Cal stood and put his arms out to her. She shuffled over, wrapping her arms around him. He pulled her close, her clean wet hair hanging loosely down her back. The smell of her soap and shampoo intoxicated him. He melted into her, kissing her neck and her collarbone, his hands wandering across her body. Maybe he didn't need to know what to say, he thought. Maybe if he could make her *feel* loved, that would be enough.

He slipped his hand under the tie of her robe, pulling the sash loose, the material falling open, exposing her perfect, naked body to him. The sight of her skin excited him instantly. She ran her hand over his hard bulge, and he wanted her right that second. His passion reaching a height he couldn't control, he moved in to kiss her.

But Dallas stopped him, putting her hands on his chest.

"Cal, thank you so much for helping me through this the last two days. It's all been so intense."

"I know, its okay." He really didn't wanna talk right that second. He just wanted to take her and make the most passionate love to her he had ever made to anyone. He had never been so turned on.

"Really, though. It was such a huge shock," she continued.

"Why don't you just call him?" Cal suggested, but when he saw Dallas's eyes narrow, he got nervous.

"What?" Dallas said, stepping back.

Cal swallowed. "I think you need to call him. Or go see him. I know how upset you were, but he seemed like he wanted to say something to you."

"He did not. He had a chance to say anything he wanted, and he just stood there like a stump."

"Well, yeah, but...he did have his kids right there. So maybe he just didn't want to get into it in front of them. I mean, I can understand that...."

She tied her robe back together. "You are really something, you know. First you say you support me, and then, when I think I can trust you, you take his side. I thought you were on my side, Cal."

Cal was stunned at her reaction. He hadn't meant to take Houston's side at all. "Dallas, I am on your side, baby. I promise. I just think all this can end now that you've seen him and he's not even with that woman. He's got a family now. Maybe he wants to make up."

"I thought you said last night that all this should be on my terms. What about that, Cal? Huh? *My terms*. But now you think that since everybody wants to forgive and forget, little Dallas should just come running. What about all those years when I was out there begging for my family to come back and nobody was listenin' to me? What about that? They don't deserve my forgiveness. They need to suffer just like they made me suffer."

"Dallas, listen. As much as I understand how you feel—and you're totally right to be upset—you have a chance to have a real family now. And children are involved. Children you see nearly every single day."

"Well, my brother made a choice years ago to cut me out of their little lives by not even tellin' me they were born. So that's not my fault."

"No, it's not. But now it's in your power to change things."

Her face exploded with anger. "Maybe you need to leave, Cal. I think you're just like everyone else. You think I need to go crawling back and beg the family that threw me away to take me back. Well, I disagree. I've been just fine on my own. And I can be again."

"Dallas, I'm sorry. I'm trying to understand. It's just that at some point someone needs to take the first step."

"I think you need to go home now. I've made a terrible mistake. I thought I finally had someone on my side, but I guess I was wrong—again. Good night, Cal." She stood with her arms crossed, waiting for him to go.

He looked at her, heartbroken. Her sadness was palpable, but he couldn't bring himself to say another word. He was exhausted himself. He turned and headed to the front door. Dallas stood in her robe, pulling the sash a little tighter with a huff, tears brimming over. Cal looked back at her one last time as he opened the front door, seeing the pain he had caused her. He stepped outside into the sleeting rain and shut the door.

Dallas cried herself to sleep. Just when she'd thought her life couldn't get any more stressful, she'd run into her brother. Now, the thought of losing Cal was sending her right off the cliff. Still, her mind drifted back to work. The parade was in a few days, but her emotions had just been through the wringer. How could she ride on that float and smile at the crowds of families with all this weighing on her? All she could think of was how Cal had betrayed her.

Of course, he hadn't really. He'd just wanted to fix her problems and make them go away. But Dallas couldn't understand that right now. She was feeling too many things at the same time: anger, guilt, resentment and sadness. She fell asleep in her robe, with wadded-up toilet paper to wipe her nose tucked in her hand. The sleet continued through the night, tapping against the windows as she fitfully dozed in and out of sleep.

When Dallas woke, her eyes were swollen from crying all night. She made a sleepy path to the bathroom and wet a washcloth.

Then she lay back down, placing the cold fabric to her blistering eyelids. She needed to get the swelling down so no one would notice how upset she'd been. Now was not the time to have a crisis, so she'd just have to ignore the one that was happening anyway.

Eventually she made her way to the shower, then dressed for work, fed Wilhelmina and headed out to her car—which wasn't there. She'd totally forgotten in all the confusion and stress of last night that she had left it at the Bama Theatre. She had also forgotten about Courtney's story.

Standing on her porch, she fumbled through her purse for her cell to call Daniel for a ride. Her neighbor from across the street waved. The one with the Times Square lights all over his house.

"Hey," Dallas shouted from across the street. "Is there any way you can turn those lights down? They shine right in my bedroom window and I can't sleep."

The man laughed. "Good! I was tryin' to get yer attention. I was hopin' you could put me on TV for all my lights."

"Well, if I don't get any sleep, *I'm* not even gonna be on TV. Just turn them off at a decent hour."

"I always heard you were a bitch. Thanks for confirmin' that." He went back into his house, and, just before he slammed the door, he turned back to shout, "And Merry Christmas to you, too!"

This day was not starting out very well.

Daniel swung by, picked her up and dropped her off at her car outside the Bama. As she unlocked her door, she heard a text message jingle in her bag. *If that's Mother, I swear I'm gonna change my number,* she thought. It was Cal.

Just making sure you got your car. I'm really sorry.

Got it, was all she sent back.

She dropped the phone into her purse and started her

car, wiping tears again from her face. Facing this day may have been her toughest assignment yet. It wasn't long before D-Day—Dread Day: the day of the play and the announcement of the new main female anchor for WTAL. Dallas began to think it could very well be the end of things as she knew them. It felt as if she was watching a crash in extra slow-motion.

It didn't help at all to see Courtney James talking to Mike the second she walked into the newsroom. She pulled herself together and tried to listen in. When she couldn't hear because they moved into Mike's office and shut the door, Dallas made her way to the ladies' room and slipped into the biggest stall, locked herself in and pressed her ear to the wall that backed Mike's office. The voices were muffled, but she could just make them out.

"Oh, Mike, I really appreciate this. Thanks for letting me know so soon," she heard Courtney say.

"No problem. I just wanted you to have a heads-up, so you can be prepared," Mike said. Dallas's stomach twisted, then dropped to her knees.

"This is a dream come true. I can't thank you enough," Courtney gushed.

"Well, I know you'll need some time to adjust. Your schedule's gonna change, of course."

Oh. My. God. He'd given the position to her already? Dallas lost it right there in the stall. She was sobbing loudly when she heard the door fling open. She froze and held her breath. Then she looked under the stall to see the shoes of the woman who'd walked in. Fake Manolo's. *Courtney.*

Oh God, she thought. She could never let Courtney see her like this. She quickly ripped off some toilet paper and wiped her face. *"Shit,"* she mumbled to herself as she fumbled around the stall in a panic. She didn't have her makeup bag with her.

"Dallas, is that you, honey? You okay?"

Courtney doesn't care if I'm okay. She just wants to rub her new anchor job in my face.

"Yes, fine," was Dallas's clipped response.

"Well, it was sounding like the end of the world in here, so just thought I'd check."

Dallas dropped her head to her hands. *Shit, she heard me havin' a fit.* "Oh, that…well, it was nothing. I'm fine. Bad breakfast burrito."

"Goodness, I'll say." Courtney said.

Dallas could hear her standing at the big makeup mirror, fumbling through all the toiletries on the counter. Dallas was trapped. In the stall. Faking diarrhea. And of course Courtney kept right on chatting.

"Lookin' forward to the parade day after tomorrow?"

"Yes." *Maybe if I don't talk much she'll get the hell outta here.*

"Oh, me, too. I'm covering the route. Aren't you ridin' on the float?

"Yes." *Please, for the love of God, leave.*

Dallas heard the water come on, the paper towel roll pulled. Then the hairspray being used. *Go. Go now,* she prayed.

"Well, I do hope you feel better, hon. Want me to tell Mike you're sick so you can go on home?"

"No! No, I'm feeling better already."

"Alrighty then. Talk to you later."

Dallas heard her heels click across the tile floor, the bathroom door open, then fall closed behind her. She leaned over and peeked under the stall. She was alone. *Now to slip out to my car to grab my makeup and fix myself.*

She left the safety of the little stall, made her way stealthily to her chair, grabbed her bag and headed outside—where she ran smack into Cal.

"What are you doing here?" she demanded.

Cal looked hurt. "Look, Dallas, I'm really sorry about—"

"I'm actually kind of busy right now," she interrupted. If she was gonna get through this day, she couldn't have another emotional conversation with Cal in the middle of the parking lot. "Is that why you came? To apologize?"

He stiffened. "Didn't you say you had something weird in your email? I'm doing what you asked me to do. I'm here to check it out," he said.

"It's fine, Cal. Really. You don't have to be here. I'll get someone else," she replied.

"There is nobody else," he said, insulted. "This is what I do. So, just show me where you sit."

"Fine, follow me."

Dallas led Cal to her desk and showed him the email. Cal clicked on it and read it, then took a few notes about the email address and other things Dallas had no idea about. While he poked around, she kept licking her fingers and trying to wipe the mascara from her cheeks. She felt her stomach churning, even though there had never been that bad burrito. She could smell his aftershave. She watched his big muscular chest rise and fall as he sat in her seat. His shoulders so broad, his hair so thick. It was all she could do not to touch him. She involuntarily raised her hand to rest it on those shoulders when she caught herself.

"Okay, I'll get to the bottom of this. But, listen, if you get another one of these, call me, okay?"

"Is it something bad? I mean, am I in some sort of danger?"

"No, you're not in danger. But I know some people at Callahan, and I'm almost certain this email has been hacked."

"Really?"

"Looks like someone has broken into their computer system. I'll make some calls and decipher all of this and get to the source. It may take a few days, or even a week, but I'll keep you posted." Cal stood up and pushed the paper with his notes on it into his blue jeans pocket before leaving the newsroom.

Dallas stood, watching him walk away. She felt even sicker inside than she looked on the outside. The pangs of not having Cal anymore seared through her like a hot laser. On top of that, she had already lost the anchor job, and now she knew some weirdo was sending her emails about the missing Baby Jesus statue. All this made her nauseous on another level, doubling the insecurities that were already building.

As she stood in the hallway watching Cal walk away from her, Daniel popped out of the edit bay. "Oh, my God. You okay?" he asked after looking at her puffy, mascara-stained face.

"No, I most certainly am not. Just a minute." Dallas bolted to her car with Daniel in tow, grabbed her makeup bag, then walked him out to the back parking lot where the news van was parked.

"Get in," she ordered as she opened the passenger door to the van.

Daniel got in and shut the door. Dallas pulled down the visor and looked in the mirror. Unzipping her makeup bag, she began telling Daniel all about what she had found out that morning about Courtney.

"No way," Daniel said in shock. "I know he hasn't decided yet. He talked about it in the early meeting before you got here."

"It's all an act. I heard him. They were in Mike's office with the door closed."

"How did you hear it then?"

"I was in the bathroom with my ear to the wall."

"Well, maybe you heard it wrong then," Daniel reasoned.

"No, I know what he said and then of course I had a conniption fit, so Courtney came into the bathroom and asked me if I was okay," she said.

"What did you say?"

"Bad burrito."

Daniel burst out laughing. "Look," he said, after Dallas gave him the death glare, "I think something else is going on. Mike wouldn't lie to us. Let's just keep doing a great job every day. I know Mike is crazy about your work. Really, Dallas, just trust me on this one."

"Fine. But it's probably just a huge waste of time. I'm just gonna get fired at the end of this." She sighed. "Where are we going anyway?"

"I have no idea. That's your job. Now, go back in there and talk to Mike."

Dallas checked her face. She looked fresh, as if her make-up had just been applied. Well, it had. She decided to just tell Daniel all about the emails later. First she had to talk to Mike.

She slid out of the van and walked back across the parking lot in her five-inch heels. She was at work, after all, and in these shoes, at least she was taller than Courtney. But when she reached Mike's office she found that he had already left for a meeting downtown, so she couldn't confront him and get any of her questions answered. She sat frustrated at her desk.

Then Courtney sauntered over, a smug look on her face.

"Well?"

"Well, what?" Dallas sat up, confused.

"Did you see it?"

"What?"

"Uh, the story I did on you?"

"Oh, uh…no. I had a late meeting at the theater." Dallas stiffened. "How did it go?"

"Well, let's go watch together. Then *you* can tell *me*."

Oh, God, I really don't think I can stomach this, Dallas thought, but she got up and followed Courtney into an edit bay anyway. Courtney hit a button, and the story began.

Dallas watched as the video showed Sara Grace singing and then rushing to Dallas and hugging her. Dallas looked at Courtney and smiled.

"Thanks. I do appreciate you not showing all the chaos."

"Don't thank me. Thank Mike. He looked at all the footage that Kevin shot, and this was his favorite clip. Since WTAL is sponsoring the play, it had to be done. Just thought you should know."

"Well, thanks anyway. They really are great kids."

Dallas walked away with a small bit of relief. It wasn't much, but she had really needed some good news. Even if it had come from Courtney James.

29

"Think we'll have another wild goose chase today?" Dallas asked with a smile, settling into the front seat of the van for the second time that morning and warming her hands against the heater.

"I hope not. There's still a few days before the scavenger hunt ends, but I really don't feel like chasing down any animals right now," Daniel said.

They were headed over to WRCT, where Lewis, Abigail and Meridee, Blake's grandmother and co-owner of the station, were meeting them. Dallas had always loved Meridee and was excited to see her. She had known her since she'd joined Blake's family when she was fourteen. Meridee was the one person in Tuscaloosa who always seemed to see the best in her. But that was her nature. She always saw the best in everyone. Dallas felt comfortable around her 'cause she had always been one of her biggest supporters. Meridee just did her own thing and never answered to anybody but herself.

Daniel parked near the two-hundred-year-old gazebo at the Brooks Mansion and started unloading the camera equipment. Lewis stepped out onto the porch.

"Hey, y'all, come on in," he shouted to them.

"Hey, Lewis. How's everything goin' today?" Dallas said.

"We're good here. We got lots to talk about, so come on in and set up here by the Christmas tree," Lewis said as he led them inside the historical old place.

Dallas and Daniel set up with the huge twelve-foot tree that would serve as a backdrop. Abigail and Meridee came down the staircase, and Dallas felt instantly better seeing them.

"Hey, baby girl," Meridee said to her, coming over for a hug. "You look beautiful as ever."

"Oh, thanks. You do, too. Hey, Abigail. Doin' okay today? Looks like you got all your feathered friends under control around here."

Abigail laughed. "Yes, so much better than the last time you saw me. I looked like I had a starring role in *The Birds* last you were here. I think Tuscaloosa got the message, though. No more live animals have shown up since your story."

"Oh, Tuscaloosa listens to her. She's our star," Meridee said, smiling at her.

"So, Abigail, what did you want the story to be about? What's our angle?" Dallas asked, sitting down on the settee next to Meridee in the foyer. Since the radio and the TV station were working as partners for the charity, Dallas wanted to make sure she got everything out to the public that the radio station needed.

"We need to get the enthusiasm up as we near the end of the hunt. Something that will stir up publicity and excitement."

"Okay. Anything else?" Dallas asked.

"The last item hasn't been found yet. We know where they all are and we know it's still right where we put it, so let Tuscaloosa know that the race is down to the final clue," Meridee said.

"Why don't I interview you and Lewis, too?" Dallas asked Meridee.

"Great idea. I'm ready whenever y'all are," Lewis said.

Dallas interviewed all of them smoothly and did a perfect stand-up.

"So remember, T-Town, not much more than a week left before the scavenger hunt officially ends, and one single item has yet to be found. Go online to see the clues. And remember, all proceeds from this contest will go to the Tuscaloosa Children's Home, a wonderful organization working hard to bring a little joy to children this holiday season. I'm Dallas Dubois for WTAL."

Dallas was helping Daniel pack up the van when Meridee found her.

"What's going on behind those pretty blue eyes today, huh?"

How in the world does she know these things? Dallas wondered.

"Oh, nothing, just a little allergies, I think."

"In the dead of winter? Come on, sugar. I've known you a long time. Now, you come with me and we're gonna have us a talk."

Technically, Dallas hadn't lied. She was referring to that chronic allergy she'd had for nearly twenty years: the Cal Hollingsworth allergy.

"Daniel, I'm gonna hang back a second. I'll see you at the van." Dallas turned and thanked Abigail and followed Meridee inside. Lewis was still out talking to Daniel, so Meridee slipped inside his large office and closed the door behind them.

"What's goin' on?" she asked.

"Well, you know the whole story with my family, right?"

"I'll never forget it. It was awful."

"Well, you know I tried to contact my brother all those times."

"I know it. I helped you write one of those letters myself."

"Well...I ran into Houston last night." Dallas choked up. She looked out the window and swallowed hard.

Meridee could see she was struggling. "Oh, sweetheart, I know that must have been so hard. You haven't seen him in all those years even once, have you?"

"No, but the worst part is—and you won't believe this—he's got two kids and they're in the Christmas play that I'm directing! I've been working with them almost every evening without a clue who they were. I had no idea I was even an aunt." Her eyes brimmed with tears. Meridee reached over and laid her hand on Dallas's hand.

"What did Houston have to say?" Meridee asked her.

"Not a word."

"Was Cal with you?"

"How do you know about Cal?"

"They don't call Lewis the Voice for nothin'."

That lightened the mood for a second, and Dallas smiled.

"Look, sugar, it's Christmas and lots of people get weird during the holidays. Hell, lots of people are weird most of the time anyway, so use my motto, don't let the crazies get you down."

Dallas decided not to tell her that she sent Cal away.

"Thanks, Meridee. I'm just a little worried about that anchor job, too."

"I've seen the billboards. The station has that whole promotion going trying to get everyone to tune in on the twenty-third to see the big reveal and find out who the new anchor will be."

"It's nerve-wracking," Dallas said standing up to leave.

"Don't worry one bit. Things will be how they're meant to be. So, you listen to me—Cal is a good man and you are doing a great job with those kids and with your reporting. Now, the rest of it with that nutty family of yours will just have to figure itself out. So, go do your thing, girl. It'll all be just fine."

Meridee stood up, all four-feet-ten-inches of her, and Dallas bent down to hug her.

"Thanks, Meridee. I always did love you."

"Love you, too, baby. Now go get 'em." She smiled a confident smile.

Dallas left the radio station thinking Meridee must have been a cheerleader in her younger days, and just how lucky she was to always have Meridee rooting for her in her career. She needed that.

She searched her purse for the list Blake had given her and decided to get back to the store to get the supplies she'd abandoned yesterday. She had a play that was opening next week and there was no time to waste.

Now, all she had to do was figure how to face Cal at rehearsal.

30

Back at the station, Dallas settled in at her desk. The newsroom was abuzz with the evening's agenda and end-of-the-day deadlines. She was going over possible stories for the next day when Julianne, the intern, came over with a notepad.

"What are you bringing for the Christmas party?" Julianne asked.

What? Dallas had totally forgotten the station party. "Oh, um, when is it again?"

"Friday night, right after the parade."

Dallas suddenly remembered. "Oh, yeah, at the Gorgas House on campus, right?"

"Yep. I'm in charge of the list, and, even though it's being catered, we need to know that you'll be bringing a gift for the children's charity we're sponsoring."

"Oh, absolutely," Dallas answered.

"Okay, boy or girl?"

"Huh?"

"Is the gift for a boy or a girl?"

Dallas immediately thought of Sara Grace. "Oh, sorry, yes, a girl."

"Thanks, see ya there." Julianne looked at her strangely before walking off.

Dallas couldn't bear the fact that Sara Grace would be alone for Christmas. She decided not only to buy something to bring to the Christmas party but *several* things, and one thing extra special for Sara Grace. Suddenly, Dallas was filled with excitement. Retail therapy was the best kind, after all, and Christmas shopping for children would be a wonderful pick-me-up after such a horrendous few days. She could already imagine the delight in their little faces as they tore the wrapping off her gifts. Maybe it was true what they say...giving actually did feel better than receiving.

Cal's stomach pitched when Dallas walked through the doors to the Bama Theatre. He'd never felt so worked up about a woman before, but Dallas just did something to him that he couldn't explain. He hoped that she'd be willing to talk to him now that she was here.

"Hey..." Cal said, not really knowing what to say.

She put her chin up as she always did and kept right on walking. "Hey," she said as she wooshed by him, making it clear she didn't have anything she *wanted* to say to him.

He felt crushed. She wasn't the only one who had let her guard down to get so quickly involved in a new relationship. Cal had been through several tough breakups in his past. He wanted the kind of love his parents and his brothers had in their marriages: the real thing. A love that lasted a lifetime.

Oh, it was easy for him to get women. He knew he was good-looking, and being a star football hero from a really wealthy family hadn't hurt either. But he didn't trust his own instincts, and it hadn't been long before he'd started doubt-ing the relationships he was in—sure they wouldn't last for the long term. Until he got involved with Dallas. With her, things were like the race cars his dad collected: they went from zero to eighty in seconds. He was falling hard for her, but now everything had fallen apart. The magic seemed all but gone. Dallas's smug attitude wasn't helping either.

As she walked past, he grabbed her arm.

"We need to talk, Dallas. Come on," he pleaded.

"Look, Cal, there's nothing to talk about. Unless you have something to tell me about the emails I'm getting, I have an incredibly busy next few days. And I'm late today as it is." She pulled away and stormed off.

But Cal wasn't the type to be hurt and not face it head-on. He was an Alabama football player, and Crimson Tide men didn't walk away from a battle. He wasn't trained that way. Head-on was his nature. He had to make a plan.

"Hey, kiddos," Dallas said from the audience seats as she approached the stage. She was determined to block Cal from her mind and get through this rehearsal.

Betty Ann and Corey ran around and got everyone to their places for the run-through. Dallas looked up at Cal and queued the music. The choir began what would be the overture and the lights lowered, and Tristan, Jay, Chris and Sara Grace took the stage to tell the story of a Victorian Christmas.

"What about the house, Miss Dallas? The gingerbread house doesn't have a roof," Tristan asked.

"It's broken right now, so for today we need to stand next to it and just pretend to go in," Dallas answered. But Chris wasn't listening and into the little candy house he went. As soon as he opened the door, the rest of the Twizzlers fell down from the collapsed roof, leaving Chris covered in candy. All the children laughed and ran over to help the giggling Chris out from under the sticky, red confections. Dallas smiled, and she and Betty Ann joined them to help with the mess. Sara Grace was laughing hard, too. The little girl spontaneously reached over and hugged Dallas tightly around the waist. Dallas was taken in the moment. The sweet encounter held her still in the chaos that had become her life over the past few days. Dallas suddenly realized she needed that affection, too. Sara Grace made her feel included and needed.

Once they'd gotten organized, the kids returned to their spots and picked up where they'd left off. When it came time for Sara Grace's solo, she approached center stage and the music began. But no one could hear her.

"Miss Dallas, I'm singing but I don't hear myself," she said, tapping the mic that was clipped to her little blue dress.

"Here, baby, let me take a look," Dallas said, walking over. She clicked it off and on. Nothing. Dallas saw Cal looking down from the balcony and then messing with some buttons on the board.

"Did I break it?" Sara Grace asked, looking worried.

"Oh, no, baby, you didn't do anything."

"Oh, here comes Mr. Cal. He'll fix it."

Cal skipped up the side stairs and was within inches of Dallas before she knew it. His sleeve brushed her hair as he reached for the broken mic. A tingle shot through her and she tried to ignore the heat it sent, but she tingled anyway.

"Here, let me see it," Cal said, taking a look. He took the back off and changed out the batteries that he just happened to have in his pocket and clipped it all back in place. "Now, give it a try."

Sara Grace sang a few words and it worked.

"See? Just a battery, sweetheart, nothing to worry about." He let his hand fall and squeezed the tiny singer's shoulder.

"Now, sing like the angel you are, okay? Mr. Cal wants to hear you all the way up there," he said, pointing to the balcony booth.

"Thanks! See, Ms. Dallas, I knew he could fix it." Sara Grace stopped abruptly and hugged Cal around the waist. "Aren't you gonna hug him thank-you, too, Ms. Dallas?"

Cal glanced over at a surprised Dallas.

"Sure," she said, uncomfortably smiling at Cal. She reached over for a sideways one-handed hug when he slipped his other arm around her waist.

"We need to talk after rehearsal," he whispered in her ear as he hugged her. He clearly wasn't going to give up.

Dallas didn't say anything. She just kept smiling as if she were the butt of a bad joke.

Rehearsal resumed, and they finally made it to the part where a live manger scene would be the grand finale. The children knew the donkey and the sheep weren't going to be there until the final dress rehearsal, but Dallas took the opportunity to remind them that they weren't allowed to touch the animals when they arrived.

Then the kids sang several Christmas carols and ended with the audience encouraged to join in the final songs.

Overall, the run-through was good and had gone off without too many hitches—except, of course, for the gingerbread house, and Dallas already planned to stop after rehearsal for the fix-it materials. She clapped for the kids and ended practice. Sara Grace ran over and hugged her as she grabbed her bag and coat.

"I love you, Ms. Dallas," Sara Grace said with a giant ear-to-ear smile.

The innocence of the moment made the words even more genuine. Dallas felt as if a warm arrow had gone through her. The child's gushing comment was the real thing. She knew she meant it. She also knew Sara Grace didn't have very many people to love. Neither did Dallas, for that matter. In that moment, Dallas knelt to one knee and, for the first time, hugged Sara Grace back, face-to-face. She held her securely, caressing the back of her head.

When she let go, Dallas looked the child in the eyes. "I love you, too, Sara Grace." Dallas smiled at her as she gazed into her eyes, making sure the little girl heard her clearly and knew she meant it. And she did. It was a moment between them that became a bond of sorts. The two of them were so similar on so many levels.

For the first time, Dallas felt real love coming from an unassuming place: from someone who didn't expect much and didn't have anything to give.

Just exactly like Dallas herself.

31

The theater was all but dark by the time Dallas gathered her things and began her walk back up toward the lobby. Cal was sitting in an audience seat, and she walked right by him without even seeing him. Only the little twinkling stars were on overhead, barely illuminating the theater. His voice came from nowhere in the darkness, like a ghost.

"Will you please talk to me?" he asked as she passed him.

"Oh, my God, Cal, you scared the crap outta me. No, really, I need to get going. I have several stops to make tonight before I can get home."

Cal stood and followed her to the front of the theater.

"If we can't work this out, you know it's just a damn shame. Things were going great," he said.

His persistence irritated and excited her at the same time. But right now she was mostly just hurt by him. She felt he'd betrayed her.

"I know. It really is a shame. And you're right, things were going great, but you are no different from the rest, Cal. Nobody has *ever* really been on my side. Everybody's always telling me to accept my family and just move on. Well, you know what? It's not that easy."

"I know, but at some point you can't hold on to all this anger anymore."

"You know what everyone seems to keep forgetting? I am the victim here. *I'm* the one that was abandoned. And now you're telling me to just call up the one person who destroyed my entire life, who wouldn't forgive me for trying to save him, and just make up?"

"Forgive? You are a fine one to talk about forgiving, Dallas. You know what? That's your whole entire problem. With your family and now with me—if somebody hurts you or makes a mistake, you hold on with a white-knuckle grip and never, ever forgive. *Forgiveness*—that's your problem."

"You can shut the hell up now. I don't need this." Dallas swallowed and held the lump forming in her throat until she was clearly out of his sight.

As she turned to walk out, Cal gave her one last parting thought. "You're only hurting yourself."

Dallas walked out into the dark, downtown street, the light poles decorated with garland and ribbon, the restaurants filling up with the supper crowds. She made her way to the art supply shop, managing not to run into any other long-lost family members along the way. She picked up the materials she needed and went on to University Mall to shop for the kids. She didn't have much money, but she knew she had to buy them some nice things, and especially for Sara Grace. Just the thought of this sort of retail therapy and she was already feeling better.

She ran into several stores and got a few things for girls, tiny bottles of nail polish and sample perfumes. Lord, if she ever did have a girl of her own, she'd obviously have her trained to be a girly-girl and ready for the pageant circuit by the time she was six. Dallas was, after all, Dallas.

She was having so much fun she decided to head over to Toys "R" Us. Oh, my, she was in pageant-baby heaven: crowns and little tiaras, toy jewelry and even little pink costumes with clouds of crinoline. She filled her buggy to overflowing and took it up front to check out.

"Sure is a lucky little girl to have you," the cashier said as she rang up the total.

"Actually, I'm the lucky one to have her."

F riday came in a flurry as everything was gearing up for
Christmas week. Dallas was in the thick of it all, and she
was crazy busy just like she liked to be. The parade would be
covered live tonight, and everyone in the newsroom was gearing up for the event. Not to mention the big staff Christmas
party following the parade.

Dallas arrived at the station early and was running around
the newsroom arranging her day when she ran right into
Courtney.

"Hey, did you hear the great news?" Courtney asked, beam-
ing.

"Um, news?"

"Yeah! It looks like we're on the float together tonight,"
Courtney told her.

"Huh?" Dallas replied, stunned.

"Yeah, I just heard."

She couldn't believe this was happening. The float was supposed to be her moment to shine—her time in the spotlight. But she figured they must have wanted to have Courtney out in the public eye, considering the announcement that would be happening next week. Still, she'd thought Mike would have at least granted her this one dignity before giving her the boot.

"Well, that should be…delightful," she replied with a bit of sarcasm. Dallas shot her a fake smile and turned away. She definitely believed in that motto: *never let 'em see you sweat.* But she wasn't about to let this go without a fight. She beelined straight into Mike's office and shut the door.

"Courtney tells me she is riding on the float with me to-night."

"She is correct."

"Mike, what gives here? I thought I was going live on the six o'clock from the float."

"You are."

"Okay, so why does Courtney need to be there during *my* live shot?"

"Dallas, I always said you had tenacity to spare, and I love that. Look at how energetic and riled up you are! Listen, I'm just having her ride on the float. She doesn't have a story and she's not busy, and I'm trying to help Tuscaloosa get to know her. So she and my ten o'clock weather guy, Marty Rains, will be sittin' on the back of the float wavin' at the people while you do your thing."

Dallas still wasn't happy. She didn't want to share anything with Courtney, especially not a spotlight like a parade. Mike obviously didn't think it was a big deal, but she needed a sympathetic ear to vent, so she went to look for Daniel down the long hallway of edit bays.

"Daniel, wait till you hear this. Courtney's ridin' on the damn float with me tonight!"

"No way." Daniel was always ready to listen.

"I know. It's ridiculous. I was looking so forward to making my one last live shot the best I could. But I guess she's already got the job, so why should I even care, right?"

"I still think you're getting ahead of yourself about that. Just go do what you do best and ignore the rest."

Dallas sighed. "You're right. Okay, I'll meet you at the setup location in a little while."

"You going to the party after?"

"Yep, wouldn't miss that. Are they still doin' the blooper reel?"

"Finishing it up right now."

"Should I be worried?"

Daniel smirked. "Everyone should be worried."

At five o'clock, Dallas pulled into her spot near the courthouse downtown. The Tuscaloosa Christmas tree was glittering with more than a thousand tiny lights. Everything was beautiful and festive. Her thoughts turned to Cal, and she gave a deep sigh. The disappointment was a weight on her as she tried to prepare for her live shot that was just an hour away.

Not many knew Dallas deeply, and Cal had been the only one to crack through her tough exterior. Deep down she was a passionate romantic, and all the twinkling Christmas lights had her longing to share these festive moments with Cal. As she sat and looked up at the fifty-two-foot-tall cedar, she recognized that she cared for him even more than she wanted to admit. But he'd let her down, and she wasn't sure how to get past that.

She got out of her car, grabbing her long, white coat and crimson gloves and scarf and headed to the venue. The parade was to begin at Greensboro Avenue and Fourteenth Street, then it would turn to head up University Boulevard. The lineup included local school choirs and marching bands, dancers, horses and more than one hundred floats, with Santa Claus and the mayor being the highlights of the evening. WTAL was set up with the satellite truck near the midway spot of the route. The theme of the parade this year was Twelve Days of Christmas, to tie in with the radio contest to benefit the children's home. Dallas knew that Vivi and Lewis would be riding in the WRCT radio float, along with some of their newest personalities, like Annabelle Harper, Abigail's sister and the host of the new *Saved by the Belle* radio call-in show.

The whole town would be out for the big event. It was safe to say, this was the biggest night of the entire Christmas season for Tuscaloosa.

"Hey, Miss Christmas," Daniel said as she approached. He was sitting in front of the control panel gearing up for the live parade.

"There was a day when I actually *was* Miss Christmas and rode on the back of a convertible in this very parade," Dallas said, removing her gloves and grabbing a ready-made hot chocolate from a nearby tray.

"I bet you were. I can just see you in that tiara."

"Those were some good times," she said, taking a sip of the warm cocoa. She held the hot sweet confection in her mouth and let it settle her.

"You need to get to the float so we can do a sound check."

"Okay, I'm ready."

She patted Daniel on the shoulder as she passed behind him. A gesture of solidarity. They had been through a lot together, and just recently she had begun to realize he had her back. Even when she was, well…bitchy.

Dallas arrived at the WTAL float and climbed up. Mike was already there.

"Hey, Dallas, come aboard," he said.

"Thanks," she said as he helped her up. The float was made

to look like a TV newsroom. And the tree on the float featured pictures of some of the foster children from the Tuscaloosa Children's Home. Dallas immediately walked over to look at them. The float was situated in between the seven swans a-swimming and the eight maids a-milking.

At least this looked as if it might be a safe spot—a good distance from the Civil War Cavalry riding their beautiful but shit-dropping horses. But then she realized that the eight maids were sitting on little milking stools and, yes, real cows were on the float. At least her float would be upwind of the cows.

Dallas got her earpiece and microphone hooked up.

"Sound check," she said into the mic. "Daniel, can you hear me?"

"Sounds great. Now, go get 'em," he said in her ear.

Courtney arrived all dressed in a dark green suit and cranberry-colored gloves. She took her seat in the center of the float, ready to start waving to her public. Dallas walked over to...welcome her.

"Hey, Courtney. Aren't you lookin' mighty Christmassy?" Dallas could hear Daniel snicker in her ear.

"You do, too, so festive," Courtney said.

"Oh, this?" Dallas asked, her hand on her coat. "No, no. This was just the preshow." Dallas removed her cream-colored coat with a flourish and got the attention of everyone in eyesight. Underneath she was wearing a short, red velvet dress with white faux fur trimming each wrist. The deep V down the back was also lined in the white, fluffy fabric. With her hair perfectly coiffed in a big and voluminous blowout, she looked like a seductive Santa's helper, a naughty Christmas elf. If she would be forced to share the spotlight, she wanted to be damn sure everyone was looking at her.

Any other reporter would have never been taken seriously in that outfit, but this was Dallas, and this was the reporter

Tuscaloosa knew and loved. Courtney was no competition, and that's just the way Dallas wanted it. Sure, she'd be freezing, but beauty was pain, she always said, especially with stakes this high.

In the minutes before the parade began, Dallas surveyed the lineup. The mayor's float was just in front of the swans, and she could see Kitty and the mayor carrying on and laughing. Just behind the maids a-milking float were Lewis and Vivi. Sonny, the police chief of homicide and Blake's baby daddy, was walking right next to the mayor's float. Farther up she saw Blake driving Vivi's powder-blue convertible with this year's Miss Christmas riding on the back. The girl was a gorgeous brunette, and she wore a white dress with a Christmas-red wrap, her crown perfectly perched on her head. The mayor had asked Blake to drive Miss Christmas for the city. And it was looking more and more like the mayor was soon to be Blake's new stepfather.

The mayor's float was spectacular. It was representing the city of Tuscaloosa, complete with a mini Black Warrior River, with water running into a recycling bin and actually flowing just like the real thing. The floor of the float was covered in the kudzu vines that ran down the banks of the real river. A park bench, where Kitty and the mayor sat, was situated just to the back of the river display, representing the gorgeous one-of-a-kind River Walk.

Everyone Dallas knew was all around her. She caught herself looking for Cal in the crowd. When she glanced back at Lewis's float, she saw Cal running their soundboard. The radio station was broadcasting the parade live from the float, and Cal was the remote sound engineer, broadcasting the events back to the station at the Brooks Mansion.

Cal caught Dallas looking his way, and he smiled at her. She grinned but turned away quickly.

By now the sun had set and all the Christmas lights were aglow throughout the festive, historic downtown.

"Okay, you'll be on in just a few minutes. All ready?" Mike asked.

"Certainly am," she confirmed with her megawatt, camera-ready smile.

"We'll let the parade begin and we'll go live soon after. Just wait for your cue."

Dallas glanced back at Courtney, who was sitting there chatting with Marty Raines, the weather guy, and every so often looking up to give a wave to everyone and no one at the same time.

It was time, and the float began to roll. Dallas was in her element with that microphone in her hand. She waved to the cheering crowds as the bands played and the dancers danced.

Just then, Courtney and Marty got up and began to walk to the other side of the float where it looked as though most of the crowd was. Dallas became immediately frustrated as she saw Courtney getting all the attention on that side of the float. She quickly ran over to that side, pushing her way in between the two of them.

"Dallas, time for the live shot," Mike announced. But Dallas was too busy waving to her adoring public to even hear him.

"Dallas!" Mike shouted.

Finally the cameraman dashed over and stooped in front of her. She realized she was on.

"Good evening, Tuscaloosa, and welcome to the thirty-seventh annual West Alabama Christmas parade. We are live from atop the WTAL float heading down Greensboro Avenue…" she began. Just that second, a loud screech interrupted her speech, and a huge redneck monster truck jumped into the lineup in front of Blake's convertible from a side street—pulling a real sleigh! The metal sleigh rungs were flinging up sparks of fire against the asphalt.

"Oh, my goodness," Dallas said, trying to keep the live shot running smoothly. "Looks like we have company."

The monster truck bounced on its massive oversize tires as the sleigh bumped and jumped over the city street. Several Tuscaloosa police officers tried to stop the driver as Sonny gave orders into the walkie-talkie in his hand.

"Anyone for a sleigh ride?" she said into the camera with a smile, attempting to make light of the situation as the cameraman captured footage of the renegade truck and sleigh.

At that second, the sleigh set off a shot of flame straight up into the air. The swans got spooked and one took off, flying over Miss Christmas and landing in the faux Warrior River on the mayor's float. More sparks began to fly from the dragging sleigh, and more swans flew out of the makeshift pond on the seven swans a-swimming float.

"Well, it looks like we only have three swans a-swimming tonight," Dallas said as one landed right at Courtney's high heels. Another landed on the mayor's float. Kitty had decided to get up and shoo them away, but just then the police were finally able to stop the truck and the sleigh, and the whole parade came to an abrupt, crashing halt, knocking Kitty off balance. With nothing to grab on to, she fell straight into the faux Warrior River.

Meanwhile, the swan on Dallas's float was dashing hither and yon and began chasing Courtney.

"Oh, my," Dallas said, smiling into the camera and trying her best not to burst out laughing. "It looks like our new reporter has attracted quite a fan club in town."

Courtney dashed around the float, trying to get away from the worked-up swan as Marty ran behind and tried to catch it. Without warning, the parade started up again, and when the float jolted into motion, Courtney lost her footing and tripped over the swan.

"Swan one, Courtney zero," Dallas said triumphantly, and Mike shot her a look.

Behind the TV float, Dallas noticed that the maids a-milking had just received a visitor, too. As soon as one of the swans joined the maids, all of the cows freaked out. All the mooing drowned out the choir just behind them. Dallas turned her attention away from the debacle and back to the camera, which was still running live.

"Wow, you learn something every day. I didn't even know swans could fly! You have it live from WTAL—the seven swans a-swimming just joined eight maids a-milking, and the cows are none too happy with these party crashers. Looks like the cows are all backing up to the end of the float trying to get away from them. This is truly the live version of Angry Birds, y'all." She laughed as she spoke, knowing this commentary would go down in history.

"Oh, my goodness. With the weight of the cows all on one end of the float, that flatbed is poppin' a wheelie as the maids try to calm their bovines."

All of a sudden, loud clopping noises were heard. Dallas looked around. It sounded like a heard of buffalo. "Oh, my God! Here comes Santa Claus, y'all—oh, and there goes Santa Claus!" she shouted as he swooshed by at top speed right in front of her. The cameraman flung the camera around just in time to catch Santa Claus flying by, hanging on for dear life as his horses pulled the sleigh at full gallop.

"Well, Santa was supposed to be the grand finale, but looks like he's ended up being the intermission. Apparently he's late to a last-minute elf meeting. Don't worry, kids. This certainly won't happen on Christmas Eve, because there are no swans at the North Pole and Santa usually has reindeer, not wild horses." She flashed her smile. "I'm Dallas Dubois, for WTAL, reporting live from downtown Tuscaloosa. Merry Christmas, y'all!"

33

Dallas was feeling pretty good about things. The parade had given her a chance to shine in the middle of chaos, to show that she could stay calm and collected, turning a crazy set of events into TV-worthy news—always a good thing for a broadcaster. She arrived at the Gorgas House on the University of Alabama campus for the annual WTAL Christmas party.

The Gorgas House was famous far and wide in the South. It was the very first building on the Alabama campus. Built in 1829, it actually opened two years before the university itself. It was famous for many things but mostly for being one of the four original buildings to survive the burning of the campus during the Civil War in 1865.

Sweeping staircases on either side of the front entrance took the visitor up to an oversize front balcony, where many an Alabama wedding party had posed for pictures.

The building sat like the jewel in the crown, at the very center of the University of Alabama campus.

Dallas admired the house once again. If she ever got married again… But she brushed the thought from her mind and walked inside. The place was already bustling with Christmas cheer.

"Oh, honey, you look adorable." Coco Channels, who'd named himself after his fashion idol, leaned in for a holiday air-kiss.

"Yes, doll, you *look* like a doll," Jean-Pierre added as he leaned over for a hug. "Your glam factor is off the charts tonight."

"Why, thank y'all so much." Dallas batted her eyes.

Coco and Jean-Pierre owned their own catering and event planning company, A Fru Fru Affair, and they'd both renamed themselves when they'd begun their business. They were loud and creative, and Dallas knew they'd recently organized all of Vivi's wedding events this past summer. They had catered the station Christmas party and they certainly didn't disappoint.

The lovely Gorgas House was covered in Christmas tinsel, upstairs and down. They even had fake snow brought in and spread all over the front grounds. Inside, yards and yards of red silk and tulle were draped all across the ceiling, and brightly colored Christmas lights were wrapped around everything that didn't move—and some things that did.

Four large cakes were spread across the antique dining table, each shaped as one of the station call letters, WTAL, and a fabulous ice sculpture in the shape of a microphone stood in the center of the room. In the corner of the room was a karaoke machine, and at the back near the kitchen was a huge screen for the blooper reel.

Dallas always hated that part of the Christmas party. She was such a perfectionist, and when she screwed up in a taped stand-up, which was rare, she always cussed like a sailor under her breath. She hated watching herself with any imperfections, especially since the blooper reel was specifically designed to make everyone laugh at the subject's expense. She dreaded the thought of the footage Daniel would be showing later on.

"Hey, Dallas, I've been looking for you," Daniel said, coming up behind her as she was checking her coat.

"Merry Christmas, Daniel." She gave him a hug.

"Merry Christmas to you, too. I loved that play-by-play of the parade! Maybe you could fill in for Lewis sometime in the Alabama booth, huh?" Daniel said, hugging her back. "You were brilliant."

"Yes, indeed," Mike said, walking up to join them in the foyer. "You were great tonight, Dallas. No one will ever forget that commentary." He rolled into a hearty laugh. "You are magnificent in the live element, no doubt about that."

"Thanks, Mike, and Merry Christmas," she said, reaching over to hug him. Midembrace, Courtney James walked up and stood behind Mike, face-to-face with Dallas. She had a sickening smile pulled across her face, and her arms crossed in front of her.

"Yes, Merry Christmas, Dallas," she said. "What a marvelous job you did tonight."

Dallas pulled away from Mike.

"Oh...thanks, Courtney. I'm so sorry about that swan. I mean, who knew swans could even fly? Are you okay?"

"Just twisted my ankle a little. That was quite the commentary you were giving, though."

"Thanks. You know how it goes—I just called it like I saw it," Dallas said, becoming a little wary of Courtney's comments. *Just where was she headed?* Dallas wondered.

"It's just too bad about the unfortunate choice of attire."

"Excuse me?"

"Well, it would have been better to look like an anchor than like Santa's little helper, don't ya think?"

She gave Dallas a sympathetic smile, then turned on her

heel to strut away just as a few of the rather tipsy staff members came in from the front grounds, covered in snow, tossing fake snowballs. A bigger fellow moved to dodge a snowball tossed by a cameraman, knocking Courtney clean off her feet. Down she went, her glass of champagne spilling all over her blouse.

Sometimes, fate was just on your side.

Dallas reached down with Mike and helped pull Courtney back up.

"Ugh," Courtney heaved as she brushed herself off. "Such teenage behavior!"

It really seemed as if Dallas was experiencing some pretty good karma for a change. She made her way to the champagne fountain for a celebratory drink. She roamed around for a few minutes in an unusually good mood, hugging and greeting her coworkers and Merry Christmasing everyone.

Just as Dallas reached the area near the big screen, Mike announced the blooper reel would be starting. She cringed and moved to the side, trying to make her way to the back, so if her bloopers were off-the-charts terrible, at least she wouldn't have to be there right in front to hear the jabs and jeers.

The reel began, and Dallas tried to pry her way to the back of the laughing crowd. She was like a salmon swimming upstream; as the party moved forward to get a better look, she was pushing against them in the opposite direction but getting nowhere.

"Next is our lovely Dallas Dubois, and I can tell you, she had quite a year, y'all," Mike said as he held the remote control in his hand. "Let's just say, this year she went for the ride of her life." He clicked a button and immediately everyone saw a clip of Dallas from the back at the opening of Lewis's radio station. She sat atop a massive mule—Daniel's idea of creative commentary—when suddenly it took off down the yard with Dallas hanging on for dear life.

"Help get me off this—*bleeeep*—thing!" she screamed as the mule dashed around wildly. Another long string of curses escaped Dallas as the mule made no move to slow down.

Everyone at the party roared with laughter, watching the big screen as Dallas shot past the camera. Trapped at the front of the room with her coworkers ribbing and chiding her, she felt like a kid in elementary school who had wet her pants while standing at the chalkboard. Instead of laughing along with everyone, she was mortified.

Finally, she was able to squeeze out a side door for some air. The night was cold and crisp. She took in a deep breath and wrapped her arms around herself, her breath making little puffs of steam in front of her. Several other people were outside drinking eggnog spiked with Jack Daniel's.

Marty Raines, the weather guy, walked right up to Courtney, who was also outside, and planted a fat kiss on her lips, then leaned back, laughing. He then wobbled over to the young female news assistant and fixed his lips right on her mouth, too. Not wanting to be the next victim of the drunken kissing bandit, Dallas bounded back around to the front of the house. But just as she was fixin' to step through the door, Marty stumbled toward her, lunging into her arms from inside, and planted a huge kiss right on her lips, lingering a tad too long.

At that exact moment, Dallas, wide-eyed and shocked at the unexpected face plant, glanced at the parking lot to see Cal getting out of his car just in time to see the big wet slobber from Marty. *Just perfect,* she thought, knowing that to Cal, it must have looked as if she was making out with Marty.

Dallas shoved Marty away, "Oh, my God! Please go get sober someplace far away from me." She looked up and saw Cal getting back into his car to leave. She ran through the side gate of the Gorgas House with no coat and only the little red velvet dress, which only barely covered her backside, trying to catch him. Sure, they were broken up, but she still didn't want him to think she had already moved on. But by the look Cal shot her as he drove away, she knew that's exactly what he was thinking.

Saturday morning came with loads of December sunshine. It was a cold day outside, but bright, glaring sun stretched its way across Dallas's yellow patchwork quilt that she used every winter. Her grandmother on her mom's side had made the quilt when Dallas had been about nine years old. Those had been the happiest of times for her, even though her dad had already left.

Back then, her mother had sung in a hotel most nights and Dallas had spent much of her time at her grandmother's house. It had been the place of stability for her, where she'd felt safe to write and create. Even as a child, she would set up her Barbies and stuffed animals and pretend to present the news. She'd written her little scripts by hand at her little wooden desk, her golden blond hair held back with a ribbon, her gleaming smile flashed to her pretend camera made of cups. She'd always known she was born to be a broadcaster.

Dallas stretched under the sunny quilt and grabbed her cell

phone, which was plugged in next to her bed. She had a text from Blake waiting for her.

Ready when you are. We'll see you at Vivi's in a few.

She was glad they'd be getting the set repairs underway, but her mind was still on the poorly timed kiss that Cal had seen last night. She felt she needed to text him, to give him an explanation of some kind. But she had no idea what to say. They weren't together anymore, but she couldn't deny that she cared deeply for him. She missed him more than she wanted to. So many times over the days since she'd sent him away, she would pick up her phone and look at it, thinking she would send a "Hey, how are you?" text, but then chicken out. Even in that moment, her heart quickened as she thought about what to say to him.

She couldn't stand it another minute. It had bothered her all night long, nibbling and gnawing her in her dreams, the look on Cal's sweet face as Marty had kissed her hard. Dallas sat up in bed and wrote a text to Cal.

Hey Cal, what U saw was not what it looked like. I'm sorry.

She hit Send and leaned back against the tufted headboard of her bed. Waiting. Waiting. She let out a deep sigh, just as she heard the text jingle.

No biggie.

That was it. He didn't say another word.

I'm not seeing him, he was drunk.

She couldn't help herself. She felt awful, mostly because she didn't want to hurt him—because she still missed him every second. But he didn't answer her that time. She sighed and rolled over, petting Wilhelmina as the cat purred and stood to nuzzle her, thinking that she had hurt Cal before, and last night's unexpected smack may have put the nail in the coffin. *Just as well,* she reasoned. She fully believed he'd sided with her family over her, and that wasn't something she could just shake off.

She padded to the kitchen and fed the kitty, made some toast and coffee and then headed to the shower to get ready for her big day with the girls.

Since Blake had offered Dallas an olive branch after her live-shot screwup the night of Dixie Dickens, Dallas decided to stop and pick up a peace offering of her own—Krispy Kreme doughnuts. She remembered distinctly from her teenaged years that when the girls gathered at Meridee's, Krispy Kremes were the official snack of the Sassy Belles.

Dallas drove out to Vivi's plantation house with the items for Blake to fix the roof of the life-size gingerbread house, a little nervous as she tried to focus on the day ahead. But thoughts of Cal plagued her all the way there. Memories of Cal holding her while she told him her deepest, most private secrets, then of running into her brother at the craft store after twenty years of silence between them.

The strangeness of this day had her stomach in knots, too. She almost had to say it out loud to believe it. "I'm going to Vivi's house, invited by Blake." That sounded crazier than putting a skank on the Sunday pulpit. But the thing was, secretly she had always wanted this: to be part of their little crowd. When Blake and Vivi had created the Sassy Belles it had been just for them and Rhonda Cartwright. Rhonda had moved away in the early years of high school, but that hadn't stopped the Belles from carrying on.

Unfortunately, Dallas could never quite figure out how to

be a girlfriend, how to have another girl's back—forever, no matter what. She didn't know how to quit competing with every single woman she met. Her mother hadn't exactly been a good role model for any of those things, and by the time she'd moved in with Kitty and Blake, she'd been too angry and scared to really try.

Today, though, she was trying really hard. Finally. And those doughnuts on the seat next to her became her secret weapon.

Blake met her on the steps as she pulled into the driveway of Vivi's. "Hey, hon, come on in," she said, welcoming Dallas right away. She knew Blake would be easy to win over after their friendly lunch date, but the bats in her stomach took flight as soon as Vivi came out of the screened door and stood on the porch.

"How are you, Dallas?" she said, though a bit stiffly. She would definitely be the tougher nut to crack.

Vivi was a fun, exciting woman. Loud and opinionated, though only about five foot three. She was covered in freckles, with a beautiful fair complexion. Her green eyes nearly matched the Christmas tree in the front hall, and her ruby-red lips were natural.

Dallas forced down the butterflies and smiled warmly at Vivi. "Oh, I'm fine, thanks. How are y'all today?"

"Good," Vivi said. "Come on in from the cold and we'll have some tea or hot cider. Oh, my heavens—look at what she brought, Blake," Vivi said happily when Dallas offered up the doughnuts. "This is wonderful, thank you." She took the treat from her and made her way to the kitchen.

Dallas relaxed—but only a little.

She'd always known it was really Vivi who had come up with the plans for the itching powder back during that Miss Warrior River beauty pageant. Who in a million years would have thought that, all this time later, Dallas would be coming out to see Vivi for help—and possibly even friendship.

Dallas stepped all the way into the house, immediately entranced by a truly Deep South Christmas. A twelve-foot tree graced the grand foyer, twinkling with tiny white lights and crimson velvet bows and garland. Old-fashioned was the order of the day, as real greenery draped in swags up the curved staircase, secured with the same red velvet ribbon. The old plantation house looked as if time had stood still there for the past hundred years.

Vivi was wonderful at crafts and had fashioned a wreath made of real magnolia leaves for every door, hanging from matching red velvet ribbon. Single candles lit every window, and her house smelled of baked gingerbread and hot chocolate and warm cider.

Dallas was enveloped in the feelings of home and family, warmth and joy, as she entered. She looked around and took it all in.

"Want some sweet tea?" Vivi asked when Dallas walked into the kitchen.

"Sure, that'd be great," she answered, sitting down at the huge oak table.

"Well, I, for one, wanna just clear the air," Vivi said as she sat down next to Blake.

Dallas was sitting across from them. It almost felt as if she was on trial. She swallowed a sip of the tea Vivi had set in front of her and tried to push down her anxiety with it.

"I have to say, I know this feels odd for all of us, what with our history and all. But I am so happy the past is in the past," Vivi said, squeezing a lemon into her tea.

Dallas was a nervous wreck. She wanted to say so much, but the knot in her stomach was growing. Dallas had been awful herself over the years, doing everything she could to use her media power to bring down Blake and Vivi when the opportunity arose. Sure, they'd been bullies, but Dallas had also been the enemy. But maybe it was time for everyone to grow up.

Dallas knew it was now or never, so she swallowed hard and threw her guarded feelings out there.

"Well, I—" She nearly choked on the words, but she cleared her throat and began again. "I appreciate Blake's gesture after Dixie Dickens, coming to say those kind words when I was feeling so low. I really do. And like Blake has said, maybe it's time, with both of you fixin' to be mothers, that we all just try to get along. I apologize for the years that we didn't."

It was the best she could do. She would never be as vulnerable with these women as she'd allowed herself to be with Cal. A huge, groveling, tearful "I'm so sorry I was such a bitch" speech just wasn't in her—and she wouldn't be Dallas if it were. What she had said hit the spot, though, and accomplished just what she had hoped; the window to friendship had been cracked open.

"Like I said the other day at the diner, I'm having this baby, and Sonny and I are getting married, and really all of this crap seems suddenly childish. I just wanna be happy now."

"Me, too," Vivi added. "And there's nothing like marriage and family to provide that. Speaking of which, how's your love life these days, Dallas? Still seeing Dan the Man?" Vivi asked, clearly happy to move the conversation to safer territory—girly gossip.

"Oh, no, that's so over." She swigged her tea a bit nervously, unsure if she was ready to confide in these women about Cal and her love problems.

"I think I saw you in Cal Hollingsworth's car a time or two. Y'all havin' a little fun on the side?" Vivi asked.

"Um, well…we're both working on this play together," Dallas explained. "He gives me a ride here and there." She smiled as the thought of him crept into her mind. But she had thrown him out. She felt a pang in her stomach, reminding herself of that.

"You know what they say...." Vivi said.

"No. What do they say?"

"Those that play together, stay together." Vivi raised her eyebrows and shot her a smile.

If only it were so easy. "Well, we're just friends," Dallas said, melancholy setting in. Were they even that anymore? She felt that pang again.

Just then, baby Tallulah woke up and let them know it with a mouth much like her outspoken mother, Vivi. She needed to eat. Now. Vivi jumped up from the table as if her fire alarm had gone off—and technically, it had. Tallulah was a little reheaded spitfire. Blake and Dallas followed her to Tallulah's downstairs crib, which Vivi kept in a nook just off the kitchen for when Vivi was working downstairs. That way she could hear the baby better in the huge old antebellum home.

"Dallas, ever thought about having babies of your own?" Vivi asked as she lifted the precious baby to her chest and the baby stopped crying.

Dallas smiled to herself. Of course she had thought of having a family of her own—but it was always more of a faraway dream, taking place way in the distant future.

Vivi readily handed the baby to her best friend, and Blake looked like a natural holding her, clearly ready for motherhood herself. Dallas was beginning to feel like a third wheel. Blake took the baby back to the kitchen, and she and Dallas sat back down as Vivi got ready to feed Tallulah. The baby was fussy, but Vivi was patient.

"So, Dallas, you never said. Did you ever think of having any children?" Blake brought the point up again.

"Oh, sure. I mean, doesn't everybody?" Dallas hedged. Just

then, the baby kicked her leg out and knocked Vivi's iced tea straight into Vivi's lap and all over Tallulah. Vivi jumped up.

"Quick, grab that dish towel," she said.

Blake jumped up, too, and reached across the table to grab the towel. With both of them tending the spill, before she knew it, Dallas had Tallulah in her arms.

It was a dramatic moment. Not for Vivi or Blake, but for Dallas. Though she was in her early thirties, she had actually never held a baby in her arms. It caught her off guard. She didn't have a second to think about it. Dallas had gone for so many years not having any real female friends. She had never even been a babysitter.

Up until the play had come into her life, she had never spent any time at all around children of any age. And she had just recently learned that she had a niece and nephew—so she'd never had the chance to know them as babies. But as she stood there cradling Tallulah, she was lost in the tiny girl's green eyes. When Tallulah stopped crying and looked up at Dallas, something about it felt just right.

Dallas would never forget that moment. To Blake and Vivi, it passed by in a flurry of activity, unnoticed as they cleaned the spill and settled back down at the table. It all took only a few minutes. But in those minutes, something in Dallas had changed. Tallulah had looked her right in the eyes and cooed. Dallas had studied the tiny baby, barely a month old, and smiled at her.

It was a pure and genuine connection. Without pretense or manipulation. Without any ulterior motives. Dallas could not remember a second of the past twenty years that felt like this. She wanted to capture it and put it in a snow globe, to look at and hold forever.

"Oh, my, look, Tallulah likes you, hon. How 'bout that?"

Vivi said, reaching back for her baby now that the mess was all cleaned up.

"That is so precious," Blake said, but she seemed to notice something was up. "Dallas? You okay?" she asked.

"Yeah…she really is just so sweet, that's all."

Just then Arthur and Bonita stepped in through the back porch. Bonita was an assistant investigator in the homicide department who worked closely with Sonny. She was a gorgeous, plus-size woman with flawless brown skin and impeccably applied makeup—and her fashion sense was to die for. On the weekends, she loved to help Arthur with his barbeque restaurant, the Moonwinx, which was right on the grounds of Vivi's plantation.

Arthur was in his early fifties and had lived at the plantation since he was a boy. His mother had worked for Vivi's family for years before she'd moved back to her hometown of Chicago and had Arthur. After she'd passed away and his father had been sent to Vietnam, Arthur had moved back in with Vivi's family and had lived there ever since. His dad had died in Vietnam, so the McFaddens and Vivi were the only family Arthur had left.

And Arthur was really the only family Vivi had, too. Her father had died when she was just a child, and her mother had always been sickly and unable to care for Vivi on her own. Arthur, who had been there since Vivi was born and had watched her grow up, had been in his second year in business at the University of Alabama when he'd decided to quit school and come back home to take care of her. He had even walked her down the aisle and given her away at her wedding the previous summer.

He and Vivi had always been close. They tended the rose gardens together, and he and Vivi ran the entire plantation, or what was left of it, together.

"Hey, little mommas," Arthur said, grinning as he came inside. "Saturday's a big ole day down there at the BBQ. Man, we got all kinds of customers."

"Oh, Arthur, that's wonderful," Vivi gushed.

Bonita sashayed over to the girls. Confused to see Dallas sitting right there in Vivi's kitchen, she shot Blake a look with her eyebrows up.

"Well, hey there, ladies. And that baby is a precious little thing. Let me see her," Bonita said as she reached across to Vivi and swaddled the wide-eyed baby up against her ample bosom.

"Ain't you just a sight for sore eyes? Hey, little baby girl," Bonita cooed as she snuggled Tallulah.

"Y'all been busy, you say?" Vivi asked.

"Oh, yeah, we have. Had us a good day for sure," Arthur said, his amber eyes twinkling.

He and Bonita made a good pair. She was about ten years younger and could stop traffic with her looks alone—and make an arrest like nobody's business.

Bonita loved her day job, and she was great at it. She was the daughter of Tuskegee professors, so she was smart and financially pretty well off. But Arthur was a perfect Southern gentleman, and Bonita said those were few and far between. After she'd met him, his sweet way and ambitious drive to open the Moonwinx had just charmed her to pieces. She'd helped him open the place last summer. They had been together for about six months now, and they were looking pretty cozy.

Because of Arthur and Vivi's close relationship, Vivi immediately treated Bonita like family. Bonita was just part of the fabric of daily life out at the McFadden Plantation, now that she was on Arthur's arm.

"Y'all still countin' on us for supper?" Bonita asked.

"Yep. Everybody's comin' tonight. We're gonna have us a

Christmas shindig," Vivi said. "Hey, Dallas, would you like to stay for supper? We'd love for you to join us," Vivi asked.

Dallas couldn't very well say no to a meal invitation, which was considered the height of rudeness in the South. Besides, it sure beat going home and staring at the phone, thinking about Cal. But she was stunned that Vivi had so easily and happily, it seemed, invited her.

"Sure, thanks so much. I'd love to stay, if you're sure it won't be too much trouble," Dallas said.

"No trouble at all. Lewis is bringing Cal, so that'll round it out perfectly," Vivi said.

Dallas froze, her stomach sinking. She knew she'd heard Vivi right. She also knew she couldn't say anything to argue it. And now she had already confirmed, so it wasn't as if she could say, *Oh, by the way, I just remembered there's a toilet I have to clean*. Nope, she was stuck as Cal's dinner date—make that *surprise* dinner date.

"Alrighty, looks like we're all set, then. Bonita and I'll get the dinner together from the restaurant, and, Miss Vivi, we still gonna have your good ole peach cobbler?"

"Yes, siree, it's my specialty. Well, borrowed from Miss Meridee, of course."

"Dallas, honey, you're in for a real treat. Ain't nothin' like suppertime out here at Vivi's," Bonita said as she kissed baby Tallulah on the forehead before giving her back to her mother. "That baby is the spittin' image of her momma," Bonita chirped.

"Oh, I can't wait," Dallas said with forced enthusiasm. "Definitely sounds like a treat for sure."

"Okay, y'all, we got us a theater project to work on this afternoon, so let's get 'er goin'." Vivi stood with Tallulah and was headed back to the little nursery off the butler's pantry when Tallulah started crying again.

"Oh, precious, it's okay." Vivi held her, bouncing, and walked back toward the kitchen. She stopped right in front of the television where the rebroadcast of the Christmas parade was being shown. Dallas's voice was giving the play-by-play commentary when suddenly Tallulah became quiet. Vivi moved closer to the TV. The baby listened, looking around.

"Dallas! Looks like she loves the parade, how 'bout that?" Vivi said, continuing to bounce.

Tallulah started to coo, and she actually smiled. Dallas was entertaining, even to a baby.

"Oh, my goodness, look y'all! Tallulah's grinnin'," Blake said, excited. Then she laughed. "I think it's the first time I've seen her really smile, Vivi! Keep her there and let me grab the camera."

Blake ran into the adjoining dining room and came waddling back as fast as she could and snapped a picture of the happy redheaded baby.

"Dallas, I think Miss Tallulah really likes you," Vivi said, looking at Dallas.

"Maybe she recognizes my voice from a few minutes ago, or just thinks the parade is funny." It still seemed strange to her that she could have any sort of real connection with a baby.

"No, she was pretty calm when you were holding her, too." Vivi smiled at Dallas as she walked back past her to put the baby in her crib.

Meridee always said Dallas had more to her than most people could see. Maybe the baby, being so new, could see through all that surface stuff, too, and just feel whether a person was good or bad. It made Dallas feel pretty good that on this one, baby Tallulah was on the same side as Meridee.

35

"Okay, Dallas, tell us what happened to the infamous gingerbread house," Blake said as the women made their way to the lovely dining room. This room, too, was decorated for Christmas with real greenery dripping over the oversize fireplace mantel.

"Well, the children got excited about being on TV, and one of my little actors decided to try his hand at being Santa. The next thing we knew, down the chimney he fell—only it wasn't a real chimney, so he kinda crashed through the roof," Dallas explained. "Now it's not worth a flip."

Blake and Vivi both burst out laughing. Dallas joined in, but she was feeling preoccupied with thoughts of seeing Cal in just a few hours. He wouldn't have had any warning that she was even going to be there—and he'd be sitting right next to her, she was sure. They'd have to pretend that they were just friends from the theater, not ex-almost-lovers. Dallas felt those familiar butterflies—the allergy was back.

"Well, I think we can put some of these pieces back together, and add these here and there," Blake thought out loud as she picked up some of the supplies that Dallas had brought with her.

It snapped Dallas back to the present moment, and she forced herself to focus on the task at hand.

The ladies worked on the gingerbread roof, and chatted as they did. Dallas let her normal capacity to fill dead air take over, as broadcasters do, asking the girls anything that popped into her mind.

"So, Blake, I saw your house is for sale."

"Yeah, it's killing me, too."

"Why? You haven't lived there in a while. I remember when I was seeing Dan, you were almost never there."

"True, but it was always my dream house. It's just beautiful and I always loved it."

"But just think of all the bad memories." Leave it to Vivi to make it all real.

"I know, especially walking in on him with Jane in my own bedroom this summer. You were there, Dallas, filming from my window, as I remember." Blake shot her a smirk.

"I'm so sorry. I don't even wanna go there."

"I know. You thought you were just doing your job. Anyway, I needed to know about all of Harry's political relationships so…"

"Yeah, Harry's *relationships*—that's a whole 'nother story, I'll say," Vivi said, helping Blake stick a piece of candy back on to the roof line. They all laughed.

"So, what about you and Sonny?" Dallas asked.

"Well, now that Harry and I have filed for divorce, Sonny and I don't have to go sneaking around anymore. We are so fine—better than fine. And this precious baby boy has made it all the more wonderful." Blake touched her stomach, smiling.

"Tell Dallas how you told him," Vivi insisted. She turned to Dallas and added, "Blake found out she was pregnant like a month after my wedding."

"It was like October," Blake began, "and Sonny and I had gone to Tannehill and were in a cabin for the weekend. My doctor called while I was there, and that's when she told me I was pregnant. I have to say, I freaked a little. I wanted to tell him so bad but Harry was in the middle of the campaign and we still had a month to go before his election, so Sonny and I were trying to keep things under wraps. I mean, Harry wasn't a prize of a husband, but of course I still cared about him—and I knew he'd be the best damn senator Alabama has ever seen—so I didn't want to mess up his chances by making the divorce and all that public. I held on as long as I could."

"You mean you didn't tell Sonny right then?"

"Nope. I have no idea how I kept my mouth shut—don't you dare say anything, Vivi Heart—or you either, Miss Dallas Dubois." Blake smiled at them as she glanced up from her work.

Dallas felt included. It had finally sunken in—this was real, and no one was fighting or even acting threatening. She liked this. *Girlfriends,* she thought, *hmph, who knew?*

"Anyway, I managed to keep it to myself for almost an entire week before it started making me crazy. So I went to the store and bought a few things to help me share my news." Blake looked up and winked.

"Well, tell us. I'm dying here." Dallas was trying to jump in with both feet. She was a little clumsy, but she was feeling a tad more comfortable with the girls opening up to her a little.

"I'm gettin' there. Okay, so I got to his place that night. Sonny slipped off his holster and laid it over the back of the chair. He put some hot chocolate on for us and we sat in front of the fire. He asked if I wanted some Baileys Irish Cream in my hot chocolate, and I said, 'No, I think maybe some marsh-mallows.' I knew he'd have to be gone a few minutes to find them. He got up and went to the kitchen, and while he was gone, I slipped the gun out of his holster and put a baby bottle in its place."

"Oh, that is so good. I love that. What did he say when he found it?" Dallas asked.

"Oh, Sonny is so emotional anyway. So he comes back and doesn't see it at first. I had to help him a little. I got up and stood next to the holster, and he just teared up immediately. I swear I have never loved anyone like I love that man."

"When are y'all getting married?" Dallas asked.

"As soon as my divorce is final. Hopefully soon. Ever since Harry won the election, he just wants it all over with, too, so he can get on to Washington."

Dallas took it all in. Happiness lived in this house. She remembered that feeling from her grandmother's house as a child, and being at Vivi's made her feel that way again. Blake and Vivi's friendship was deep and full of love. She wanted that, too. She wanted to be surrounded with family. She thought of what Cal had said to her about forgiveness, but after everything that had already happened, she knew it was probably too late this year.

"Y'all, I am starvin' to death. Let's get the dinner show on the road," Vivi said. The girls had worked the afternoon away, and the scent of ribs and baked beans were in the air from the Moonwinx out in the side yard. They had been smelling the delicious aroma all day long, and finally all the teasing their noses had taken was over.

"Hey, ladies, y'all come on in here for some good ole supper," Bonita said, coming in through the front door with a platter of ribs.

"Oh, my Lord, have mercy," Vivi said, running into the kitchen to hold the door open for her. "I gotta put the cobbler in the oven, I clean forgot about it."

"We got stuffing and mashed potatoes, too," Arthur said. "'Tis the season, y'all."

"And we got us some cornbread, too," Bonita added.

"Yeah, we're gonna have us a feast," Vivi said. Tallulah was just waking up from her nap, and Vivi went to her little crib and gently picked her up and swaddled her. Everybody was in the kitchen milling around. Vivi and Lewis's dog, Harry the Humper, followed Arthur inside.

Lewis had brought the dog home the same day he and Harry had made amends last summer. The canine humped everything in sight, so Vivi had called him Harry the Humper. He often stayed right alongside Arthur, who constantly fed him rib bones from the restaurant.

"Go on now, Harry, you stay outside for now," Vivi said, shooing the beautiful golden retriever out back. "I love saying that—*get outta here, Harry.* It gives me quite a bit of satisfaction." Vivi laughed along with Blake and Dallas. She always had her best friend's back.

With all the commotion, no one heard Lewis and Cal come in. They both suddenly appeared in the doorway from the kitchen to the dining room.

"What are y'all doin in here, havin' a party?" Lewis came in and made a beeline to Vivi and Tallulah. He kissed Vivi as if he hadn't seen her in a month of Sundays. Then leaned down to the baby.

"C'mere and see Daddy, my little princess," he said, taking the baby girl into his arms. Lewis leaned into Tallulah and cooed and kissed the baby, the joy dancing all over his lit-up face.

But Dallas and Cal didn't see any of it. They were locked

on each other, both of them in shock. Neither of them knew what to say, but someone had to say something. Dallas swallowed hard, her mouth dry and sticky. She hadn't been very nice to Cal the last time she'd seen him.

"Dallas…I, um…had no idea you'd be here," he said.

"Neither did I until this afternoon. And I just found out you were coming. It was all kinda spontaneous," she said, then took a deep breath and smiled a small smile. Almost like an apology.

She was trying so hard to fit into this group, but this was only making things more difficult. Cal put her on edge in a different way than he used to. Oh, she was still highly attracted to him, but now she felt pangs of guilt. But being typical Dallas, she tried not to show it.

"What can I do to help out here?" she said, turning her attention back to Blake and Vivi.

"Here you go, set the fixin's out on the table," Bonita said, handing her the coveted secret barbeque sauce that was Arthur's family recipe. "You stay here long, I'm gonna definitely put you to work." Bonita always had that "get things done" attitude.

"Do I hear somebody bossing folks around?" Sonny's deep baritone rolled into the near-bursting kitchen.

"Oh, baby, so glad you're here. I missed you today," Blake said as he leaned down and hugged her, kissing her intensely, dropping his hand down her backside and squeezing her ass. Blake and Sonny oozed passion…and heat—even though she was pregnant. Dallas saw that. And everyone could feel it the minute he walked into the room.

"Hey, Bonita, sounds like they got you doin' what you do best—runnin' the show." Sonny laughed and gave Bonita a hug.

Most of the food was on the table, and the cobbler was in

the oven as everyone gathered the glasses for iced tea. Every single seat would be full, just the way Vivi liked it.

Lewis was still the only one at the table who knew Cal had been seeing Dallas. He hadn't told a soul, since Blake and Vivi would have given her an earful about that for sure if they knew. But from the winks and nudges he was giving Cal, it was clear that Cal hadn't mentioned they *weren't* seeing each other anymore.

Dallas squirmed in her seat, thinking it was only a matter of time before Lewis burst with the news. Cal looked at her apologetically. If only he had known she was gonna be there, he could have warned Lewis to be quiet.

But it was too late.

"Hey, did y'all know these two here are our newest love-birds?" Lewis announced, nodding toward Dallas and Cal.

Cal shook his head at Lewis, but it was already out there. Dallas felt nauseous. Her heart rose in her throat as Vivi gushed, "Oh, you little liar. I thought you said y'all were just friends. Now we know, missy."

Oh, God, Dallas thought. They looked at each other, and without words, in one split second, they agreed they were in this together. Like it or not.

36

Dallas had no intention of allowing this to become the bridge for Cal to just walk right back into her life. No way, she told herself. Cal had made his choice, and she knew if she let him back in it would just make her weak. And she had no time for weakness right now, with the play and her job and her family all weighing on her shoulders. Nope, she'd just make sure she did only what was necessary tonight to avoid any drama, and then she'd get the hell outta there.

"So, you and Cal are finally dating. That is the biggest news of at least the last two months," Blake said. "Why in the world didn't you say something earlier?"

"Well, we…we haven't really been seeing each other too long." Dallas smiled and kept taking things from Bonita and passing them to the table.

"Well, I'm sure both of y'all are fully aware by now, Dallas has always had the biggest crush on you, Cal," Blake continued. "Good Lord, she would nearly break out in hives when she saw you comin' toward her in school."

Dallas felt her face grow hot. *She may break out in hives any second,* she worried. She just smiled an uncomfortably strained grin and kept busy passing food.

Across the room, Cal seemed to be enjoying this.

"Yeah, I knew that. I still make her excited," he teased.

What the hell was going on? Dallas set the last thing down on the table with a bang. She shot Cal a look. So Cal wanted to have a little fun at her expense? Not gonna happen. If it was going down like this, Dallas was *all over* that competition. Competition was her middle name.

"Oh, sweetheart, Lewis said the other day it was *you* who had the crush on *me.* Isn't that right, Lewis?"

"Yeah, he sure did," Lewis agreed, taking the bait. "He would get all excited every single time he saw you cheerin' in that little cheerleader outfit from the sidelines." Lewis grinned at Cal, who turned three shades of crimson. Dallas winked at him. She would always love being on top.

They all sat down to supper, Vivi holding the baby. Lewis had pulled the crib up into the doorway to the butler's pantry so he and Vivi could take turns tending her. Arthur and Bonita took such pride in all the food. They sat next to each other, smiling and laughing and touching each other through the meal. And Blake and Sonny were so in love, everyone could feel it. Their relationship was so close and intense it was palpable. Dallas was seated, as she suspected, right next to Cal.

"How long y'all been seein' each other?" Vivi asked.

"Oh, not too long, really." Dallas was trying to keep the answers short.

"Well, y'all make a gorgeous twosome, I'll say," Bonita said.

"Don't they just," Vivi agreed. "And they sure will make such pretty babies, too."

Dallas actually choked on a rib. She threw back a gulp of tea and tried to smile.

"Oh, Vivi, don't embarrass them like that. They're just get-tin' started," Blake said, shaking her head at her best friend.

"Oh, no, I don't mind." Cal scooched over and slung his arm around Dallas, knowing it would only make her more uncomfortable. But he didn't seem to care. "I think you're right, Vivi. She will certainly make some pretty kids, that's definitely a given."

Ugh! What is he doing? Dallas felt his arm snug around her shoulder, and he had moved his chair so close she could feel his thigh rubbing against hers. She was growing hotter, in more ways than one, by the second. She wanted to slap him and passionately kiss him at the same time. That's pretty much how she had always felt about him.

"Well, thanks for the compliment, but I don't see babies in the near future for me."

"Oh, now I disagree. You were pretty good with Tallulah today," Vivi chimed in.

"You were, Dallas. I saw that myself," Bonita said.

"Well, maybe with the right person."

"Oh, I think you've got the right person. I can feel the heat all the way over here," Vivi said.

Supper was finished, and the cobbler came out of the oven, a sweet and delicious confection. Cal walked out to the front porch with Lewis and Sonny. Arthur and Bonita took the plates and trays back down to the restaurant and never came back up to the main house.

When the kitchen was clean, Dallas sat back down to talk with Vivi.

"Vivi, I know you both have already helped so much with repairing the set for the play, but you're such a good seam-stress, and I was wondering if you had any scraps or material to make me a pair of angel wings?"

"Sure, I know I've got stuff all over this house. We can find something for sure. Whadya need it for?"

"I have the cutest little soloist from the children's home, and she's really something special. I want to do something to help her stand out during her big moment, and she would look precious in some angel wings."

"Oh, honey, that's such a sweet idea. Let's run upstairs while Tallulah is asleep and dig through my old craft closets."

The three women got up and made their way up the gorgeous curved staircase to a spare bedroom that hadn't been used in ages. There was barely any furniture in the musty room. Vivi had kept it closed for years, she explained. The door creaked loudly as she pushed it open. The women walked inside, the full moon casting stark shadows across the hardwood floor. Vivi walked over to a small, rickety wooden table and turned on the dim light.

"This had been Daddy's office when I was little. I spent a million hours in here playin' dress up. I think we closed it off right after he died…" Vivi trailed off in the dust of a memory

Blake and Dallas walked around the room, their footsteps echoing in the near-empty space. Dallas looked out the window that overlooked the side of the house. She could see Arthur and Bonita sitting together in the light of the restaurant's kitchen. They were laughing, Bonita throwing her head back at something Arthur said.

"Vivi, you okay?" Blake asked, moving up behind Vivi.

"Yeah, it's just strange, you know. I haven't even thought about this room in so long, never mind been in it." She walked over to a scratched-up, rolltop desk still sitting in the corner of the room. It sat in front of a huge window overlooking the new pond Vivi had put in last summer.

"Daddy would have loved this view. Too bad he didn't

get to see what this place turned into. I think he would have been happy."

"Oh, sweetie, he would have been so proud of you—and that precious baby, too."

Vivi pushed up the rolltop, and memories from someplace long ago fell and scattered across the desktop, some dropping to the floor.

Dallas moved over to be with the other women. She and Blake watched Vivi slowly finger through her father's things, holding them as if they were buried treasures in her gently freckled hands.

"Daddy left me so early. I wish I had known him a little longer."

She picked up an old photograph and studied it. It showed Vivi sitting in her dad's lap holding a huge stick of cotton candy. The wiry red curls dancing atop her head made her look like Little Orphan Annie. They were sitting in front of a Ferris wheel, the neon colors glowing behind them. Dallas could tell the photo was taken at the West Alabama Fair, a magical place when you were a kid in Tuscaloosa.

Vivi laid the photo back down in a little box, then she opened the drawers and pulled out another box.

"I've never seen this one before," she said. She sat down on the bare floor to spread out the box's contents.

Dallas and Blake sat down beside her. Vivi pulled out her father's pipe and smelled it. His wallet was in the box, too, still holding her baby pictures. There was a ring she didn't know anything about and also an old envelope that was wrapped with a leather string tied in a knot.

"What is this?" Vivi asked.

"Open it up and let's see," Dallas prodded, her curiosity getting the better of her.

Vivi untied the knot, and a collection of yellow parched papers fell into her lap.

"This is Daddy's will, I think," Vivi said after a cursory glance. "I've never seen it before." She stilled herself as she read her father's last wishes.

As she rustled through the papers, Blake, being a wills and estates attorney, couldn't help herself, so she picked some of the papers up, too. Dallas wasn't exactly timid, and, at the risk of looking nosy, the reporter in her took over. It was like a complete investigative team looking for clues into a man's life.

Suddenly Vivi stopped cold and inhaled sharply.

"Oh, my good God in heaven. Blake! Please tell me, am I readin' this right?" Vivi's hand trembled as Blake took the page from her and read it.

"'And as for my land and home,'" Blake read aloud, "'and all the surrounding acreage, I leave it all, as is, to my nephew, Arthur Perkins.'" She read it again. "My *nephew,* Arthur Perkins." She lifted her eyes from the page to look at Vivi, who seemed as though she'd had the wind knocked out of her.

Within a few lines of text, Vivi had learned in the flash of a second that Arthur, her longtime friend, was really her blood cousin. Not only that, but he also owned the entire plantation that she had always called home. And he had for over twenty years.

Suffice it to say, angel wings were not in the near future. At least not the kind you could make.

37

The women sat in total silence. What Vivi had just found out could and would change her life. She'd thought the whole place still belonged to her mother, who was still alive and staying in the fancy retirement home in town, Splendor Acres. They had a financial adviser who paid all the taxes on the home, and Vivi had always thought she would inherit the home and property after her mother died.

But this discovery would change every single thing she knew to be true about her life and her relationship with Arthur.

"Surely Arthur must know about this," Vivi said, tears now spilling down her cheeks. "They would have to have told him about it after my father died. How could he keep it from me all these years? It's like he's been lying to me. How can we go on now that I know he hid this from me my whole life? How could I ever forgive him?"

"You know Arthur, Vivi. I'm sure there's a good reason he

never said anything. You have to go talk to him. Now. It's best to get it out in the open." Blake held Vivi as she tried to convince her.

Dallas sat still, listening to the two of them—and watching Vivi about to throw away her most important family connection, next to Lewis and the baby, right out the window.

"I can't, Blake, I'm too upset," Vivi sobbed. "I have never, ever been mad at Arthur. Not even once. I am hurt to the bone. But he's been hiding the truth from me all along. He owns this whole place and—and he's my own cousin and he didn't think I should know! Why? Did he think I couldn't take it?"

"Maybe he was protecting you," Dallas offered.

"From what? I needed to know this, don't y'all think?"

"Oh, Vivi, you have to go to him right away. You don't have a choice. All this pain is just gonna snowball on you and before you know it, you won't even be the same person," Dallas explained, talking from experience.

"She's right, Vivi," Blake said, rubbing Vivi's back.

"No. I just can't right now. I'm so mad at him for keeping this from me. He was the most important person in this world to me, till Lewis and the baby came along, and still, I love him like an older brother. But now? Keeping this from me all these years is such a betrayal. I can't even begin to forgive him for this."

"Vivi, listen to me, you have to talk to Arthur and make this right. I know you're mad, but you know Arthur's heart. He would never do anything to hurt you," Dallas said, her own pain taking over the moment. "If you don't, you'll be ruining your own life. Resentment is a poisonous thing. It will spread through your whole life and change you from the inside out. You won't be the same wife to Lewis, the same friend to Blake, and you especially won't be the same mother to Tallulah. That baby deserves to have her real mother, not the shell that will be left after all that anger destroys you." It had never been so clear to Dallas before, but maybe she just needed to see the situation from the outside to understand exactly what she needed to do.

Blake sat with her mouth open. "I couldn't have said it better myself. Now, go on down to see Arthur. We'll go with you for support."

Vivi sniffed and wiped her nose with her long cardigan. "I guess there was always the little hint of this hangin' overhead," she said.

"Whatdya mean?" Blake asked her.

"Daddy's brother, my uncle Henry, was killed in Vietnam, too—just like Arthur's daddy. I guess this means that…Uncle Henry must have been Arthur's dad."

The boys had gone into the living room and were watching some game on TV. Vivi decided not to upset the entire apple cart till she had talked to Arthur herself, so the three of them headed down to the side yard without disturbing them. It was dark and freezing outside, a clear night with a trillion stars shining overhead. As they neared the Moonwinx, they could hear Arthur and Bonita laughing.

"How do I even begin this conversation? 'Oh, by the way Arthur, I just learned you're actually my cousin and you own my plantation…?' That's not gonna cut it."

"No, just show him those papers in your hand and see where it goes from there." Blake squeezed Vivi's hand, and Dallas took the other. And to Dallas's surprise, nothing felt the least bit strange about that.

All three of them stood at the closed door to the Moonwinx. Vivi sucked in a deep breath and knocked, in case Arthur and Bonita were playing more than cards. Vivi was trembling.

"Hey, what are y'all doin' here? Lawd, y'all gonna freeze out here—not a one of ya with a coat. Get on in here." Arthur swung open the little screened door, and they all went inside the little restaurant. The restaurant was mostly for pickup and take-out orders, so there wasn't much seating, but they pulled up a few spare chairs around a table.

"What do I owe the honor of this here visit?" Arthur asked, smiling at them all. Vivi instantly teared up and shoved the yellowed papers under his nose.

Arthur looked down, and Bonita handed him his little gold-framed reading glasses. He sat quiet for a second, but they could tell he knew right away what he was looking at. Bonita got up and stood behind him to read over his shoulder. Arthur didn't say a word. Vivi waited, her breath choppy and measured.

"Tell me about that if you can, please, Arthur." She sniffed. "I need to know."

"Oh, Vivi, come 'mere to me, baby girl." He reached over, and they embraced. "I never, ever meant to hurt you."

"Well, it's too late for that. I just don't understand. Why would you keep this from me?"

Bonita sat back down next to Arthur, her mouth still not closed.

"I'm so sorry. I wanted to tell you so many times, but I was afraid," he said.

"Afraid of what, for heaven's sakes? Me?"

"I didn't want anything to ever change 'round here. I loved it all the way it was. It was all just a piece a paper to me. I don't need all this," he said, gesturing to not only the restaurant but the land around them. "You were too young to be granted the ownership in name, and your momma was too sick to take it on. Your daddy left it to me and it was understood, though it ain't there in writing, that I would make sure it belonged to you after your momma dies. Nobody would make a fuss about it if I just gave it to ya. And that's what I was plannin' on doin."

"Arthur, I'm not even carin' one little bit about all this property. What I'm talkin' about is that all these years you knew we were blood kin. I needed to know that. I don't have any blood relatives at all besides Momma, and she doesn't even recognize me anymore. I had *you* all this time and never knew."

"Baby girl, this don't change nuthun'. Look at us. We always been family." He smiled and a tear fell down his cheek. "I was afraid if I showed you this, somethin' would change, and nuthin' round here ever needed changin'. I love you like you're my baby sister, and no little old blood test or piece of paper gonna make me love you any more than I already do. You're my family, Vivi, blood or not. It don't make no difference."

The relief and happiness on Vivi's face was obvious. "I love you, too, Arthur." She melted into his embrace.

Bonita had tears streaming down her round cheeks, and Dallas and Blake sat next to Vivi wiping their eyes, too. The emotions were palpable in every corner of the little restaurant.

Dallas's heart and mind were suddenly the clearest they had ever been in her whole entire life.

"Will y'all excuse me? I got some of my own business to take care of."

38

Dallas couldn't get back up to the main house fast enough. She ran with her arms folded and her head down, fighting the December cold. All she could think of was Cal, and the words she had said to Vivi were replaying on a loop in her head. All that talk of forgiveness. Cal was right. He had been right about everything, and she needed to find him and tell him right away. To tell him how sorry she was.

She reached the front porch and dashed inside, going from room to room, looking for Cal. Not in the kitchen, or the front hall; she called out for him, her desperation mounting.

"In here," he shouted from the cozy living room where he was parked in front of the big screen with Sonny and Lewis, a Budweiser in hand.

She let out her breath as soon as she reached the doorway to the room. It was a sigh of relief. She looked at him sitting on the couch next to Sonny, his long legs outstretched in front of him, crossed at the ankles over the cushioned ottoman. He looked so handsome to her, his dark golden hair, messy and out of place. He was wearing blue jeans and a dark pine-green sweater. He looked relaxed as he sat there with all the men watching a football game. At that moment everything clicked, and for the first time she truly knew she was in love with him. For the first time, she could finally admit that to herself.

"Cal, can I talk to you, please?"

"Uh-oh, big guy's in trouble," Lewis said, grinning.

"Oh, yeah, here it comes, you can see it," Sonny added.

Cal got up, slightly confused, but made his way over to Dallas. She took him into the kitchen and sat down with him at the big oak table. The lights were low; only a small lamp illuminated the room from a corner near the fridge. Dallas sat close to him. She hadn't even questioned how he might feel until just now. Maybe he wouldn't even want her back. Maybe he thought she was too rigid, and he had been wrong about her. Dallas only knew that she was sorry and that he was right: she had a definite problem with forgiveness. But that was about to change.

She swallowed hard and looked deeply into those gorgeous gray-green eyes.

"Cal, I need to say something, and I just need you to listen." She paused and smiled a nervous smile.

"Okay..." he said.

"I want to say that...I'm really, really sorry for all the things I said the other night. I never meant to hurt you. I didn't want you to leave."

"Well, you need an Oscar, then, 'cause you sure threw me out like you wanted me to go. Asking someone to leave when you really want them to stay? That's kinda confusing, you know," Cal said with a small smile, his sarcasm breaking the ice a little.

"I know it. I'm so sorry. I'm really sorry," she said.

"Okay. I understand." He let out a breath and looked at her sweetly. "I know you have been under a huge strain and with your mom and brother and all…"

"Well, I just wanted to say I was wrong."

"Wow. Do I need to call the TV station and get this on the ten o'clock?"

"Okay, stop it. I mean it. I was wrong."

"About what?

"All those things you said at the theater. I haven't been able to stop thinking about it. You said I had a problem with forgiveness, and I've decided that you may have been right." She cleared her throat, hoping he would just stop talking and kiss her.

"Oh, does that mean I'm forgiven?"

"Yes! Come on, Cal. I…well, I just wanted you to know how I felt." She began to think he wasn't going to just jump up and hug her, like she wanted, and she wondered what else she'd have to do to convince him. But suddenly he leaned over and kissed her, holding her head close to him with one hand, his other hand resting on her cheek. He kissed her long and passionately, slipping his hands under the nape of her neck and under her hair.

"Oh, Cal, I've missed you so much. I was so crazy to push you away."

"I've missed you, too, but it's okay now. You're here with me, and it's okay."

She continued to kiss him, her hungry mouth open and lusting for him. She crawled her hands through his thick, gorgeous hair. "Cal, I will never send you away again. I promise. I promise."

Just then Sonny walked into the kitchen for a fresh beer.

"Lord, you two. Get a room," he said, opening the fridge that was right next to them. He shot a conspiratorial grin at Cal. "Hey, Dallas, seen *my* girl anywhere?"

"Yeah, she and Vivi are over visiting Arthur."

"So I guess I'll just have to wait my turn for the make-out sessions." He winked at Cal and headed back to the big TV.

"I have my car here," Dallas said. "Let me take you home."

"You sure you wanna take me *home?*"

"I remember one night you were going to show me your man lair before we got interrupted...."

"You just let me say goodbye, and I'll meet you at the car."

"Okay, me, too."

"What were y'all doin out at Arthur's, by the way?" he asked as he got up, dropping his hand down and squeezing her butt on the way out of the kitchen.

"I'll fill you in while we drive. It's a long story."

Dallas felt as if a weight had been lifted. She couldn't remember ever feeling this happy—this free. She felt open and truthful. True to herself. Finally.

Now, she really needed to show Cal just how sorry she was.

"Wow, that is amazing," Cal said once Dallas had told him the whole story of Vivi and Arthur. "But now it all makes sense."

"I know, and it has a fairy-tale ending, too, don't you think?"

"Yeah. I know how you like the whole 'happily ever after' thing, don't ya?"

"Well, of course I do. Especially the part where the prince kisses the princess awake."

"We'll just have to see if we can work that in for you." He glanced over and winked at her.

Dallas let Cal drive her car to his house. They had said their goodbyes, and she'd loaded up the gingerbread roof that Blake had fixed into the trunk. As they drove, she reached over and settled her hand onto his thigh, as if she was claiming him. He was hers and that felt right. She had admitted her mistakes and apologized—everything seemed to be falling into place.

Except she couldn't bring herself to tell him she loved him. She'd gone into the kitchen with the intention of telling him, but something had made her hesitate.

Dallas felt differently about Cal than any man she had ever been with. Yes, she'd told her other husbands she'd loved them, but that had been more frivolous—expected. It certainly hadn't been deep or real. And she had always been overly careful not to get too emotional, not to let them inside. But then Cal came along, and he was the very first man—the very first person—in her whole life since her family split up who she had let completely in, penetrating the walls until nothing was between them. Only truth.

"Oh, by the way, I've been meaning to tell you about this, but with you not talking to me and all…." He flashed a teasing smile. "I was able to trace those emails. Just as I suspected, they aren't coming from Callahan Enterprises."

Wrapped up in her own little dream world, Dallas had almost forgotten all about the emails and the missing Baby Jesus case. "Oh, yeah? Where are they coming from, then?" Dallas asked.

"They're coming from a frat house on campus. The Wi-Fi this hacker's using is addressed right at the fraternity—they weren't very careful about it. I've got a little more digging to do, but I'll get to the bottom of it in the next couple of days."

"Ms. Peaches was right then. She really is something else."

"What do you mean?" Cal asked.

"She's the lady with the missing nativity statue. She told me a bunch of fraternity boys took her plastic Baby Jesus last year, too, and ran it all over campus. Some kind of pledge thing, I think. I bet those boys are just trying to get on TV," Dallas explained.

"Maybe, but I have a little more digging to do. I know that

frat house pretty well," he added and glanced at her. "It used to be *my* frat house."

"Oh, wow. Was this a prank back when you were there, too?" she asked.

"No, not this exactly, but we did have Christmas pranks as a freshman we were told to pull. So I'm gonna check it out on Monday. See if I can get this wrapped up for you."

Dallas smiled at him and laid her head on his shoulder.

Cal drove through town and over the Warrior River, heading toward Lake Tuscaloosa and the Townes of North River. Dallas was excited as they approached his house. She knew this was where so many coaches and higher-ups from the University of Alabama lived. "Upscale" barely did it justice. Cal had definitely come from money, she realized. Not that it mattered by this time, since she had completely fallen for him, but, man, this was the cherry on top.

Dallas felt as if she was a princess being stolen away to the castle as Cal turned into the circle drive of his home. She sat still looking at his place, which was perfectly decorated for Christmas. The front yard displayed decorated Christmas trees on either side of the entrance. The front steps beckoned you to a porch that was covered in tiny twinkling white lights and festive red velvet ribbon wrapped around all six columns, top to bottom. The home was new, but built to look like the gorgeous antebellum homes of Tuscaloosa. Cal walked around the car and opened her door.

"Here we are," Cal said, helping her out of the car. "Home, sweet home."

"Oh, Cal, it's beautiful."

"I just bought it last spring when I moved back to Tuscaloosa to take over the computer science division. I've always loved living at the lake anyway—grew up out here."

"Oh, really? Where?

"North River Yacht Club."

Dallas's eyebrows went up. "Okay, tell me really, what exactly did your daddy do before he retired?" She knew North River Yacht Club wasn't where the average person in Tuscaloosa lived. Business owners and doctors, maybe. The reporter in her was ever curious.

"Who said he retired?"

"Come on, Cal," she begged.

"Ever heard of C&H chips?"

"The potato chip company?"

"Uh-huh."

"That's *your* family? Wait—that's Callahan Enterprises! Oh, my gosh, are you Callahan?"

"Not the original—that's my dad. After playing football, he started making the food people love to eat at games. He did pretty well." Cal was always so understated. She had gone to school with him for years and never knew about this. But she had never allowed herself to really get to know him, and she certainly had never run in his circle.

"No wonder you wanted to get to the bottom of those emails so bad. Why didn't you say something?"

"Well, we weren't back together till about an hour ago, so I really didn't need to." He smiled at her.

Cal was more reserved than the men Dallas was used to dating, and this hint of the mysterious attracted her like never before. He wasn't a braggart. He never felt the need to announce his pedigree.

Cal opened the front doors to a grand foyer and beautiful, wide staircase set to the right side, draped with green garland and tiny lights. At the top of the stairs was a landing with a huge window overlooking a pool, gazebo, and leading out to a private dock and Cal's speedboat. The landing had an overlook with a spindled railing, where a magnificent Christmas wreath hung, greeting guests just below in the entryway.

While Vivi's house was the perfect picture of old money in Tuscaloosa, Cal's home was opulent—the picture of the new wealth growing there.

"Have a seat in there and I'll get us a drink. What's your pleasure?"

"Anything with a splash of Jack," she answered.

Dallas walked into the large family room off the kitchen, and sat in front of the oversize fireplace. Cal had the whole room decorated for Christmas, the mantel with greenery and a display of nutcrackers, and a fifteen-foot tree in the corner next to the massive wall of windows looking out on the lake. Pictures hung all around of his family, his mom and dad, two older brothers and their kids. Family was obviously very important to him. Cal had a picture of his dad taken during his dad's football days at Bama. Cal was the spittin' image of his daddy, long and lean and gorgeous.

His home was masculine, but Dallas could tell someone had decorated this place for him.

"Where in the world did all the decorations come from?"

"I had some from when I was teaching in Georgia, but my two older brothers and their wives and kids came over for a blowout decorating party a couple of weeks ago. They said it would be a shame if this place wasn't in the holiday spirit," he said, returning with the amber drinks in highball glasses.

"It sure is gorgeous," she commented, looking up and down the room.

"It was great having them all over here. I'm so glad to be back home where everybody is. I was a fish outta water in Georgia." He handed her the glass.

"Well, get over here and let me resuscitate you," she teased.

Cal set his drink on the mantel and fixed a fire for them in the grand fireplace. She loved watching him work with the wood. It took him only a minute or two to get the fire going, then he grabbed his drink, and he settled in next to her on the couch. The firelight illuminated the room, the only light besides the glistening lights of the Christmas tree.

They each took a sip of their Jack and Coke as she snuggled into him. Putting his drink down on the coffee table, he turned to her and kissed her lips softly. Then gently taking the drink from her hand, he set it down next to his.

"Dallas, I missed you. I thought after that night in the theater we were done."

"No, baby. I could never get you and the things you said out of my head."

He dragged his mouth down her neck and rolled his tongue under her jaw. Then, kissing her collarbone, he made his way into the neck of her sweater. Dallas sat up from the back of the couch and slipped off the soft creamy V-neck and tossed it to the floor, revealing her vanilla-colored lace bra. Cal slipped his fingertips around her ribs, grazing her skin, giving her instantaneous goose bumps. He slid his hand under the small of her back and, straddling her, pulled her down on the sofa, underneath him.

Cal relaxed on top of her as she slid her hand up under his sweater, untucking his T-shirt at the same time and pulling them both over his head in one slow movement, his bare skin now on hers. He reached under her and unhooked her bra, then tossed it to the floor. Both of them naked from the waist up, flesh to flesh, he cupped her breast with one hand, resting his lips on her nipple. She arched upward, giving him all the permission he needed.

Dallas dragged her nails gently up his back and back down, slipping them inside the waistband of his pants and cupping his ass, giving it a gentle squeeze. He continued to lick her breast, her nipple now wet, stiff and sensitive to his tongue. She kissed him passionately, her open mouth so hungry for him. She had been with plenty of men in her life, but she could never remember being taken like this, aroused like this. Maybe it was because she was finally really in love with the man on top of her. And the emotional connection was something entirely new for her.

She slid her hand down his belly, pushing gently underneath his jeans and cupping his erection in her hand while softly biting his bottom lip. At the sound of his groan, she unzipped his jeans, his dark boxer briefs easy to pry open as she gripped him more firmly.

Cal crept his large hand down to the button of her jeans, loosening them—she felt them slide down her hips and legs until they fell off her ankles to the floor with everything else. He tasted every inch of her—from her lips past her breasts, licking her abdomen, then circling her navel with his wet tongue. He slipped his fingers underneath her lacy red panties, exploring her most tender space with gentle, teasing strokes.

Without warning, he stopped and scooped her up in his arms and carried her up the wide staircase and to his bed.

Dallas had never even been carried over a threshold, let alone carried up a grand staircase to a king-size bed. Cal's bedroom was lit softly. Moon shadows danced across the sheets as he gently laid her down, then crawled on top of her. She hooked her fingers under his briefs and pushed them down his toned and muscular thighs. His body was like one she had never seen before. He had been an athlete years before, but he still looked every inch a football star.

Cal pulled at the waist of her panties and slipped them down around her ankles. She gave a kick, flinging the red lace toward the window seat as she wrapped her bare legs around him, pulling him closer, his excitement nudging against her.

She reached down and felt him become more rigid in her hands. His tongue followed the curve of her breast as he slipped his fingers inside her.

She breathed heavily into the crook of his neck, and pulling him into her, she raised her knees as an invitation to what they both had been so hungry for. He softly parted her silky thighs and plunged inside her, his head falling into a cloud of her perfumed hair on the pillow.

With each thrust, she fell into ecstasy with him. His breath was rough as he laid his cheek on her breasts, burying himself in the warm, wet grip of her body, and she arched her back, opening herself to him like she never had before.

Together they fell into a desperate but perfect rhythm, and in the midst of a passionate kiss, they seized together in a rush of sensation neither of them had ever felt with another person.

Afterward, they lay entwined in each other's arms.

"You are so beautiful, Dallas. I see you now, inside and out."

"You certainly do," she said, holding him tightly to her.

"No, I mean it. There's so much more to you than anyone has seen, and I love that." He hesitated then, and she could tell he was trying to decide whether or not to continue.

"Dallas, I have to tell you something." He drew in a deep breath. "I love you."

"Oh, Cal." She wrapped herself as much as she could around his naked body, still on top of her, and buried her face into the crook of his neck, kissing him softly over and over. "I love you, too," she whispered against his skin. "I knew I did deep down inside since the night you left."

"That's when I knew it, too," he replied. "I've never felt such a connection with anyone ever, Dallas." He stopped and kissed her again, then smiled as he looked down at her lying beneath him.

It was the biggest moment in her adult life—to allow someone to have all of her, not just the physical but complete access to the emotional side, as well. She allowed Cal to see her at her most vulnerable, and, most important, she allowed herself to trust him. She was ready to let him in. He wasn't just anyone. She felt he was hers, and she belonged to him. Completely.

Dallas woke up around three-thirty in the morning. It took her a second to remember where she was. But one turn of her head and she saw that the sweetest man lay asleep next to her, his dark golden hair mussed, his naked body like a perfect muscled god stretched out across the stark white cotton sheets. She snuck quietly out of bed and tiptoed into the bathroom and shut the door.

The marbled vanity stretched over the side wall with sconce lighting on a dimmer switch. She slid the switch up, barely lighting the room in a dim ivory wash. The travertine floor, heated, felt delicious in the cold, wee hours. Dallas saw the massive walk-in closets that doubled as dressing rooms, the deep oval tub, and she was in heaven. She really felt like a princess sneaking through the prince's castle. She washed her face and headed back to the opulent but comfortable bedroom.

The most stunning feature in the oversize bedroom was the huge arched window seat overlooking the lake. It was as if it were calling to her. She grabbed a shirt of Cal's that was lying on an overstuffed chair and slipped it over her naked body as she sat down in the window. The moonlight washed the room in dusky blue shadows.

"Hey, whatcha doin', baby?" Cal sat up in bed.

"Just sittin' here, lookin' out the window. Lookin' at you." She could see him in bed from her spot, and she smiled at him. "I can't believe I'm here. I'm really happy, Cal."

"Oh, baby." He patted the bed and scooted over. She looked out the window once more, then slid into bed next to him. Pulling her into the crook of his body, he buried his face in her hair, snaking his arms around her tiny waist.

Dallas woke up exactly in the same spot, with Cal snuggled behind her. This was real. It was her life. She couldn't remember ever feeling so relaxed. She could feel Cal up against her back, and it felt so good. Somewhere along the way the ground had suddenly shifted. She knew everything was different now. From this day on, everyone would look different—everything would feel different and taste different. *She* was different.

"You awake?" Cal whispered.

Dallas turned over to see his precious, boyish face looking back at her. The man underneath that sweet face had totally changed her life, and he didn't even have any idea he had quite literally performed a miracle.

"I am," she said grinning at him, "wide awake—for the first time."

"Sleep okay?"

"Only the best night of my entire life, so I guess that's pretty good, huh?"

He nuzzled her and kissed her cheek. "Hungry?"

"Starved. Some old athlete gave me quite the workout last

night," she teased. "I'm glad I left extra food out for Wilhelmina. I had no idea I would be invited to a sleepover."

"Well, how 'bout some quick pancakes, then we get over to your house and check on the kitty?"

"Sounds like a plan."

"By the way, I love this new sexy nightgown on you." He rubbed his hands up underneath his old button-down polo, caressing her sleep-warmed skin.

"Want it back?

"Only if that involves you taking it off."

"That's an even better plan...."

They played in bed, reliving bits and pieces of the night, before she hopped up and snatched the sheets off his naked, rock-hard body, dropped them on the floor and ran downstairs. He grabbed his pajama pants off the closet floor and ran after her.

She was giggling as she ran down into his kitchen—and smack into Cal's brother. Then in ran Cal at top speed right behind her, laughing loudly until he caught sight of his brother.

"Oh, Cam. Hey. We, uh...I...didn't know you were gonna be here..." Cal said awkardly.

"No, man, I'm the one that didn't know. I am really sorry for interrupting. Hey...aren't you that TV reporter?"

Dallas blushed as she pulled Cal's shirt a bit lower on her exposed thighs.

"Cam, meet Dallas Dubois, my girlfriend. Dallas, this is my oldest brother, Cam. He's Justin's dad. You met Justin that night at Dixie Dickens," Cal reminded her.

"Oh, right. He looks like you. It's nice to meet you. I need to just...uh, run up and grab my...clothes." She smiled demurely, trying to slip out by walking backward.

"No, no, please don't bother. I'm leaving right this second. Cal, man, I had no idea or I'd never have let myself in. Just, um, call me later. Wanted to see if you wanted to come over and watch the game tonight, but, hey, looks like you might have other plans." Cam winked and started walking toward the front hall.

"Lemme walk you out," Cal said moving toward the front door in his red-checked pajama pants.

"Nice to meet you, ma'am," Cam said to Dallas. "I'm sure we'll see each other again soon."

Dallas was halfway up the stairs when Cal returned from seeing out his brother.

"Is it safe?" Dallas asked from the landing.

"Coast is clear."

"Oh, Cal, I'm sorry."

"Don't give it another thought," he said, leaning over and kissing her. "He has a key, and ever since I moved back, they've been worried I'd get lonely here in this big place all by myself."

"Aww...poor baby. I don't think you look too lonely."

They enjoyed a relaxed morning together, making pancakes, drinking coffee and then cleaning up the kitchen. Then Dallas went upstairs to get dressed. She picked up her cell phone and checked for messages. She unlocked the screen and let out a big sigh: her mother.

Dallas, please. Christmas is less than a week away. I want to see you.

"What's wrong, baby?" Cal asked, coming into the room.

"Nothing. Just..." Should she bring it up and spoil this perfect morning? "Just my mom." There it was. Out there to ruin the day. She drew in a deep breath. "She wants to see me," she said. It was as if her balloon had popped.

Cal seemed reluctant to speak after what had happened the last time.

"Honey, it's okay. I know I have to address this. I'm just scared," Dallas admitted.

He walked over to her, both of them standing in front of the arched window seat in bare feet. He pushed her long hair behind her ear.

"I love you. I'll be with you for whatever you decide to do. You don't need to be scared anymore, baby." He smiled at her and kissed her softly.

Dallas's life felt almost complete. The final piece of the puzzle was within her reach. She could feel it just in front of her. Now it was just a matter of grabbing it.

41

Dallas and Cal arrived back at her house after noon. She unlocked the door, kicked off her shoes and went straight to the kitchen to feed Wilhelmina. The kitty heard the rustling and the can opener and ran in to greet her momma, purring and rubbing up on her legs with her huge white tail.

"Hey, little girl, Mommy missed you," Dallas said sweetly, bending over with Wilhelmina's food and giving her a rub down the back.

Cal stayed behind in the living room, turned on her fireplace and plugged in the little Christmas tree. Dallas reappeared in the kitchen doorway.

"Can I get you anything?" she asked him.

"Just you. Come sit with me by the tree," he offered, holding out his hand to her.

Dallas shuffled over to him in her sock feet and snuggled into his side. The warmth and amber light created the perfect setting for Dallas to get out in the open all that was on her mind. She wanted to talk about what she knew she needed to do—speak to her mother—but just the thought of that whole Pandora's box started to make her stomach twist into knots.

What would she say? It had been so long, and the pain sometimes felt insurmountable. It had been easier to keep ignoring it. That is, until the Vivi and Arthur thing. Dallas had realized deep in her heart that forgiveness was truly the only way out of all that pain.

It wasn't just her mother she had to worry about, though. The even bigger issue was her brother. She had continued to direct her niece and nephew in the Christmas play over the past week since she had run into them at the craft store. They didn't realize anything was out of the ordinary, since Houston must still not have told them anything, but she always felt a little anxious around them, knowing they were her own flesh and blood. She looked at them differently now, knowing all she had missed.

She wanted so badly to end all this—this twenty-year silent moratorium. But the old familiar voices would whisper in her ear, *You didn't start this, they threw you out.* The words stopped her every single time from listening to her heart and just picking up the phone.

"Tell me what's goin' on in there," Cal said as he kissed her forehead.

"I know I just need to do something," she began. "After all that happened at Vivi's, I know if I can just forgive all this stuff from so long ago, things might be different."

"Well, baby, then do it. What's holding you back?"

"I'm afraid, Cal."

"And that's totally understandable. You've had no basis for trust with either of them. It's true what they say, trust has to be earned. And believe me, they haven't done anything to earn it yet. This time *they* are coming to *you*. I mean, didn't your mother tell you Houston wanted to see you, too?"

"Yeah, but he's never reached out himself. And then he didn't even say a word that night in the craft store. I have no idea how he feels at all."

"It doesn't matter, you know? You have to forgive him, too, if you really want to finally be free of all this."

"A part of me doesn't wanna give them the satisfaction, you know?"

"I know—but then you'll always wonder what if. I'm sure you've been wondering that already with your mom calling and texting all the time. If you think about it—what have you got to lose? They've already hurt you about as much as they can, right?"

Dallas nodded.

"And think about *this* for a second. Just what if it turned out really good? You'd have a whole helluva lot to gain."

She lay back into him and twirled her hair, thinking through everything over and over.

"Aren't you wondering?" Cal asked her, trying to guide her toward a long-awaited resolution.

Dallas didn't answer.

Ghosts of her happy childhood invaded her mind, images of her with her mom and brother during Christmastimes long ago. Then, the haunting images of her alone in Blake's house, in Blake's family, where Blake was the star of the show. The letters she'd sent to her brother, and the agonizing wait for a response that had never come.

"I *have* been wondering. One thing in particular, though, has been really bothering me."

"The night we ran into your brother?"

"No, it's my mom. She keeps calling and texting and every time she says, *It's time.* What do you think she's talking about?"

"I don't know. But I do know one way to find out." He drew in a deep breath and looked sweetly at her. "Do you think you're ready?"

"I'll never be ready, really, but she is right about something. It's definitely time to try."

Cal smiled at her and handed Dallas her cell phone. Dallas found the number from the missed calls and pushed Call with her trembling fingers, biting her bottom lip.

It was ringing. She inhaled deeply.

"Hello? Mom?"

D allas showered and got dressed in a hurry. She was on
her way to face her past. Her brief phone conversation
with her mother had made her even more anxious.

"What am I doin', Cal? I'm not even gonna know what to
say. Houston doesn't even know I'm going over there," Dallas said, pulling up her boots. "I told Mother not to say anything...that I might change my mind." She was sitting on
the end of her bed talking ninety miles an hour. Nerves had
taken over what started out to be a calm day. But it was now
or never. She knew she needed to try to put the pieces of her
family back together.

"Is she going to be there, too?" Cal asked. "I know you
didn't talk to her for very long on the phone."

"Yes, she'll be there, but I just wanted to make sure Houston wanted this, too. I mean I only saw him that night at the
store. He's rejected me for all these years, so it's hard to imagine that he wants to reconnect now. But Mother said that the

whole time she had been trying to contact me was not just for herself but for him."

"Why didn't he try himself?"

"She said he thought I'd never respond, since he never did."

"What in hell made her think you'd respond to *her?*"

"She would do anything for Houston. If he was afraid to contact me for fear of rejection, he'd go to her, and she'd do anything he asked her to. She wouldn't care how many times I said no, she'd bother me till I said yes. It obviously worked." Even though Dallas was going to try to find forgiveness in her heart today, it was impossible to prevent at least a little bitterness from creeping up.

"Don't forget, you hold all the cards here. If you get the least bit uncomfortable, we can go. You just give me a look or a nod." He smiled and reached over and squeezed her hand, but noticed she seemed to have something else to say. "Did she say something else, baby?" Cal asked.

"Yeah, she said something else—she said she loved me." Dallas looked at Cal, her eyes glistening with emotion. "If she really did, though, how could she throw me away? I asked her that and she started to cry and said she was so sorry. But how can I trust that when I know she will do anything for Houston and has never felt the same for me?"

"For now, we'll just give her the benefit of the doubt. Let the past be the past and we'll see what happens. You're in charge. Don't forget that."

Dallas liked how Cal said "We." There was security in that.

She stood up from the bed and pressed her jeans down with the palms of her hands.

"Here I go," she said.

"Look at me," Cal said, taking her face in his hands and looking her right in her eyes. "This is yours today. You have all the power. You can say yes or no to any of it or all of it.

You can accept as much as you want of them. You're just going to hear them out. Then you won't let them leave any questions unanswered."

"Thank you. What would I do without you?" She leaned into Cal and hugged him.

"I'm right beside you," he promised. "Ready?"

Dallas nodded and slid her fingers through Cal's.

"Okay. I'm ready."

The ride to her brother's house was quiet. Dallas sat in the front seat of Cal's car, nearly squeezing his hand blue as he drove halfway across town to the south side, near Hillcrest High School. His old model Porsche 911 pulled into the driveway on Magnolia Circle.

Houston's house was big, though not like Cal's. This lovely area of town was the perfect spot for families, with great schools and the sort of neighbors who would host backyard barbeques. It occurred to her she didn't even know what Houston did for a living. She didn't know her brother anymore. He was a complete stranger.

"Okay, I'm ready," Dallas said as she opened her car door.

She stood on Houston's driveway, knowing things would certainly be different from back when they were young. She had never seen Houston's adult home. She had missed him falling in love with his wife, Amy. She hadn't been part of his wedding—she hadn't even known he'd had a wedding until recently. Every single thing would be new to her as soon as she crossed that threshold just inside his front door.

Dallas was also about to see her little actors from the play, Anna Beth and Austin, and she knew that in just a few minutes their lives would change, too, when they learned she was their aunt.

If life could be like a fairy tale, she wouldn't be alone anymore, she'd finally have her family back. But she knew fairy tales were just that, and so she prepared herself to take what she could get.

She held Cal's hand as they walked up the sidewalk and rang the doorbell of Houston's home. She could see the big family Christmas tree through the front window. The thought crossed her mind for a split second to turn back to Cal's car and run. She stood nervously at the door, shifting her weight. The huge wreath on the door prevented whoever opened it from seeing who was there ringing the bell. Dallas could hear a dog barking, and the children laughing—and the footsteps of whoever would click the lock and finally open the door, changing all of their lives forever.

43

Dallas tightened her grip on Cal's hand just as Anna Beth
swung open the door.

"Ms. Dallas! Look, Austin, our teacher's here." She wrapped
her arms around Dallas's waist in excitement. "Look, it's Mr.
Cal, too!" She ran off to find her brother, Austin, just as Amy
rounded the corner from the kitchen drying her hands with
a dish towel.

"Come in, come in," she said, a puzzled look on her face.

Just then, Houston came in from up the hallway. He froze
at the door, and Dallas could see their mom just in the other
room. LouAnn smiled at Dallas, looking relieved that she
had actually shown up, then she rounded up Anna Beth and
Austin and took Amy and headed out of the living room and
into the kitchen.

Cal gave Dallas's arm a squeeze. She smiled a small smile
and nodded, letting him know she would be okay. He walked
on into the kitchen behind LouAnn and Amy to give Dallas
and Houston their privacy.

As soon as they were alone, Houston stepped toward his estranged sister and hugged her, tightly, for several seconds, as though he'd never let go. Both of them began to sob. All of those years of anger and resentment seemed to melt within their embrace. "Dallas, I don't know where to begin. All I can think to say is that I'm so sorry," Houston said. "I am just so sorry for everything."

"I know, and I'm sorry, too. But…I tried to write to you. Did you get any of my letters?"

"I did. I was just so stupid back then, and so was Mother for allowing me to act that way." His face was streaming with tears as he led her to the living room and sat down on the couch.

"I just want you to know, I realize now that you were a child and you thought you were saving me. But I was just a kid back then, too. I know that now, but so much time had gone by that I just didn't know what to say anymore. I had no idea how to make up for what I've done to our family," he sobbed.

Houston swallowed hard, trying to pull himself together. Finally, he managed, "I've missed you. Do you have any idea how much I've missed you?" He hugged Dallas again. "I want to know every single thing I've missed."

"Looks like I've missed even more," Dallas said as he held her. "Whatever happened to whatshername?"

"Oh, Eleanor? She eventually divorced her husband, then ran off with someone else. She was exactly what you said. But I was too young and full of myself back then to see what was right in front of me. After all those years passed and she was gone, I was afraid to try to contact you. You had stopped writing, and I knew I deserved what was happening. I was afraid you'd never speak to me again, and rightfully so, but I couldn't bear to face the rejection. I know how selfish that must sound."

"So, you never even tried? Of course I would have been

so mad at you, but even with all that, I would have forgiven you. In the end we would have had our family back together. I've always thought, since all these years had passed, that you were still mad at me. I've felt disowned and thrown away. With Mother not talking to me either, I thought for sure you must have married the witch and you were somewhere living happily ever after."

"My ego was my worst enemy. Then my pride got in the way. Back then I couldn't be wrong about anything, but the price I paid in losing you wasn't worth any of it. I lost my little cheerleader. My very best friend."

Dallas was so emotional, she could barely hear him as she laid her head on his chest and they both sobbed.

"I love you, Dallas. Let's not lose another minute."

"I love you, too, and I'm sorry it took me so long to forgive you."

"Now it's time to forgive Mom, too," he said.

"Let's not get carried away, here."

They laughed, easing the tension of the moment a little.

"I know she's a tough one. She was the parent, and it was her job to help us figure all that out. But I know she's sorry, too. She has lived with the guilt of it all for so long, and she's wanted us all back together for years."

"Why did she wait until now to try and make it happen? I mean, I really appreciate that you two didn't live in silence forever, and I'm grateful that we're here today, but it's been twenty years, Houston. Why is it so important to her that we reunite all of a sudden?" Dallas asked.

"She didn't tell you?"

"Tell me what?" Dallas sat up and wiped her tears with the sleeve of her sweater.

"Mom had a major health scare last month."

Dallas was stunned. Her mother's weary-looking appearance that night at her house made more sense now. "I had no idea. Is she okay?"

"Yeah, she's fine. But it really took a toll on her and made her think about everything." Houston relaxed his back into the sofa and held Dallas's hand as he explained. "She's agonized over this split for so long. The truth is, all of us have been so scared and, really, so stubborn. So, when she thought she was sick, she thought she'd lost her opportunity to bring us together. But then she found out the tests came back negative, and it was like she had another shot at life. This is all she's been thinking about since then. It's like we've all been given a second chance to finally get it right."

"That's why she's been tenacious in calling me."

"Well, you didn't get that trait outta the clear blue, you know." He raised his eyebrows at her and smiled. "Want to go meet the family?" he asked her.

"I most certainly do," Dallas said, smiling. "But what will you tell the kids about why they never knew I was their aunt? I don't know about you, but I'd rather they didn't hear all about what happened. I want to have a clean slate with them, if I can."

"I'll tell them we all just found out. For now that should work. I know they'll be asking questions soon enough, but by then I'll have thought of something."

"And Amy?"

"I told her a little bit the other night after we ran into each other. I'll fill her in on everything else after the kids go to bed tonight."

Houston stood up, still holding her hand. "Dallas, I've really missed you. Let's make an agreement. Never again, okay?"

"I promise, never again. If either of us ever have a problem or get mad, we'll just scream it out like all families do. I'm so happy I have you back. I never want to lose my family again."

Her eyes brimming with happy tears now, she finally had her hero back. And it didn't even take her a second to find that forgiveness and that trust she was so worried about. It was right there all along, just under the surface, waiting for the moment when it would all be okay again. They embraced again, holding each other tightly before heading into the kitchen.

Now she had to face her mother. After all those years apart, she harbored much more anger toward LouAnn than Houston. She felt her mother was much more responsible for what had happened. But now, as they walked into the kitchen, Cal, LouAnn and Amy all sitting at the table watching Anna Beth and Austin play in the backyard, she knew it would all be okay. Her eyes met LouAnn's as she stood and hugged her only daughter, both of them crying tears of joy and regret. Dallas had never even realized she had so much emotion inside her, since she'd been shoving it down for so long. But over the past month, her firewall had begun to crack, and today the entire thing had come crashing down. She was just beginning to see that maybe fairy tales and Christmas wishes actually do come true.

44

"How do you feel, babe?" Cal asked as they walked back to his car.

"Like an entirely new person," Dallas answered, exhausted from the entire experience, but feeling content with how well things had gone.

Amy had already had lasagna in the oven, so after Houston and Dallas had talked, she'd asked Dallas and Cal to stay for dinner. Dallas had had a heart-to-heart with her mother, then they'd all sat together and told the children. Christmas magic was most definitely in the air.

The fireplace roared into the late evening as Dallas and Cal had sat next to the Christmas tree and the family had shared stories of their childhood and also of the times they'd missed. Dallas had held Anna Beth in her lap on the floor, Austin sitting in his dad's lap next to her. Dallas had looked up at her mom, and LouAnn had teared up every now and then throughout most of the night. "I have my babies back with me," she'd kept saying, as though she had still been trying to wrap her head around it. It was just too good to be true for her. For all of them.

"It's so strange, though," Dallas said as she buckled up.

"What?" Cal asked.

"Just how quickly everyone forgave each other. We had gone for so long, everyone in so much pain and being so stubborn. But the second the dam was broken, we just let it all go. We picked back up like all that anger was never even there."

"That's what forgiveness does. It can melt everything. Trust me, I know."

"How do you know? Did something like this happen to you?"

Cal hesitated. "I, uh...I do have a little experience in the forgiveness zone, I guess."

"What happened?" Dallas pushed.

Cal was driving north on 359, but instead of heading home, he drove over the bridge and on into downtown and parked near the old historic clock. He turned off the car and sat still for a few moments, cleared his throat, then turned to Dallas.

"I was just a kid myself when I learned about what a lack of forgiveness can do to a person. I had the best uncle in the world. He and my dad were best friends, practically inseparable. They started Callahan Enterprises together. But by the time I was a young teenager, they'd had a major falling-out. Suddenly my uncle, who I loved like another older brother, was out of the family. Up till then, I couldn't remember a Christmas that he wasn't the life of the party. He'd always taken a special interest in me. Uncle Calvin thought for sure I'd grow up, play a little Bama football, then join him and my dad in the C&H business."

Dallas sat, listening intently. She could see Cal's eyes brimming with tears. "What happened? Did they ever make up?" she asked softly.

He drew in a deep breath, his mouth contorted with emotion, "No. They didn't have the chance. My uncle died before they reconciled. My dad tried in vain to get Calvin to forgive him and come back home before my grandmother would die of a broken heart. She hated seeing her only two kids not speaking. It went on longer than the twenty years your family didn't speak. My uncle never trusted my dad again. Then, when I was in high school, he died suddenly of a massive heart attack. Their relationship will never be fixed now, and my family has to live with that forever."

Dallas leaned over and kissed his cheek. "I had no idea," she said, realizing they had much more in common than she'd thought. "No wonder you kept pushing me," she said. "You knew firsthand the destruction all that anger can cause. I love you, Cal. I'm here for you, too, if you need me. What did your dad do that had your uncle so upset?"

"In the early years of the company my dad took a loan out against it and didn't tell my uncle. My uncle ran the finances and when he found out, he accused my dad of embezzlement. That infuriated my dad. My dad came clean about the loan but then my uncle decided he could no longer trust my dad with any money. It got really ugly and my uncle left the business and they never spoke again. When he pulled out it caused a financial hardship for the company, but my dad worked hard to save it. He saved it all right, and then it began to thrive. I always believe he succeeded just to make his brother sorry he pulled out. Either way, they never made up and now they never will."

Dallas sat still as she listened to all Cal had buried and felt for him. "I love you so much. I'm so sorry."

"Thanks, baby. I love you, too," he said. "It's all water under the bridge. Now let's get you home. You have a big week ahead and you'll need to rest up after that emotional night." Cal smiled.

"I know it. The play is Saturday night and Christmas is only a week away."

"And don't forget the announcement of the anchor seat, too."

"Oh, please don't remind me. I'm a nervous wreck," she said as Cal started the car.

"No matter what. You'll be fine. Tuscaloosa loves you." Cal reached over and squeezed her thigh as he drove her home. "So do I."

Dallas flew into the newsroom of WTAL on Monday morning, ready to show her stuff. This was crunch week. Even if she did believe the job had already been given away, she sure didn't want to be one of those two reporters who would lose their jobs at the end of this. She was running late, but she managed to get there just before the nine o'clock meeting. She took her seat in the conference room just as Mike began the assignments for the day.

"Dallas, I need you to run out to see Ms. Peaches Shelby again. She has gotten what she thinks is the last of the pictures of her Baby Jesus statue. We need to try to see if we can wrap this before the end of the week."

"Great, no problem," she replied. Then she leaned over to Daniel and grumbled, "It's showtime, and I get the Baby Jesus."

"Courtney," Mike continued, "there's been a police chase on Skyland. You need to go out to the station and talk with the officer who handled the call." Mike shoved the papers to her across the conference table—right under Dallas's nose.

Though Dallas had a new attitude and a weight off her shoulders in her personal life, careerwise she was still as full of tenacity and ambition as she'd always been. She told herself that, until the anchor position was officially announced, she'd keep right on making sure her work was the best it could possibly be. She'd push ahead as if she still had a chance, even if she was only covering Ms. Peaches.

After Mike gave out the rest of the assignments and they all cleared out of the office, Dallas let Daniel know she had to quickly check her emails, but that she'd meet him out by the van. She didn't even sit at her desk. She just leaned over and scrolled the messages, looking for anything from Callahan Enterprises. There it was. She clicked on it. It was written as a poem, just like the last one.

Notre Dame has touchdown Jesus
To help them get their kicks.
But the Crimson Tide has Baby Jesus
In the arms of our St. Nick.

Dallas hit Forward and sent the email straight to Cal's personal email, then scribbled the clue down on a piece of paper and shoved it in her coat pocket.

"Daniel, I gotta good feeling about today," she said as she clicked her heels across the pavement in the back parking lot to the news van.

She told him the update on the poems coming from Callahan Enterprises, and about their email system being hacked.

Dallas checked her phone. Cal had sent her a text.

I think I've got your answer about those emails. I'll let ya know.

Dallas thought about the frat boys who Cal would be cornering about this. He was an alumnus, and a pretty prestigious one at that, plus he was a professor there. It wouldn't turn out very well for those boys when they were caught. But maybe Ms. Peaches would at least have her beloved Christmas decoration back. That was the hope anyway.

They drove down Fifteenth Street and turned up Hargrove Road to Glendale Gardens and Ms. Peaches's house. The cold air hit Dallas in the face with a slap as she stepped out of the van and touched her heels to the driveway. She glanced over to the manger scene to see the still-empty manger and no Baby Jesus.

"Hey, y'all," Ms. Peaches called from the front door. "Come on in outta this cold. I swear this weather keeps changing every day, and I can't keep up with it. One day we need short sleeves, the next day we need a scarf and gloves."

"Hey, Ms. Shelby. Good seein' you again," Dallas said as she stepped inside the small but well-appointed house. "I hear you have some new pictures to show us." She followed Peaches into the dining room where all the pictures were laid out on the table in the order they'd been sent in. It was as if Peaches was trying to put together a jigsaw puzzle.

"So I am beginnin' to think we got us a pattern here," Ms. Peaches said. Daniel turned on the camera and began shooting.

"What do you think you can decipher from this collection of photos?" Dallas asked. She wanted to hear what Ms. Peaches had to say before she showed the poem. She had a theory about what was going on, but it would sound better if she could get Ms. Peaches to elaborate on it.

"Well, I think this all may have something to do with the fact that Alabama is going to the National Championships."

Dallas agreed, but she continued to push Ms. Peaches in the right direction. "Why do you think that?"

"Well, look, here," she began. "We got all these pictures here, most of them having to do with football. And yesterday, the most recent ones came in and look where they are with my Baby Jesus." Peaches shoved a picture over to Dallas, who held it up for the camera.

"We have here the most recent photograph Ms. Peaches Shelby received in the mail just yesterday. Clearly we can see the Baby Jesus statue has recently visited the Bryant Museum on campus and had its picture taken with the National Championship trophy, the crystal football. Ms. Peaches Shelby seems to now believe that with all the pictures she has received in the mail, maybe the hoax all has something to do with the upcoming championship game."

Dallas finished up the bridge stand-up for the middle of the story, then asked Peaches back to the living room to answer a few more questions.

"What do you think these pranksters are trying to tell us, Ms. Shelby?" she asked, holding the microphone to Ms. Shelby's mouth.

"Well, I actually think they're trying to say somethin' good here, like Alabama's got the Good Lord's blessin' or somethin'."

"So, all in all, you don't really think this is being done maliciously?"

"No, not anymore. For sure at the start I thought that—I figured they were disrespecting Jesus by prancing that statue all over town. If they were tryin' to be mean, the pictures would all be mean-spirited. But they're not. They all have a definite message about football, and I'm pretty sure Jesus likes football and especially our Crimson Tide."

Dallas struggled not to laugh. That was just a pure Southern mind-set. In Tuscaloosa, everything was about football— even, according to Peaches, Baby Jesus.

"Well, that is a great attitude to have, Ms. Shelby. If this is about the championship, I guess we'll know more the closer we get to Christmas."

"Can I please say somethin' to those boys, just in case they're watchin'?"

"Absolutely, go right ahead. Daniel's still rolling."

"Y'all, if y'all can hear me, I know you're running around campus with my Baby Jesus, but whatever y'all do, just make sure it's back by Christmas Eve." She smiled and nodded her head, as if to say, *Okay, I'm done.*

"Okay, Daniel, let's wrap this outside," Dallas said as she stood up.

"I wanted to show you this, Ms. Peaches," Dallas said as she pulled the poem from her coat pocket. "It's an email I got from whoever it is that has your statue. I was hoping the pictures today would correspond with it, but it's not quite a match," Dallas explained.

Ms. Peaches read the poem and shook her head. "Surely Santa Claus don't have my statue." She laughed, then stood up and thanked them both as they all headed outside to the front porch. They got outside just in time to see the mailwoman, who was putting her mail in the box for the day.

"Y'all wanna wait and make sure we don't have somethin' new for today?" Peaches asked.

"Sure, might as well," Daniel said, putting down the camera. "Lemme get it for ya," he offered.

He brought the mail back from the box at the street curb and handed it to the older lady.

"Yep, here we go," she confirmed. "This envelope here looks just exactly like the other ones that have come. Let's see what we get today."

She stood in the cold under the graying skies and ripped open the manila envelope.

"Just like I thought, we got us some new pictures," she said, pulling out the single photo from inside.

"See there, y'all! I was right!" Peaches announced triumphantly. "They got my statue over at the stadium. Y'all, let's get a move on and maybe it'll still be there."

They all ran to the news van, breaking all kinds of rules to let Ms. Peaches ride with them.

"We're getting an exclusive, Daniel," Dallas said excitedly, her heels spiking into the damp grass as they crossed the yard.

Jumping inside, they slid the doors shut, and Daniel ripped backward out of her driveway and drove out of Glendale Gardens for the short ride over to the stadium.

"May I see the picture, Ms. Shelby?" Dallas asked, turning to the back of the van.

"Why, sure you can, honey. You've been here the whole time."

Dallas took the photo and studied it. Surely Ms. Peaches could have been a detective. It certainly looked as if this prank had everything to do with Alabama's national championship bid. The picture showed the Baby Jesus statue in the arms of another famous statue, cast in bronze right in front of Bryant-Denny stadium—the statue of coach Nick Saban. The caption in the photo read, "The Crimson Tide has the Lord's blessing for the number one spot in the nation!"

"That's it!" Dallas said. "Baby Jesus is in the 'arms of St. Nick'—Nick Saban, our famous coach!"

It may not have been a police chase, but in a football city like Tuscaloosa, Dallas had the biggest exclusive in town. She might even get the live shot for the day with this—if she played her cards right.

Daniel whipped into the parking spot at the stadium, and even from the lot they could see the plastic statue still in the arms of the statue of the famous coach.

"Y'all! Look! It's my Baby Jesus. I'll have Him home for Christmas." Peaches was so thrilled, she could hardly contain herself.

Daniel and Dallas jumped out of the van, Dallas helping Ms. Peaches down. Ms. Peaches took off running as best she could to the famous Walk of Champions where the statues of all of the University of Alabama's famous coaches were standing in bronze. Daniel rolled the camera, getting the perfect shot of Ms. Peaches's run toward her treasured nativity decoration.

Dallas had called Mike on her cell as they'd made their way over to the front of the stadium. She'd filled him in on all the details. "Mike, this is an exclusive and I believe it should be the live shot tonight."

"I think you're right. Get all you can for now, and we'll send the live truck over for the shot tonight."

Dallas hung up the phone, grinning from ear to ear. "Yes!" she shouted as she stuck the phone back into her coat pocket. She told Daniel what was going on.

"Perfect!" he said. "Right place, right time, and you knew exactly what to do with the story. I do like the way you work," he said, giving her a high five.

"No, the way *we* work," she corrected. "I couldn't do this without you."

That evening, they picked up Ms. Peaches and made their way back for the six o'clock shot. They had to call the fire department to climb a ladder to get the statue down. The Tuscaloosa newspaper showed up and got the photo of the year—a studly fireman climbing the bronze statue to retrieve the plastic Baby Jesus.

She caught Cal standing in a crowd that had gathered to watch the decoration being taken out of the arms of the Saban statue. He watched her do her thing with a huge smile on his face. He had his nephew Justin standing right next to him.

"Looks like Baby Jesus will be back in his manger at the home of Ms. Peaches Shelby for Christmas Eve, safe and sound. The plastic statue certainly got a grand tour of the campus and, according to the pranksters, who still remain at large, has bestowed the Lord's blessing on our Crimson Tide. Notre Dame may have touchdown Jesus, but it looks like Alabama's got the ultimate blessing. For WTAL, I'm Dallas Dubois."

Cal walked over to her and hugged her and shook Daniel's hand. Everyone was jubilant, milling around the famous Walk of Champions and chatting.

"I do love watching you work," Cal said, giving her a squeeze.

"And I love showing off in front of you," she shot back with her eyebrows raised. "I can show you some more of my talents later if you like."

"I finally got to the bottom of this whole prank," he said. "I think you need to walk over here with me and see for yourself what happened." He led Dallas over to the parking lot where Justin was standing with Cal's car.

"We found your fraternity boys," Cal said looking at his nephew. "Go ahead, Justin."

"Ms. Dubois, I'm the one that's been sending those emails," he said bashfully.

"You? My, my. You are quite the poet, I'll say. Why in the world did you do it?"

"Well, it started off as just a freshman prank. The guys did it last year, but we wanted to top them—to really stand out— so this year we put the National Championship twist on it."

"Not only a poet, but very creative," Dallas said, teasing him. "But I still don't understand. Why send me the emails? And why use your grandfather's company to do it?"

"Well," Cal interrupted, "it looks like part of the prank included an attempt at matchmaking. Apparently he thought if he could force us to spend some time together, we might actually start liking each other."

"Oh!" Dallas laughed. "What made you think we didn't like each other?"

"Well, Uncle Cal said so at that Dixie Dickens thing," Justin offered.

Cal took a step back and looked worried.

"Oh, really? Hmm," Dallas said, smiling at Cal with her eyebrows up. "Well, I think maybe this whole plan actually worked. Whadda'ya think, Cal?"

"You know…maybe it actually did," Cal smiled back at her.

Justin caught them exchanging looks. "Oh, seriously? You two are dating now?" He burst out laughing. "That's two for two, then. This prank is going down in history!"

Cal moved next to Dallas and snuck his arm around her waist. "He thought if he sent them from Callahan Enterprises, then I'd get involved and, well, we'd spend time together trying to figure out why the emails were coming from my family's company. So he and his frat brothers ran around with Ms. Peaches's statue, took the pictures and then tied the matchmaking part of the prank in by sending you those emails. He thought he had a slam dunk until he remembered his uncle Cal here is a computer hacking specialist." He smiled and shook his head.

"I'm really sorry, and we'll apologize to Ms. Shelby, too. Maybe we can offer her yard service or something to make up for it."

"Good idea," Cal said. "Now get outta here and go talk to her. I'm sure she won't press any charges if you tell her everything."

"Justin's a good kid," Cal said as his nephew walked away. "He's a lot like me, pretty good with those computers."

"Well, I don't think he meant any harm," she agreed. "Plus,

I guess we actually have a reason to thank him, since he did, technically, get us spending more time together."

"Speaking of time together, don't think I've forgotten about having dinner served *on* you…." Cal squeezed her hand.

"I'm game for that, but I need to talk to you about something before I become your dinner plate." She smiled.

"Really? Me, too," he answered. "I have an idea that I wanted to run by you. Maybe we could go out to dinner and talk, then head back home for dessert…on you."

He looked as if he had just figured out the secret to something. She couldn't wait to see just what was on his mind. And tell him of her brilliant Christmas idea.

46

"Hungry?" Cal asked as he started the car.

"Famished. Where do you wanna go?"

"Oh, I was thinking about the Cypress Inn, whadya think?"

"Are we celebrating something?" Dallas asked with excitement.

"I think we have a lot to celebrate," he said, smiling at her as he headed left on Fifteenth Street and over the Warrior River Bridge. He held her hand all the way, talking about all that had happened and the big event at the end of the week: the production of *Sleigh Bells* and then the announcement of the anchor seat.

Her family had said they would all be at the play to see Anna Beth and Austin, and to be there for Dallas's directorial debut. Dallas wanted so badly to spend as much time with them now as possible. She wanted to invite everyone to eat together after the play, but she remembered hearing her mom say something about the family Christmas dinner that night and she didn't want to intrude or disrupt the children's tradition, whatever it was. So she hadn't said anything.

But there was something even bigger she had been thinking about. In the mix of everything going on this week, Dallas had decided she wanted to have Sara Grace spend Christmas with her. She had bought her so many gifts, and she wanted to give the little girl a real Christmas morning. She wanted to tell Cal all about it, too. She hadn't gone to the proper people about it yet, so she thought she might run it by Cal at dinner first just to see what he might think.

Cal seemed to have something else entirely on his mind. He had become quiet on the drive along the river to the beautiful restaurant. He turned into the drive, rolling down the hill toward the wooded lot on the riverbanks. The Cypress Inn looked like a lodge, stunningly decorated for Christmas, a huge tree in the lobby and wreaths on the glass front doors. A wide planked porch wrapped around the right side and was dotted with rocking chairs. It was a quiet, tranquil setting and boasted just about the very best menu in town. The hostess seated them at a window table with a view of the river.

Dallas finally broke the awkward silence. "What's on your mind, babe? You've been so quiet."

"I've been thinking a lot and...I was wondering if you'd like to spend Christmas with me and my family?"

It hadn't even occurred to Dallas that he'd want her spending time with his family, meeting his mother and father and all the rest of the bunch. She just hadn't really considered it, especially since she planned to start arrangements to take Sara Grace in for a few weeks.

When she didn't respond right away, Cal looked disappointed. "It's okay if you're not ready. I understand."

"No, baby, no, it's not that I don't want to. Maybe I should tell you what I've been thinking and see if you still think it's a good idea, me spending Christmas at your house." She hesitated, hoping he wouldn't think she was crazy. She took a deep breath and just threw it out there.

"Cal, I was thinking of arranging for Sara Grace to spend Christmas with me. Do you think I'm crazy?"

Cal smiled at her, giving her a look that told her he was completely in love.

"Not crazy. Brilliant. I love that idea! It's perfect."

"Oh, I'm so glad you think so. The play is Saturday night, and I just couldn't stand the thought that it would be the last time I'd see her. And the idea of her being alone on Christmas morning—well, anyway, I plan to begin the arrangements first thing in the morning."

"What about the question I just asked you? Wanna spend Christmas with me? And I don't just mean the family dinner. I'm talking about coming over Christmas Eve to spend the night, so we can wake up and have a proper Christmas morning together."

Dallas felt her heart melting at the thought. "Well, now that you know I might have Sara Grace, is that still okay?"

"Of course it is. Actually, makes it even better. I have a massive house and only me there, so she can have her pick of bedrooms, and I think she'll love that big ole tree, don't you?"

"Oh, my gosh, this is so awesome. I can't wait. Yes, yes, we will spend Christmas with you. Oh, Cal, this is gonna be the best Christmas ever."

After dinner, Cal drove Dallas home. The conversation was excited now, with all the plans they were making for Christmas.

"Why don't you invite your mom and Houston and his family over to my house, too? Tell them they can choose the day so we don't interfere with their own traditions. But I was thinking that since Sara Grace already knows your niece and nephew from the play, it'll be nice for her to have some other kids around to play with."

"Fabulous idea. I will call Houston first thing in the morning."

Just as Cal turned onto Dallas's street, they were startled by flashing red lights and loud sirens. A police car whizzed by them, stopping in front of the house with the Times Square Christmas lights. As they got closer, they realized the front porch was on fire. A WTAL news van pulled up in front, and one of their night reporters jumped out and raced over to her neighbor.

"Good Lord. I'm gonna run over and see what happened," Dallas said, barely waiting for Cal to put the Porsche into Park.

"Scott!" she shouted to the reporter. "What happened?"

"Hey, Dallas. What are you doing here?"

"I live right there," she said, gesturing to the other side of the street.

"We got a call about a house fire. We heard he was trying to deep fry the turkey on the front porch, but he slid the whole bird in frozen. He forgot he had to defrost it. Whole damn thing exploded."

"The guy's an idiot. He has so many lights, you can see this house from space," Dallas said.

"Well, if not then, you certainly can now." They both laughed just as the owner, Eddie Crawford, came over to talk to them. The firefighters had managed to save the house before any real damage was done. The porch was all but gone, though, but that couldn't be helped.

"Hey, Mr. Crawford." Dallas smiled as he approached Greg.

"Damn fryer. Nuthin' in those damn directions said a thing about havin' to thaw that freakin' bird out first."

"Well, you *did* want your house on TV, so I guess it will

be now," Dallas said, happy to have had the last laugh. "Scott, I'll leave the rest of the story up to you." She patted Scott on the shoulder and walked back to her house across the street.

"What the hell happened?" Cal asked as he got out to meet her.

"That guy's been so rude, trying to get me to do a story on him and all those blasted lights. He was trying to deep fry his turkey, and it all went up in smoke, so to speak."

"Well, I guess that means his lights won't be on tonight." Cal smirked. "Now let's go see what fires of our own we can start inside...." He winked as they walked inside.

Cal closed the door and pulled the blinds.

It was already Thursday, and Dallas's week had gone by in a blur. For Dallas, this job had always been a passion. When someone asked you, *If money weren't involved, what would you do for free?* Dallas would always answer: TV news. It always felt less like work and more like fun. She loved being out on the front lines, connecting with the people of Tuscaloosa and making sure everyone was informed. Broadcast news just pulsed through her veins. The fame was an added perk, the icing on the cake.

Rehearsals had been pretty uneventful in the week leading up to the opening, with only minor glitches here and there. But the soloists were ready, and the gingerbread house was finally intact. No one could even see the glue that held the new roof in one piece. Blake had done an excellent job of putting the whole thing back together again.

Dallas sat at her desk on pins and needles, waiting for word from the children's home about Sara Grace. She had gone down to the facility on Tuesday to file all the proper papers. She was supposed to hear today, as they had done a rush job for her since it was Christmas and because of who she was in town. Fame, even a little bit, always helped. She was staring at the phone when she got a brilliant idea.

Blake always knew how to pull strings in the legal world, and her grandmother, Meridee, knew everyone in Tuscaloosa. Maybe they would be able help. She picked up the phone and called Meridee first.

"Hey, Miss Meridee, this is Dallas. How are you doin' today?"

"What a nice surprise! I'm doin' better than a witch in a broom factory, darlin'. How 'bout you?"

"Oh, great. I was wonderin'…you happen to know any of the higher-ups over at the children's home?"

"Honey, I sit on the board myself, so I'm sure I do. Lemme think—oh, Margerie Hinton works over there, and last I heard they had made her one of the executives. Why? Whatcha need?"

"I am trying to arrange for a little girl who's in my play to come spend Christmas with me. Her name is Sara Grace."

"Oh, I know that child. She's been there since her momma died, poor thing. I'll tell ya what, you let me get on that and I'll call you right back," Meridee said.

"Thanks so much! She and I have gotten so close. This would mean so much to me."

"No problem," Meridee said. "Hey, I'm havin' a Christmas party here tomorrow night. Why don't you come and bring that new man of yours?" Meridee asked.

"How did you know I was seein' somebody?" Dallas asked.

"Child, I have lived here far too long not to know pretty much everything, so y'all come on. I'll call you back now in a few. Don't you worry. I'm sure it'll be okay. Always is. Bye now." And she hung up. Meridee was relaxed and confident.

Dallas leaned back in her chair and exhaled. She knew deep down Meridee was right. Things were somehow always okay in the end. She could see it all now, the party, the play, Cal and Sara Grace and her family...*This may be the year even I believe in Santa Claus,* she thought.

It wasn't too long before her phone rang. She jumped, startled back to reality from her daydream.

"Hello?"

"Hey, hon, it's Meridee. It's all gonna be okay. Ms. Hinton said they were working on it right this minute, and they'd have it all set by the end of the day."

"Oh, my Lord, thank you so much. I am so grateful for this."

"No, baby, the home is so grateful to you. Little Sara Grace needs this so much."

"Do you think they could let me tell her instead of them? I just want to surprise her."

"Oh, yeah, I don't see why not. Lemme get Margerie back on the horn and I'll call you back."

She hung up. Dallas sat on the edge of her seat, literally crossing her fingers like a schoolgirl. A minute later her phone rang again.

"Hello?"

"All set," Meridee announced.

"You are the best! Thank you so much."

"You're welcome, baby girl. Now, what about tomorrow night?"

"You can count on it. Cal and I will be there for sure. Can we bring anything?"

"Just yourselves and be ready to party. We do Christmas up big at my house."

"Okay, see y'all then—and, Meridee, I appreciate this more than you know."

They hung up and Dallas was elated. She picked up the phone and immediately called Cal, an ear-to-ear grin plastered involuntarily across her face.

"Hey, baby, guess what? We got her! Yes! I'm having a girl for Christmas and it feels wonderful!"

48

"Thanks for picking me up. I am so ready to get out of here for the weekend," Dallas said, sliding into the front seat of Cal's Porsche. It was Friday night, and the air was so damp and cold she could see her breath as she spoke.

"No problem, babe. This'll be fun. A little distraction before your big night tomorrow," Cal said, pulling out of the parking lot of WTAL.

"I know. And I love Meridee's house. It was my favorite thing about being Blake's stepsister all those years. Well, it was the *only* good thing, actually. At least I always knew Meridee liked me."

"I have heard her parties are legendary. Lewis went to a few after Harry and Blake got married, since he was Blake's brother-in-law. Actually, I hear he and Meridee are pretty close"

"Well, they must be if they own that radio station together," she replied. "I'm so nervous about tomorrow. There's so many things happening all at one time. Abigail called me from the radio station today and said they will announce the winner of the Twelve Days of Christmas contest right after we take our final bow, then Mike's coming up to represent the TV station sponsorship, and then the mayor's gonna speak. I hope I haven't passed out by then."

"No, sweetheart, you'll be in your element, everyone clapping and looking at you. And I'll be enjoying every second, knowing I get you all to myself after we get home—well, after we put Sara Grace to bed. Does she know yet?"

"No, I wanna tell her right after the play. Ms. Hinton is packing up her things and will have them waiting in the dressing room. I went out last night and bought her some new clothes and a new pajama set for Christmas morning. Oh, Cal, isn't this awesome?"

"Yes, baby, I am the happiest I've been in a long time."

"Me, too."

They pulled into the upward slant of the cracked driveway at Meridee's old house in Glendale Gardens. She lived just down the street from Peaches Shelby. Dallas could see Ms. Peaches's manger scene all lit up with her Baby Jesus safely in the little plastic manger.

"I can't wait to see everyone," Dallas said as she got out and headed toward the screened-in porch. She and Cal entered the front door to Christmas carols being sung a cappella. Everyone had a highball glass with rum or Jack in hand, and Meridee had a necklace on that lit up with little Christmas lights. The main living room displayed a beautiful Noble fir tree filled with old decorations from all the years of history the house held. The scent of alcohol, evergreen and Meridee's signature scent, Charles of the Ritz, filled the happy home. A large grand piano sat in the far left corner of the room, near the dining room, just begging to be played.

"Hey, y'all! Get your asses in here and have a drink," Lewis said as he swung by, dancing with baby Tallulah in his arms.

"Hey, Lewis. Hey, baby girl," Dallas said, grinning at the little redheaded baby as they passed.

"Hey, man, Merry Christmas," Cal said, patting Lewis on the back.

"Be right back, baby," he said to Dallas. "Rum or Jack in your Coke?"

"Jack, sugar," she answered with a grin. Cal kissed her on the lips and then headed to the kitchen to get them both a drink.

"Hey, Meridee, aren't you so pretty and festive?" Dallas said, hugging her. "Thanks so much for inviting us—and for everything, really."

"Oh, honey, you are certainly welcome for everything. Now, come on in and have somethin' to eat. Rum balls, cheese balls, sausage balls—hell, we got all kinds of balls here!" She winked and threw her head back, laughing her trademark rolling laugh, and walked away, toasting Kitty and the mayor as she passed by. Meridee was truly one of a kind.

"Hey, Dallas, child. How in the world are you? You were amazing the night of that Christmas parade, by the way," Kitty said. "Mayor Charlie here and I watched the playback the next day and laughed our asses off."

"Yeah, honey, you were terrific. I never laughed so hard," Mayor Charlie said, then threw back a big swig of Jack, straight up.

Just then, Cal walked up with the drinks and handed one to Dallas. Blake and Sonny joined them, and there were hugs all around. Everyone exchanged Merry Christmases and started telling stories. Dallas was lost in what she knew would become a new memory in the warmth of this magical home that Meridee constantly opened to everyone.

Soon Arthur and Bonita arrived, joining in the laughter and eating, hugging everyone hello. Everyone in Blake's circle was there. It was the way Dallas remembered it, except now *she* was part of the circle, too, with Cal by her side. This time she felt as if she belonged. She was finally a real part of this amazing family, something she had secretly always longed for. She could feel the joy warming her from the inside out.

"Hey, how are y'all tonight?" Dallas asked as she joined Vivi and Blake in the kitchen.

Vivi was holding Tallulah and bouncing her on her hip. "I'm so sorry about the other night," she said. "When I got up to the house after visiting Arthur's, you and Cal had left."

"I know it. I'm so sorry, but I realized something very important when you were talking to Arthur. I had to go fix a few things in my own family, so I left the second I figured it all out," Dallas explained.

"I totally understand. And, listen, you really said a lot of important things that night. It really helped. I mean it. Forgiveness is freedom, and it really brings such peace. I hoped it worked for you, too."

"Oh, yeah, honey. It did."

"It has for me, too," Blake added. "I even forgave Harry after that night for all his fooling around during the campaign. He looked at me and wondered what the hell had happened to me, but I just went right along like it was nothing. And get this, y'all. Jane was standing next to him, and so I looked into her beady eyes and said, 'You know what? I forgive you, too… bitch.' I whispered that last part under my breath, though."

All three of them burst out laughing just as Bonita and Arthur walked in.

"'Scuse me, Miss Vivi. I believe I need a word with you if y'all don't mind." Arthur was grinning ear to ear and offering his arm to Vivi. She handed Tallulah to Blake and wrapped her arm through Arthur's as he led her to the front room. He looked back over his shoulder and gestured to the women to follow him. With everyone in the living room in front of the tree, Meridee dimmed the lights, the Christmas tree glittering in the darkness. Arthur took a small wrapped present from inside his jacket pocket.

"Vivi, I love you and Lewis and that sweet baby girl more than life itself, and I want you to have this from me to you. Merry Christmas." Arthur's eyes glimmered in the dim light.

Vivi opened the little box and a tiny slip of paper was folded up inside.

"What's this?" she asked as she opened it. Then her mouth dropped open, and the tears began to overflow, spilling down her rosy cheeks. "Oh, Arthur, how—" She stopped. She was overcome. She put her other hand over her mouth. Lewis walked across to her, slipping his arm around her waist and peering at the piece of paper. His mouth dropped open next.

"Arthur? Are you sure?" Lewis asked.

"I am indeed. It was the plan all along, and I was savin' it till Christmas, but I knew tonight we'd all be together."

Vivi turned the paper around so everyone could see. "Look, y'all. It's the deed to the McFadden Plantation. I own my own house!"

Everyone clapped and hugged. Vivi leaned over to Arthur and hugged him tight. "What about you? I mean the place is worth a fortune. Don't you wanna sell it? At least let me pay you."

"It was never mine to sell, Vivi. I was just the guardian of it till you got married. I promised your daddy I would take care of it till you either got married or let me know you weren't ever plannin' on marrying. I knew the minute you started seein' Mr. Lewis that you'd be marryin' that man, so I just waited for the right moment. Besides, haven't you heard of the

Moonwinx BBQ? I hear they're so successful, they're fixin' to franchise that place all over Tuscaloosa. I'm doin pretty good these days," he said, winking at her.

"You know, I think we need to co-own all this land," Vivi offered. "It's decided. Blake, please draw up the papers. I am deeding all the property for the Moonwinx right back to Arthur."

"Oh, now, Miss Vivi that ain't necessary," he said, shocked.

"I know it, but it absolutely is important to me, and it would be to Daddy, too. So it's done. It's mine to do what I want with, and this is what I'm doin'." Vivi smiled and handed the deed to her lawyer and best friend, Blake.

Arthur and Vivi embraced under the lights of the tree. Everyone smiled, collectively wiping away tears. Blake slipped her arms around Sonny as he leaned down and kissed her, everyone caught up in the tenderness of the moment.

Cal pulled Dallas into him closely and kissed her. "I love you. This is just as it should be."

"I love you, too." she said, kissing him back softly.

"Okay, y'all, that's enough of the boo-hooin'," Meridee announced. "Time for more booze. Hey, anyone here play the piano?" Meridee asked.

Dallas nudged Cal, and he raised his hand.

"Good, get over here and let's get this party started," Meridee said.

Cal sat down at the black antique grand piano and started playing "Deck the Halls," everyone singing. Blake and Vivi ran into the kitchen and came back in a jiffy with three amber-colored mixed drinks.

"Bonita, one for you. Dallas, one for you," Vivi said handing out the drinks to the two other women. "And Blake, honey, you get the mocktail. Sorry, Momma."

"Sassy Belles, for us all," Blake said, raising her glass of the signature drink of their little club. The other women joined her, clanking them together.

"To new beginnings," Dallas said.

"To new beginnings," they all repeated.

49

Dallas woke early Saturday morning. Too early. She turned over, pulling the covers up under her chin, the night before still clinging to her. She kept her eyes closed in hopes she'd just drift off again—but it was no use. The anxiety fell over her, heavier than her grandmother's homemade quilt. She placed her arm above her head on her pillow to pet Wilhelmina, who always slept on the pillow right above her head, nuzzling her head most of the night. Her soft purr was Dallas's lullaby.

But it wouldn't help her get back to sleep on this heavy morning. Dallas had a lot to think about, but she decided to only focus on the happy things for now. Later on, the nerves about the anchor job and the play would take over anyway. For now, she wrapped her mind around Sara Grace's arrival.

In the spare bedroom, Dallas hung the new clothes in the closet and put a princess tiara on the bed. She had wrapped her presents and hidden them in a hall closet to bring to Cal's for Christmas morning. New sheets and a pink striped comforter made the bed just perfect for a little girl. Since tonight was only the 23rd of December, Sara Grace would spend her first night with Dallas at her little house near the campus. Although Dallas and Sara Grace would be at Cal's for Christmas Eve and Christmas Day, Sara Grace would be with Dallas through New Year's, so she would need a room there. Plus, she wanted to spend some "girl time" with Sara Grace so they could get comfortable with each other. She looked around the room, satisfied with herself. She knew Sara Grace would be comfortable there.

"Come on, Wilhelmina. Mommy's got breakfast," she called to the kitty from the kitchen.

She fixed herself some toast and coffee, then headed to the shower. *My life will change again today,* she thought, stepping under the spray of steaming hot water. *But no matter what happens tonight,* she reasoned, *when it's all over I will be coming home with Sara Grace and Cal. I have no control over whatever else happens, so I have to let it go.* But Dallas relinquishing control…? Well, that might take another Christmas miracle entirely.

The weather had turned nasty outside; another ice storm was predicted for the evening. Frigid winds blew damp and cold, as the gray skies grew thick and puffy. Darkness fell early. Dallas asked the parents to leave the children at the theater with her after rehearsal, so none of them would get caught in the ice and cold outside.

The dress rehearsal was now over. The live animals, who were outside in makeshift pens under tarps until showtime, were perfectly tame and ready to be led onstage by two crewmen dressed as shepherds. It was only one sheep and one donkey, so the menagerie would be easy to control.

Dallas sat with Cal alone in the sound booth on the balcony. The empty theater was quiet; the little lights of the pretend stars twinkled overhead. Ms. Betty Ann and Corey had the children in one of the practice rooms having a snack. The show was scheduled for seven-thirty, so everyone had time to rest. Since it was five o'clock, some of the parents had gone for pizza.

"They looked great today, babe. You've done a great job," Cal said, leaning over and kissing her forehead.

His warm lips sent a spike of heat through her cold body. *You know it's the real thing when even a kiss on the forehead gets you excited,* she thought.

"I'm so glad I have you, Cal. You are just what I've needed for so long. I can't believe we didn't try this me-and-you thing before." She smiled and kissed him on his lips and held it there.

"I have no idea, but evidently the timing was everything. I can't imagine what I would do without you right now. You know what? It's all gonna be fine. All this will be over soon, and, by midnight, we'll have tucked in a little girl and we can have a drink in front of the fire at your house. Sound good?"

She nodded. Cal had a way of keeping things simple. That was a good thing, since Dallas's life was always somewhat dramatic. But her heart was as big as her hairdo, and Cal had figured that out just in the nick of time. They needed each other, and each of them sweetened the other's life like perfect sweet tea.

"Let's go check on the kids and the animals and make sure everyone's ready to go," she suggested.

There were two hours left till showtime, but Dallas needed to run off all those nerves. Cal followed her down the stairs and into the theater auditorium, then up the makeshift ramps that were created for the kids to go into the audience safely to sing "We Wish You a Merry Christmas." They were to walk up and down the aisles, throwing little candy canes out to everyone at the end of the play.

"Hey, my superstars, how's everybody doing?" Dallas said cheerfully as she walked into the practice room.

The children got excited, and all jumped up to hug her and Cal. Cal sat down at the piano nearby and played the theme song from the Charlie Brown Christmas show and everyone started dancing. Betty Ann jumped up and grabbed Corey, swinging him around.

"Ms. Dallas, I need to tell you something," Corey said to her, and Betty Ann spun him past.

"Sure, honey, shoot," Dallas said, dancing with little Tristan with the big blue eyes and dark curly hair.

"I wanted you to know, I really enjoyed working with you. You're nothing like what I thought," he said over his partner's shoulder.

"Oh, really?" she teased. "What did you think I was gonna be like?"

"I meant…you're just really down-to-earth, not like a TV diva or anything." He smiled, trying to wiggle free of old Betty Ann, who was having a great time making a spectacle out of him for the kids.

"Well, thank you, Corey. If you need a recommendation letter or something, I will be happy to write you one. You have been wonderful and so patient with the kids—and with me."

He stopped dancing and came over and hugged her. Little Tristan danced off with Sara Grace. Everything was going along just fine until suddenly the lights went out.

In the back part of the theater behind the stage, it was pitch-dark. Betty Ann felt her way to a shelf where they kept an emergency flashlight and flicked it on.

"Okay, everybody, listen to me," Cal said, jumping into action from the piano bench. "Don't be scared. We're all gonna follow Ms. Betty Ann to the green room up front. There's a generator light on up there, and maybe we can see the street outside so we will know when the lights will be back on. So, everyone hold hands and walk slowly. Ms. Betty Ann and Corey will take us up front."

The green room was what they called the lobby, and that's where all the concessions were stored. A small, dim light was on in the corner as Betty Ann led the way out of the room, to the stage, down the ramp, up the aisle and into the green room. Corey took over from there.

"Okay, y'all have a seat in a big circle and stay put. We'll pass out some snacks and wait safely for the lights to come back on. It shouldn't be too long," he said, looking at Dallas for reassurance. She only wished she could give him some. It was nearly six o'clock, and people would be arriving to get a seat in the next hour.

The kids sat patiently for all of about fifteen minutes. Then someone needed to go potty. Then someone else. And before they knew it, six or seven kids were in the bathroom. When they came back to the green room, they would ask for a drink. Then a snack. After they got a snack, they wanted to run around and play hide-and-go-seek. Sugar Babies was not a good choice of snack for a cloistered group of children.

Betty Ann and Corey tried to sing songs and keep the kids seated in their circle, but as the minutes slowly dragged by, the kids were getting more and more antsy.

Then came a knock on the front glass door. Cal ran over and opened it. Vivi and Blake stepped inside, shivering from the cold night air. Vivi had a huge, black plastic garbage bag slung over her shoulder like Santa Claus. Dallas walked over and helped them both through the dark over to the concession stand.

"I brought you a little something," Vivi said as she opened the garbage bag.

Dallas stood next to her as Blake looked on from behind.

"I wanted you to know, I didn't forget," she said as she pulled a pair of perfect white angel wings shimmering in the dim light with iridescent glitter. "They're covered in *Belle*rina Dust, It's for good luck. We'll tell you all about it."

"Oh, Vivi, they're so beautiful! Thank you so much," Dallas said. She was overcome by the gesture.

"You still needed them, didn't you?" Vivi asked.

"I certainly did. Sara Grace," she called out to her little soloist. "Come see what Miss Vivi brought you for tonight."

Sara Grace came running over, excited to see the large white wings made of translucent white fabric and secured tightly to wire in the shape of wings. They were trimmed with white faux fur and covered with glitter. Sara Grace didn't close her mouth all the way across the room.

"Are these really for me?" she exclaimed.

"Yes, baby. Miss Vivi made them just for you." Dallas took them and helped Sara Grace slip them over her arms. They were perfect.

"You look beautiful," Dallas said.

"Thank you so much," Sara Grace said to Vivi. "Are you Ms. Dallas's friend?" she asked.

Vivi and Dallas looked at each other and smiled.

"Yes, I am," Vivi answered. "I hope you like them. They're yours to keep if you want them."

"Yes, I do! I mean…thank you." Sara Grace ran off to show the other kids her new prize.

"Is she one of the kids from the Children's Home?" Vivi asked Dallas.

"She is, but she's not in a foster home at the moment."

"You mean she'll be at the Children's Home over Christmas?" Blake asked sadly.

"Actually, no," Dallas answered. "I'm taking her for Christmas. She'll be with me and Cal."

Vivi and Blake looked at each other. Clearly, they had never known *this* Dallas.

"Those wings are great," Cal said as he approached the women. "Lewis never told me you were so talented, Vivi."

"It's nothin'. I just threw 'em together when I was up with Tallulah last night. I sang to her while I glued everything together. I think the glitter amused her. Pageant baby in training."

It occurred to Dallas at that second, watching Sara Grace scamper around in her wings, that this theater was where the awful itching powder incident had taken place almost twenty years ago. My, how far they had all come since then. This was most certainly a peace offering from Vivi, right in the place where the war had begun all those years ago. And the olive branch was angel wings.

"When do we expect some lights in here?" Vivi asked.

"I just talked to the power company," Cal said. "They're working on it. I told them we have a play with a ton of people expected in an hour. I don't know what we'll do if we're still dark at seven-thirty."

Just then a group of parents knocked on the glass doors. Cal walked over and held the door for them.

"Look, y'all, pizza!" he shouted. The kids jumped up and ran to the parents with the hot, delicious food. Two parents brought in warm boxes of Krispy Kremes and sat them on the concession counter.

"Perfect, pizza and doughnuts for kids who are locked in a small area," Blake said sarcastically. "Now that was brilliant."

"At least it'll keep 'em busy," Corey said, coming over to get some paper plates from behind the counter.

"Yep, and then they'll be high as kites, wound up like Bessie-bugs and still locked in this room," Vivi said.

"Well maybe we can get them fed and calm by the time the lights come back on." Dallas went around the counter to help Corey.

"I have an idea," Cal said. "Let's line up some cars and turn on the headlights. Maybe we can at least have enough light to see what we're doing in here."

Several moms went out and started up their cars so as not to drain the batteries and did just that, illuminating the lobby with spotlightlike brightness. It was terribly uncomfortable but better than one dim light in the corner. They needed to be able to see the kids in case somebody wandered off. The harsh light revealed the lobby, now a disaster of candy wrappers and smashed, stepped-on chocolate ground into the beautiful tapestry carpet.

It was now six forty-five. The ice storm had held off for the most part, but the theater was still pitch-black. How in the world would they get the play on with no lights? Dallas grew more and more nervous, knowing the whole event might have to be postponed. Her mom called and said she and Houston and Amy were on their way. Dallas knew it was only a matter of time before all of the audience would be making their way inside from the lobby.

"Okay, listen up, everyone," Dallas announced. "We need to clean this all up the minute you've all finished eating. Corey and Betty Ann will lead you to the bathrooms to wash up. Each of them has a flashlight, so stay close to one of them. Come back and help gather all the trash and throw it away in the big can behind the counter."

The children were giggling and fidgety, on a sugar high they might never come down from with all the candy and then doughnuts. Dallas could only hope everyone would remember their lines.

"Cal, do you know anything about generators? Maybe we can rig us something up just in case," Dallas said with a desperate look on her face.

"I know a little but not enough. Let me go see what I can do," he answered, heading up the stairs from the lobby to the sound booth.

Cal was gone about ten minutes when Corey shouted, "Hey, look, we have lights on the stage!" If nothing else, the footlights were working. Cal came down from the balcony smiling. Dallas walked over to him and hugged him happily. "You really are the genius I heard you were," she said, kissing him.

"Well, I try," Cal said modestly. "But we won't have any lights in the auditorium, and I know that's gonna be a safety issue. So let me just call the power company back. We got about half an hour before the show's supposed to start. The audience will be here any minute." He stepped aside to make the call.

Dallas felt defeated. She knew they really couldn't have the play if the auditorium had no lights, and there were no lights in any of the bathrooms.

"Maybe we can just delay the beginning," Betty Ann said, trying to console her. By now the kids had settled back down, all looking sleepy, which was not good either.

"Okay, they said about half an hour and we'll be back in business," Cal said.

"Half an hour? We'll just have to announce the delay as the guests arrive at the box office," Dallas said.

Which was right this minute.

Vivi stepped into the box office and took over, leading everyone inside the lobby. Mike Maddox from the TV station and Abigail Harper and some others from the local media arrived, ready for all the big announcements coming at the end

of the performance. Dallas talked to them for a minute before Corey led them all to their seats by flashlight. The green
room was bursting at the seams by seven-twenty. The lady
who usually ran the box office was scared to drive over because of the weather reports of the impending ice storm, so
Blake and Vivi worked with the growing crowd while Dallas and Cal held down the fort with the kids. Still, no ice was
falling from the sky and no lights were shining inside. It all
seemed like a major bust.

"May I have your attention, everyone?" Dallas called out
to the crowd. "Things aren't looking so good right now. Mr.
Hollingsworth has just checked with the power company and
they are running behind. All of downtown is dark, and it's
already seven forty-five. We have decided to postpone the
play." Dallas dropped her head in disappointment as she spoke.

Everyone shouted aww's and booed, but she and Cal and
Betty Ann didn't know what else to do.

"Hey, wait a minute! I see the streetlights back on down the
block," shouted Betty Ann, peering out the front doors. Then
suddenly, the lights in the green room flickered, and Cal and
Dallas glanced into the auditorium. The tiny star-lights came
up, and the whole place was instantly a Christmas wonderland.

"Okay, scratch that," Cal announced. "We're on in twenty
minutes. Everyone take your seats." He pulled Dallas into him
for a passionate good-luck kiss and smiled as he rushed up the
balcony stairs, skipping every other one with his long legs.

"Ms. Dallas." Sara Grace tugged at her skirt. "I'm gonna
get to be an angel tonight on the stage. I'm so excited!"

Dallas turned and bent down to look into her eyes.

"Me, too, baby. Let's go get ready. Surely nothing else can
go wrong."

Finally, after all the rehearsals, the Christmas production of *Sleigh Bells* was underway. The music began, the lights went up and all the children entered the stage singing. The audience applauded like crazy. Dallas stood to stage left in the wings. Betty Ann and Corey worked straight across from her on the other side, ushering the kids on and off through their scenes of an old-fashioned Victorian Christmas.

Everything was running so smoothly, Dallas thought this may be the most flawless performance of all. Chris and Jay came forward to do their puppet performance with their German nutcrackers, and even that went off wonderfully. Then Sara Grace approached the microphone, her little angel wings situated perfectly on her back. The music began for "I'll Be Home for Christmas," and her voice matched her wings. She sang like an angel.

She glanced over to Dallas who was mouthing the words to the song along with her. She gave her a little smile. When

Dallas looked up and out into the audience, she saw her mother and brother. She locked eyes with them and began to tear up. Her family was there, and this year she actually *would* be home for Christmas. Her brother gave her a thumbs-up, and her mom blew her a kiss. Dallas could barely contain herself, tears streaming down her face as Sara Grace finished up.

"Ms. Dallas, what's wrong?" Sara Grace asked after she bowed. The audience was standing now and applauding her.

"I'm fine, sweetie, just tears of joy. I'm so proud of you," Dallas said, sending Sara Grace back out for a second bow. The little girl in the perfect angel wings bowed over and over and waved to the crowd.

During intermission the manger scene was set up, the shepherds leading the donkey and the sheep to their spots. All the children were supposed to be Christmas caroling along the snow-covered Victorian street when they come upon a manger scene along the path. That would lead in to "Away In a Manger" as the last formal song, then all the children would head into the audience singing "We Wish You a Merry Christmas" as they threw candy canes. It was almost over and Dallas could finally breathe.

But then, Jay and Christopher got their hands on those nutcrackers.

Just as the manger scene was revealed and the children passed by and broke into the song, Dallas could see Christopher give Jay the nod and each of them stuck their nutcracker puppets right on the butts of the two live animals, chomping down. The donkey and the sheep both took off running as the children screamed and jumped back, clearing them a path. The animals ran down the ramp and into the shrieking audience, spooked beyond control.

The shepherds took off after them.

"Stop that donkey!" Dallas shouted. All the children were

laughing as the sheep let out a *baaaah* so loud it drowned out the music. The audience scrambled up, standing on their seats and trying to stay out of the way of the donkey and the shepherds. Finally, with the animals wrangled, Dallas walked to center stage to make an announcement. "So sorry, folks," she apologized. "We had no idea the manger scene would become a rodeo, and as if that weren't enough, now for the finale." Cal immediately started the music, and the children all began "We Wish You a Merry Christmas" and headed down each side of the stage, throwing candy canes.

Anna Beth and Austin stopped by Dallas as they started down the aisle, Anna Beth pulling at her skirt. Dallas bent down as the child whispered in her ear, "I'm so glad you're my aunt," she said softly and kissed Dallas on the cheek.

Dallas smiled at her. "Me, too," she said.

The entire audience broke into the song, singing along with the children and catching the candy canes. The children made their way back to the stage as the song finished, all lining up and holding each other's hands for their bow. The audience stayed standing and clapping as the kids bowed, and Dallas made her way on stage with Betty Ann and Corey.

Sara Grace pulled Dallas into the lineup next to her, Dallas now in the center as the audience kept clapping. Cal made his way up the ramp and stood to the side, clapping until Tristan went over and dragged him center stage next to Dallas. Cal slipped his hand into Dallas's and clasped her fingers within his. He leaned over to her and kissed her cheek and squeezed her hand as the audience applauded. The stagehands shook the snow overhead, and the flakes fell as the children bowed. The entire stage looked like a snow globe that had just been shaken, and despite the mishaps, Dallas couldn't have been more proud.

The mayor stepped out and stood next to Dallas and put his hands in the air to quiet the crowd.

"Okay, y'all, that was wonderful, rodeo and all! Can we quiet down to a low roar? We have so many people to thank. First and foremost, I wanna thank Dallas Dubois and Cal Hollingsworth for devoting their time and energy to our kids. Ms. Betty Ann and her assistant, Corey, too. Y'all have done a fantastic job. The city and the Tuscaloosa Children's Home have benefited greatly form your efforts. Now, may I introduce the public relations representative for WRCT, Abigail Harper, and the owner, Lewis Heart!"

Everyone applauded at the mention of the Voice of the Crimson Tide.

"Thank you, Mayor," Lewis said as he and Abigail stood at the mic.

"We're here as one of the sponsors of this fantastic play," Lewis began. "Our Twelve Days of Christmas contest was held to benefit the Children's Home. We'd like to announce the winner." He handed the mic to Abigail.

"Well, we are happy to announce that our winner is right here tonight as a member of the cast. Sara Grace Griffin, you have won the iPad!"

Abigail handed the child the prize.

"Thank you so much," Sara Grace said as she took the gift. "Mr. Cal, thank you for helping me," she whispered to him, so no one could hear her. But Dallas heard. She looked at Cal and smiled. No wonder she'd found that little toy drummer boy in his car that night.

"And," Abigail continued, "I'd like to thank the anonymous Santa who donated iPads to *every* child that will be spending Christmas in the Children's Home. It is an unprecedented gesture." All the kids from the Children's Home who made up the cast and choir jumped up and down, screaming with excitement.

Dallas looked at Cal. He was grinning ear to ear. *Could it be?* she wondered. She leaned over to him. "That's not you, too, is it?" she whispered. He stood silent, smiling.

Just then, Dallas caught Mike coming out onstage from the wings. He held a piece of paper in is hands as he approached the mic. Dallas felt her gut tighten, and her hands suddenly felt shaky. In all of the excitement, she had put this moment on the back burner. The announcement of the anchor successor was seconds away. She had wanted this job for as long as she could remember. Just then, she caught a glimpse of Courtney standing on the other side of the stage in the wings. *Oh, God,* she thought. *It's her, for sure. She's all dressed up and ready to meet her public.*

"Thank y'all again for all the support you have given us as we have worked for the wonderful Tuscaloosa Children's Home this year," Lewis wrapped up, presenting a check to Ms. Hinton from the home. He handed the microphone to Mike.

"Good evening, Tuscaloosa. I'm Mike Maddox from WTAL-TV, the sister sponsor for this great production. First, I want to thank our star reporter Dallas Dubois, who volunteered her time and creativity to your children here, all while continuing to hold down her full-time job at WTAL every single day." Everyone applauded and whistled for her. Cal, standing at her side, dropped her hand and clapped loudly. "You have definitely embodied all that we expect from a reporter and more these last few weeks, stepping in without warning for the ailing Ms. Fairbanks. Now, let me present this check to the Tuscaloosa Children's Home on behalf of WTAL."

He handed the check to Ms. Hinton while the crowd applauded again.

"Now, as most of you know, we will be announcing a new six o'clock anchor this month. I've decided tonight is the perfect opportunity to introduce you to your new anchor. As of January first, keep an eye out for none other than your favorite director, Ms. Dallas Dubois!"

Dallas stood there smiling, but not moving. Her nerves had taken over and she hadn't even heard a word. She started clapping, thinking she was clapping for Courtney.

"Babe, it's you," Cal said, nudging her. "*You* are the new anchor."

"What?' she asked, confused.

"You, babe, it's you. You're the new anchor!"

Dallas suddenly registered that every single person was standing in the audience, all clapping for her. She was stunned, but she forced her legs to move and walked over to Mike.

"Oh, Mike, thank you so much. I can't believe it!" She looked out into the roaring crowd and waved. Her mom blew her a kiss and clapped. Houston wiped a tear from his cheek and blew her a kiss, too. Her whole family was there. She looked out and saw Vivi and Blake, with Sonny and Lewis, baby Tallulah, Arthur and Bonita, Meridee and Kitty all clapping for her and smiling. She just knew she was gonna wake up any minute.

"You deserved this, Dallas," Mike said. "You've been working for this spot for years. I am happy to be here to give you this promotion in front of the town that loves you so much."

"But what about Courtney?" Dallas asked, unable to stop smiling as she spoke.

"Let me have your attention, please. One more announcement," Mike said to the crowd. "Let me also introduce Courtney James as our new morning anchor. The WTAL Sunrise Show also begins January first."

Courtney walked out and waved, staying only for a moment before she headed off into the wings.

Now I understand. The whole new schedule was for her morning show, Dallas thought to herself.

Everyone started gathering their things as Sara Grace tugged once more at her skirt. Dallas looked down and saw the little girl was crying.

"What's wrong, baby?" she asked.

"I'm not gonna see you anymore, and I'm gonna miss you," Sara Grace said, her cheeks streaked with tears.

Dallas looked at Cal and smiled. "I think we need to talk to you, sweetheart," she said. Cal knelt down right there at center stage. He was on one side of Sara Grace and Dallas was on the other. Cal smiled at Dallas and nodded his head.

"I have a surprise for you," Dallas said.

"What is it?" she asked, still unable to fully catch her breath.

"How would you like to spend all of Christmastime with me?"

"Really?" Sara Grace squealed with joy. She threw her arms around Dallas in a huge bear hug.

"How would you like it if we spent some time with Mr. Cal, too?"

"I can't believe this is real," Sara Grace said.

"Well, it sure is. It's all set. You can come home with us right now, if that's okay with you," Dallas said hugging her again.

Sara Grace was practically bouncing with joy. Dallas clutched the child's little hand and Cal held the other. The three of them stood and walked into the wings. All three of them knew they had their Christmas wishes in their grasp.

Dallas glanced out and saw Meridee still standing there with Blake and Vivi and Kitty. Meridee winked at Dallas, then leaned into the other women. "I always knew that girl was good. And I'm never wrong when it comes to people."

Meridee smiled as the women all headed up the aisle together and out into the cold Christmas air of downtown Tuscaloosa.

★ ★ ★ ★ ★

Acknowledgments

How do I begin to say thank you to all the wonderful people who helped make this book possible? I am so grateful to: My beautiful, brilliant new editor, Michelle Venditti. Your insight is priceless, your patience immense and your hand-holding such a tremendous a comfort. With your ability to teach me as we go, and my ability for quick study, we are an amazing team. I am so lucky to have you!

To the rest of my MIRA family, including the talented cover design team of Michael Rehder and Quinn Banting. The covers are gorgeous and so Southern. I'm super proud of them! And to my fantastic PR team, Michelle Renaud and Lisa Wray, where would I be without you and all your tremendous efforts? You all went above and beyond for me. Thank you so much! And thank you to Jennifer Musico at Kaye Publicity. You have been nothing short of wonderful to work with!

My wonderful mother, Betty, who's nonstop cheerleading keeps me afloat and at the computer even on days when I'm not sure what I'm doing. I have never known what it feels like to be alone—because I always know I have you with me, pulling for me, giving me ideas and reminding me to just keep my eye on the ball. You have given me everything, and I can only pray I am half the mother to Brooks you always have been to me. I know how to love because I am loved by you. You will forever be the wind beneath my wings.

Brooks, my precious son, you love me genuinely every day and make sure I know it—every day. When I'm happy I see it glimmering in your eyes, too. I love sharing life with you! Thank you for your constant support. I love you more than I could ever say.

My husband, Ted. Thank you for loving me, supporting me and drying my tears. You take care of me in ways I never could have imagined. I'm so happy I married my best friend all those years ago. I know I must be quite a handful. I love you so very much.

To all my friends and family for always encouraging me, pushing me and believing in me and for the endless amounts of love I get every day. I have the very best Sassy Belle sisters in the world. Susan, my strong, beautiful, determined sister, you are a role model for so many. You kicked cancer's ass and smiled while doing it! I admire you more than I can say. Lynn, my smart sister, so strong and beautiful, I will always need you in my corner—where you have been since you were fourteen years old. What would I ever do without you? Joyce, also so strong and beautiful—thank you for everything through all the years.

Huge thanks to my mother-in-law, Peggy Ishler Bosse. Without your careful editing and listing of questions, where would these books be? You have been a priceless help to me, and I thank you from the bottom of my heart.

To my precious, priceless agent and close friend, Elizabeth

Pomada. Thank you for being one of the first to believe in me, for editing the books even when you weren't well, for always telling me to keep writing. "Onward," you cheered…and onward we flew—together! Thank you for telling me you are my biggest fan and for the warm friendship you always offer me. You are wonderful.

To Jeremy West, visionary genius, web designer, social media expert and dear friend! I could never have waded these waters without you.

My extended family, I love you all so much and thank you for all the constant support. And, of course, my hometown of Tuscaloosa, Alabama. As always, I hope I make y'all proud.